Jon had touched her—in a very possessive, male way

Gabby's heartbeat thumped in her ears as she marched to her office. She could still feel the heat of his big hand burning through the seat of her khakis as he'd steadied her on the ladder.

It had taken every ounce of self-control to tell him to unhand her. What she'd really wanted was to grab him by his shirt and... well, explore all those urges his touch had instantly brought to life.

While she might not like him, she was wise enough to understand that it wasn't always about liking the other person. Sometimes it was about pure animal attraction.

And when it came to Jon, it was very clear the animal in her liked the animal in him.

Dear Reader,

I loved writing *The Last Goodbye*—which is Tyler's story—and I loved, loved, loved writing Jon's story in *One Good Reason*. I didn't set out to write a sequel. I created Gabby as Tyler's conscience and friend, but somehow, almost as soon as she appeared she morphed into an ex-girlfriend who, maybe, still cared too much. Then I gave Tyler a brother, because I didn't want him to be alone in his childhood, and along came Jon.

By the time I'd finished Tyler and Ally's story, I knew that Jon and Gabby had to meet each other. A guy like Jon, with hyperprotective instincts, and a woman like Gabby, who is determined to make her own way in the world, seemed destined to be together from where I sat. Not that either of them were ever going to be aware of that! That would take all the fun out of it.

I'd like to think that while *One Good Reason* has some definite heavy moments—an abusive parent is no laughing matter—there is plenty of light and tenderness and love and hope amongst the hard stuff. People are hugely resilient, and love is a great healer.

I hope you enjoy reading Jon and Gabby's story. I love to hear from readers via my website at www.sarahmayberry.com.

Until next time, happy reading!

Sarah Mayberry

One Good Reason
Sarah Mayberry

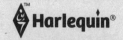

TORONTO NEW YORK LONDON
AMSTERDAM PARIS SYDNEY HAMBURG
STOCKHOLM ATHENS TOKYO MILAN MADRID
PRAGUE WARSAW BUDAPEST AUCKLAND

Recycling programs
for this product may
not exist in your area.

ISBN-13: 978-0-373-78469-1

ONE GOOD REASON

ABOUT THE AUTHOR

Sarah Mayberry lives by the seaside in Melbourne, Australia. She has recently married her partner of eighteen years and is enjoying their new home and fabulous but exhausting garden. Her goal for the next year is to learn how to prune the thirty-two different fruit and nut trees on their property and to be more organized. When she's not writing, she loves to cook, sleep, shop, read and watch movies. She really wishes going to the gym made it onto the "loves" list, but she makes herself go anyway. Long live ice cream!

Books by Sarah Mayberry

HARLEQUIN SUPERROMANCE

1551—A NATURAL FATHER
1599—HOME FOR THE HOLIDAYS
1626—HER BEST FRIEND
1669—THE BEST LAID PLANS
1686—THE LAST GOODBYE

HARLEQUIN BLAZE

380—BURNING UP
404—BELOW THE BELT
425—AMOROUS LIAISONS
464—SHE'S GOT IT BAD
517—HER SECRET FLING
566—HOT ISLAND NIGHTS

I have to thank my husband for his endless patience with me while I was writing this book. That deadline was some doozy, my darling, but you fed and watered me and mopped my fevered brow and I thank you from the bottom of my heart for your kindness and support.
Where would I be without you?
In my book, you are the ultimate hero.

I also want to thank Wanda
for her endless faith in me—
you said I could do it and I did. Phew!

PROLOGUE

January

JON ADAMSON WOKE WITH A START. Someone was in his room. A heartbeat later, he was on his feet, fists raised, every muscle tense as he squared up to the intruder.

"Mate." His brother held up his hands, took a step backward. "It's just me."

Jon dropped his fists. "You should have knocked."

"I did." Tyler's gaze flicked to the half-empty bottle of bourbon beside the bed. "Several times."

The light was hazy in the room. Jon tried to guess the time. Nine in the morning? Ten? He reached for the jeans he'd dumped at the end of the bed when he'd finally crashed last night.

"I was up pretty late."

He wasn't about to offer explanations for the bourbon or anything else. A man could have a few drinks at the end of the day. Besides, Tyler was the younger brother—it was Jon's job to be the heavy, not the other way around.

"What are you doing up this way?" he asked as he stepped into his jeans.

Jon had been back in Australia, living in their late father's house in the rural Victorian town of Woodend for eleven months now. Tyler lived an hour and a half away in Melbourne, so the two of them didn't cross paths very often. Not that that would have changed even if they were geographically closer. They'd never been the kind of brothers who lived in each other's pockets—witness the ten years Jon had spent in Canada.

"I hadn't heard from you for a while. Thought I'd better check in."

Jon pulled his T-shirt over his head, aware of the unspoken questions behind his brother's words.

Why didn't you return my phone messages? What's going on?

"I've been busy."

"Yeah, I saw that. When did you knock down the wall between the kitchen and living room?"

"Figured both rooms would benefit from the light. It's all about open plan these days."

"What happened to tidying up the yard and giving the place a lick of paint before we listed it?"

"If you're that desperate for the money, I can get a valuation done. Pay out your half."

"It's not about the money."

Jon walked toward the door. "Yeah? What's it about, then?"

Tyler followed him to the kitchen. Jon had pulled up the old linoleum tiles and the boards were rough beneath his feet. He sidestepped the hole where he'd removed a rotten plank and crossed to the sink. Turning on the tap, he sluiced handfuls of cold water onto his face.

Tyler was looking around, inspecting the gaping holes in the plaster where the kitchen cabinets had once hung. The only remaining features of the original kitchen was the sink unit, the freestanding stove and the fridge. And they'd be gone any day now, too.

"I suppose you've gutted the bathroom, too?"

"Everything except the toilet and shower recess."

Tyler's gaze was knowing. "Wouldn't it have been easier to knock the place down?"

"I'm fixing it up for resale. We both agreed it needed work before we put it on the market."

"Mate, you're demolishing it from the inside out."

"The kitchen needed updating. The bloody thing hadn't been touched since the fifties. And the bathroom was leaking into the subfloor. You can see the joists I had to replace if you want to."

Tyler didn't say anything, but he didn't look away, either.

Jon could feel his hackles rising. Tyler was making a big deal out of this, reading things into Jon's actions. Whatever Tyler thought was going on, he was wrong. Way wrong.

Jon crossed his arms over his chest, widened his stance. "I'm doing you and Ally a favor. You'll make a lot more with this place fixed up than you would have if we'd put it on the market as it was."

"Will you quit it with the money? I don't give a damn how much we make. I'm here because of you."

"I'm fine."

"Yeah? You looked in a mirror lately? When was the last time you shaved or had a haircut?"

Jon brushed a hand over his bristly jaw. "I've been busy."

"Too busy to eat? Because you look like a bag of bones."

"I'm *fine*."

"Which is why Ally got a call from Wendy in the middle of the night on Monday, telling her it sounded like you were holding a demolition derby."

Wendy was the next-door neighbor. Until this moment, Jon had thought she was all right. He'd even tried to talk her into bed a few times, but she was seeing some computer guy.

"I was taking the wall out," Jon said.

"At two in the morning?"

"If I woke her, I'll apologize."

"And what about all the bottles in the recycling bin?"

Jon's eyes narrowed. His brother was quite the amateur sleuth. "I'd say that gets filed under 'none of your business,' same as everything else."

"Doesn't work that way, sorry. I'm not going to stand by and watch you kill yourself over an old bastard who wasn't worth it."

"This has nothing to do with him." But he could barely get the words past the sudden tightness in his throat.

"You think if you change enough of this place it'll change what happened?"

"I think you've been living with an advice columnist for too long."

Tyler eyed him for a long beat. Then he tilted his head to one side and nodded slowly, a gesture which Jon read as conceding defeat.

Good. He didn't need a keeper.

As for the things Tyler had said… This had nothing to do with the old man. It had nothing to do with anything.

"I told Ally you wouldn't listen," Tyler said.

He crossed to the kitchen door and collected something from the hall.

An overnight bag.

It took a moment for the penny to drop.

"No," Jon said.

"I figure if we both pitch in, we can get this place finished in a few weeks. Get it on the market. Then you can go back to Toronto or wherever. Get away from here."

Jon swore. "I don't want you here."

"Tough."

"I don't need a babysitter."

"Then stop acting like you do."

Jon breathed in slowly through his nose and out through his mouth. It didn't make much difference—he still wanted to smash a hole in something.

He strode across the room, picked up the overnight bag. Started for the door. Maybe once he'd tossed Tyler's gear into the street his brother would get the message that his intervention was neither welcome nor necessary.

Tyler blocked his path. Jon stopped short of barging into his brother's shoulder. He met Tyler's gaze. There was determination there. And something else.

Compassion.

It made Jon's hand curl into a fist.

"Get out of my way."

"I'm not leaving unless you come with me," Tyler said. "Come to Melbourne, move into the spare room. Get away from this place."

"Get out of my way."

Tyler didn't move. Jon reached to push his brother out of his path. Tyler resisted, grabbing a fistful of Jon's T-shirt as he attempted to hold him off. Years ago, Jon would have been able to shift his brother easily, but Tyler was a man now, and they'd both inherited their father's big build.

Jon braced his legs, shoving harder. Tyler shoved back. For long moments they struggled, locked together. In any other fight, it would have come to blows by now, but Jon was not going to throw a punch at his brother.

Not in this house.

"Move," Jon demanded.

"He's dead. And even if he wasn't, he's not worth it. Not in a million years."

A surge of anger gave Jon new strength. He wrenched his brother to the side. Shoved past him and into the hall and out the door.

The air was cool on his face, the grass still damp from the morning dew. He dropped the bag on the ground and stood half-turned away from the house, chest heaving from the exertion, aware of his brother in the open doorway, watching him.

This wasn't about his father. Jon refused to let him hold that much power over him. He was simply making the most of the house. Fulfilling its potential. It was what he did—he was a builder. He made homes for people. Until recently he'd co-owned a construction company in Toronto. This was business as usual.

His gaze found the recycling bin, filled to overflowing with various liquor bottles.

Too many bottles for one person. Way too many.

He swore. Ran a hand through his hair, fisting his fingers in it and pulling so tightly that it hurt.

Why couldn't Tyler have left him here to rot, or whatever it was he was doing? Why couldn't Tyler have left him to battle it out on his own with the ghost of a dead man?

He laughed, a short, hard bark of bitter amusement.

If this really was a battle, according to the tide of bottles spilling onto the lawn, he was making a pretty poor showing. He was in full retreat, utterly routed, on his way to surrender.

Tyler's hand landed on his shoulder.

"Let's patch it up and sell it. Then never look back."

Jon knew his brother was right but he hated the understanding in his voice. He twisted from under his brother's grip. Moved away from him.

"We should focus on the kitchen, knock it off first. The bathroom won't need too much time if we stick to the original layout."

Carefully not looking at his brother, he strode toward the house.

CHAPTER ONE

March

GABBY WADE BELTED OUT THE chorus to Sinéad O'Connor's classic "Nothing Compares 2 U" as she pulled into her usual parking spot in front of T.A. Furniture Designs, her voice echoing loudly in the small space. She waited until the final notes of the song had faded before turning off the ignition with a contented sigh.

There was nothing better than a really good angst-ridden ballad to kick off a Monday morning, and no one was better at it than Sinéad. Gabby grabbed her bag then twisted to collect the jumbo box of doughnuts from the backseat. The smell of chocolate and strawberry wafted to her as she walked toward the showroom door. It was barely eight o'clock, so the entrance was still locked, and she balanced the box on her knee as she struggled to get her key in the lock. The doughnuts nearly hit the dust before she got the door open, but she managed to keep her grip on them. Not that it would have made much difference to the guys—they would probably eat cardboard if it had chocolate frosting on it. A little gravel would hardly put them off.

She locked up behind her, then passed through the showroom, making a mental note to rearrange the display sometime this week. Even though she was officially only the office manager, she'd been stepping into sales a lot more lately and a static showroom wasn't doing anyone any favors.

Heaven knew, Tyler was too distracted these days to notice those kinds of things. It was just as well she had his back.

The sharp whine of a power saw hit her as she entered the workshop. Dino was ripping some red gum, and Paul was setting up the router to bevel the edge on a cherry dining table. Carl was marking up some wood, squinting like crazy because he still refused to admit he needed glasses.

"Morning, boys," Gabby hollered over the noise.

Dino grunted without looking up, while Carl ignored her altogether. Paul glanced up briefly, throwing her a token wave. She waited for his brain to register what she held in her hands.

One cat-dog, two cat-dog, three—

His head whipped up again and his mouth curled into a sweet smile. "Is that what I think it is?"

"Yes, my gallant prince, it is. Two dozen of

Krispy Kreme's finest for the fairest gentlemen in all the land."

The saw stopped abruptly. Suddenly all eyes were on her.

Nothing like refined sugars and fats to get a man's attention.

"Gabby, you're a gem." Dino started toward her, dusting his hands together.

"What he said," Carl echoed, his eyes on the box as he followed in Dino's footsteps.

"Try to leave some for Tyler and Kelly," Gabby said.

Paul took the box from her hands. "Of course. We're not animals."

Dino had a doughnut in each hand.

"I'll take your word for it," she said.

Dino laughed sheepishly as she turned toward her office. Then, as though it had only just occurred to her, she swung around.

"I almost forgot—we really need to get that boardroom table out tomorrow. So anything you guys could do to finish it would be really appreciated."

Dino froze midbite. "So these are bribe doughnuts? Nice. How cheap do you think we are?"

"I got chocolate custard, your favorite."

Dino's aggrieved look faded a fraction. "Fine. We'll do what we can. But no promises."

Gabby hid her grin as she walked to her office. If she knew Dino—and after three years of being Tyler's office manager, she was pretty confident she did—the table would be ready for the afternoon's deliveries. And all it had cost her was a trip to Krispy Kreme.

United Nations, eat your heart out.

She pushed open her office door—and froze.

A complete stranger—a man—sat at her desk, his back to the door as he used her computer.

She stared at his broad shoulders, strong neck and close-cropped dark hair. What the hell was he doing in her office? Making himself at home in her chair?

"Um, excuse me…?" she finally said when she'd gotten over her initial surprise.

He held up an imperious hand, not even bothering to glance over his shoulder to see who it was. "Won't be a minute."

She stared, incredulous, as whoever-he-was continued to tap at the keyboard.

Was he for real?

"Of course. Make yourself at home. Maybe you'd like a coffee while you're at it?"

He did glance up and she found herself staring into a pair of dark gray eyes.

"Tyler said I could jump on to check a few things. I'll be out of your hair in a second."

His voice was low and deep, a subterranean rumble along her nerve endings. Between it and those eyes and the shape of his jaw and face, it wasn't hard to work out who he was: Jon Adamson, Tyler's brother.

He turned to the computer and Gabby found herself staring at his shoulders again. He was bigger than Tyler, broader. She knew he was older by a year or so, too, but apart from that, the only things she knew about Jon were that until recently he'd been living in Canada, that he'd missed Ally and Tyler's wedding because of some business commitment there, and that the past few months he'd been in Woodend while he renovated the family home prior to sale. Correction, she knew one other thing—he was rude. Because surely even the most insensitive person could guess that invading somebody's personal space then virtually ignoring them when they discovered you was not exactly the way to go about winning friends.

She crossed her arms over her chest and waited. And waited.

And waited.

After what felt like an age, Jon hit a key on her computer and pushed away from the desk.

"Thanks for that," he said as he stood.

He was a little taller than Tyler, and now that he was facing her she noted further similarities and differences between the brothers. His cheekbones were pronounced like Tyler's but sharper, and the lines around his eyes and mouth were deeper. His jaw was the same strong, sure arc, his chin as determined, but his eyes were a much darker gray, the color of storm clouds instead of Tyler's unusual quicksilver.

Her gaze swept his body, taking in his pristine white T-shirt and his equally crisp-looking jeans. Both new, unless she missed her guess. Only his boots looked well-worn. She refocused on his face, noting his clean-shaven jaw and the military neatness of his buzz cut.

He looked…newly minted somehow. But in a raw, spare kind of way.

She was aware of him checking her out, too, and for a crazy second wished she was wearing something other than a faded T-shirt and jeans and that she'd gone for a proper haircut instead of trimming her fringe with the nail scissors this morning.

She shook the thought off quickly—all signs pointed to the fact this man was an ass, and she didn't give two hoots what an ass thought of her.

Not even one hoot.

"You're Gabrielle, right? Jon Adamson." He offered his hand.

She let him hang for a moment before sliding

her hand into his. It seemed only fair, since he'd kept her hanging.

"It's Gabby."

His palm swallowed hers, and she felt the roughness of calluses against her own soft skin.

"You all finished now?" she asked. "I don't want to cramp your style."

He gave her an assessing look. "Like I said, Tyler didn't seem to think you'd mind if I used your office for a few minutes. But if I've stepped on your toes, I apologize."

His tone was very even, very calm. As though she was the one who was out of line here. She felt herself bristling even more and was forced to admit that maybe she *was* overreacting a little. After all, he'd simply borrowed her computer, with her boss's permission. Nothing to get her panties in a twist over.

Except...

He was too big and too strangely familiar, and yet not, and she felt...invaded and a little overwhelmed by his unexpected presence.

She wanted him gone. Wanted her space back.

"I was a little thrown, that's all."

"Again, sorry if I stepped on your toes."

He moved out from behind her desk and she took a hasty step to the side to avoid brushing against him as he headed for the door.

She watched as he strode away, his broad shoulders dipping from side to side like a cowboy as he walked. Only when he was gone did she take a seat in her chair. It was warm from his body and she shifted, feeling invaded all over again.

Why he couldn't have used Tyler's computer, she didn't know. Or at least Tyler could have given her a heads-up, told her he'd loaned her office to his brother.

Can you hear yourself? Anyone would think you were eighty-two, not thirty-two. Next you'll be talking about young people today and how things were different in your day.

Gabby took a deep breath and let it out. She'd already acknowledged she'd overreacted. Yes, Jon could have handled the situation better, too, but she was blowing the whole incident out of proportion. It was a blip on the radar, nothing to get worked up over. He was probably only visiting the workshop for a few minutes, using the excuse of checking out his brother's business to abuse the facilities. The odds were good she'd never see him again.

Launching her email program, she started reading the latest batch of orders and enquiries, absently running her fingers through her short dark hair. She was about to respond to a complicated request from one of their corporate customers when Tyler appeared at her door, a mug of coffee in hand.

"You got a minute?" He propped a shoulder against the frame. As usual, he was dressed in faded jeans and a black T-shirt, the color a perfect foil for his silver eyes.

It was impossible to look at him and not think about his brother. The resemblance was that strong.

"As in a genuine sixty seconds? Absolutely. Anything more than that and you'll be paying me overtime tonight."

"Dream on," Tyler said with a snort of amusement.

He sat in her visitor's chair, his big body loose and relaxed. Gabby studied him for a beat, fascinated despite herself by the change in him over the past year.

The easy laughter, the softness in his eyes, even the way he moved—Tyler was a new man since he'd met and married Ally.

Happier. More content. Less single-minded and closed off.

It was good to see. No, it was better than good— it was great. Tyler deserved some peace and comfort in his life.

She frowned at the wistful note to her own thoughts.

That'll be enough of that, young lady.

"Don't get too comfortable," she said. "I wasn't joking about being snowed."

"You can work through lunch."

"Your turn to dream on. You know nothing gets between me and my food. Come on, spill. Quit chewing up my valuable time."

"It's no biggy. I need you to add my brother to our insurance policy."

Gabby sat a little straighter. "What?"

"Jon. My brother. He's going to be helping out here at the workshop for a while."

"But—" There were so many objections crowding her throat she couldn't decide which one to voice first. "But he's not a cabinet-maker or a French polisher, is he?"

"He's a builder, and he's good. He'll pull his weight."

"So, is this a temporary thing? A couple of weeks? A month?" Gabby asked.

"It's for as long as it needs to be."

"What are you? Yoda? *As long as it needs to be?* What the hell does that mean?"

Tyler sighed. "Sometimes I forget what a pain in the ass you can be. Can't you just do what you're told for a change?"

It stung. Useless to pretend it didn't. She was only looking out for him. Worrying about his business. And he thought she was a pain in the ass.

"Fine. I'll add him on as a permanent employee." She picked up a pen and poised it over her notepad, ready to take down his instructions verbatim, since that was clearly the kind of employee he wanted her to be. "Anything else I can do for you?"

"Gabby. Come on. Don't go all cat's-bum-mouthed on me. You know I was only joking."

Nice to know he found her hurt feelings amusing.

"Way to smooth talk me, silver tongue."

"I'm sorry I called you a pain in the ass." He said it like a dutiful schoolboy reciting his times tables.

She raised her eyebrows.

"And the cat's bum comment was completely uncalled for," he added.

"No kidding. And good work with the sincerity there, too. It's really convincing."

Tyler grinned. "Are we friends again?"

Friends.

For three years, they had been a lot more than friends. He'd been her lover, had practically lived at her place. She'd built all kinds of white-picket dreams around him. Then she'd realized that he was never going to share himself with her in the way she needed, and she'd pulled the pin on their relationship. He'd been angry at first. Convinced that she was asking for something he didn't have to give. But after a while they'd settled into a friendship and she'd come to work for him.

Then he'd fallen in love with Ally and given all of himself to her freely and openly without a second's thought.

"Your minute's up," she said.

Tyler laughed. Despite the fact that she was still annoyed with him, she couldn't stop her mouth from twitching in response to the rich sound.

He pointed a finger at her. "I saw that."

"Stop pretending you're charming, because you're not. You can't ask for my opinion and advice one minute and then tell me to pull my head in the next."

Tyler must have picked up on the seriousness of her tone because his smile faded.

"I was only joking, Gab, okay?" He was sincere this time, his eyes very sober.

She nodded, feeling ridiculous for being so prickly. She blamed the stranger she'd found at her desk this morning—Tyler's brother had thrown her off her pace and she was still trying to regain her equilibrium.

"I'll get the paperwork sorted today. What do you want me to set up as far as payroll goes?"

The million-dollar question—exactly what was Tyler paying his underqualified, transient brother?

"I'll take care of that."

She frowned, but this time she didn't say anything. Before she'd joined the business, Tyler had handled the administration himself, so he was more than capable of adding an employee to the payroll. Why he suddenly chose to do so now when she'd been taking care of it for years was a whole other issue.

"Right. Then I guess we're sorted," she said.

"Good stuff." Tyler stood, lifting his coffee mug in a casual salute before heading out the door.

She focused on her work, pushing all the nagging voices in her head to one side. At the end of the day, the name on the sign was T.A. Furniture Design. He was the one taking the risk, therefore he got to make the decisions.

Meaning she was going to have to get used to having his brother around.

It was an unsettling thought. Which was stupid. She got along with all the guys; she'd always been the kind of woman who got on well with men. They ragged on each other, told jokes, had the occasional beer together after work. They were her mates. And despite their not-so-great start, there was no reason why she wouldn't rub along fine with Jon, too.

No reason at all.

JON TURNED OFF THE ORBITAL sander and ran his hand over the tabletop. In the very early days of his apprenticeship he'd dabbled in furniture making, but he hadn't had the patience for it then. Now, he felt the smoothness of the wood beneath his fingers and felt a definite sense of achievement and satisfaction.

He was about to switch the sander on again when someone touched his arm. He looked up to see his brother standing there.

Jon slid off his ear protectors. "What's up?"

"It's quitting time. In case you hadn't noticed."

He glanced around in surprise. He'd been so lost in his work that he hadn't registered that the rest of the guys had gone home for the day.

"Right. Well, I've still got a way to go with this." Jon indicated the tabletop.

"You can finish it tomorrow. We're ahead of deadline on that job."

"I told Dino I'd have it ready for him in the morning. I'm happy to lock up if you want to head home."

"Gabby usually does that. She's still working."

"Is that safe?"

Tyler raised his eyebrows. "You worried she doesn't know how to handle a lock and key?"

Jon ignored the joke. "What if someone was hanging around? She probably doesn't weigh more than a hundred pounds."

In fact, his brother's office manager was so slight it had taken him longer than it should have this morning to figure out that the slim woman glaring at him was an adult, let alone Tyler's right-hand woman. With her boyishly short hair and jeans and T-shirt, she'd looked more like a skinny teen than a woman who helped run a multimillion-dollar business.

"Don't ever let Gabby hear you say that," Tyler said. "She'll tear you a new one."

"It's the truth, isn't it? She'd be toast if someone tried to overpower her."

Tyler groaned. "Definitely don't say *that* to her."

Jon gave his brother a look. "You're serious?"

"Gabby prides herself on her independence. Hates it when people do things for her that she can do herself. If you'd met her mom, you'd understand. Really scary lady."

Jon shrugged. "Fine. She can lock up, if that's what floats her boat."

Tyler pulled his car keys from his pocket. "Swing by the house on your way home if you change your mind. I've got some of that German beer you like and Ally's cooking lasagna."

Jon gave a noncommittal shrug. He knew Tyler was being hospitable, but the last thing Jon wanted was to sit on the sidelines of his brother's life and play witness to his happiness. Not that he begrudged Tyler any of what he had—the business, his home, Ally. He simply didn't need the reminder of all the things he'd messed up in his own life.

Plus it would make it a hell of a lot harder to stick to his self-imposed sobriety if he had to sit around and watch his brother knock back beers all night. And his abstinence would make Tyler curious.

Jon simply didn't want to go there. Yes, he'd had a wake-up call about his excessive drinking, but that didn't mean he wanted to talk about it or advertise it.

"I guess I'll see you tomorrow, then," Tyler said.

"Sure."

He didn't go immediately, and Jon sensed there was something else on his mind. Jon reached for the sander, checking the tension on the clamps. After a long beat, he heard the metallic clink of his brother's keys and when he glanced up Tyler was heading for the door.

Not for the first time, Jon wondered whether accepting his brother's offer of a temporary job had been a good idea. He didn't need the money—he'd sold out of his construction business and had a sizable chunk of change in his bank account—but he also didn't need to be sitting around staring at the walls while he worked out what to do next. Taking up Tyler's offer to work for him once they'd finished renovating the house had seemed like the best option—it was either that or continue the downward slide toward oblivion in the bottom of a bottle.

There was no denying that the notion held a certain appeal—the end of the struggle, all the crap cloaked in a warm, fuzzy haze of alcohol—but he could still hear his father's voice in his head, telling him over and over how worthless he was and how he'd never amount to anything.

He flat out refused to let the bastard be right.

He started the sander again. The vibrations traveled up his arms as he moved along the grain. Slowly, the tension banding his shoulders relaxed and he lost himself in the simplicity of the task.

He had no idea how much time had passed when the sander suddenly fell silent. Instinct made him look over his shoulder. Gabby was standing beside the outlet, her handbag on her shoulder. He pulled off his ear protectors.

"Sorry. I tried shouting and you didn't hear me."

She didn't sound sorry. Didn't look it, either, her arms crossed tightly over her chest.

"If you're ready to go, I already told Tyler I'm happy to lock up," he said.

"But you don't know the alarm code."

Purely out of habit, his gaze dipped below her neck. She was small on top, one of those petite women with tiny breasts and narrow hips. She probably didn't even need to wear a bra.

Basically the exact opposite of the kind of women he found attractive.

"I will if you tell me."

She frowned. He wasn't sure if it was because of what he'd said or if she'd caught him looking.

"What? You think I'm going to rip my own brother off?"

She stiffened. "It's a complicated system."

"I'll take notes."

She pushed her handbag strap higher on her shoulder. "All right. The keypad's in the showroom." She said it grudgingly. Reluctantly.

He followed her, aware of the tension radiating off her in waves. Man, she was one uptight chick. Tyler seemed to rate her highly, but personally Jon couldn't see the appeal. Humorless, defensive, prickly—she was the very definition of hard work, and he didn't do hard work when it came to women. Not that that would ever be an issue with Gabby—everything about her screamed not available, not interested, not ever.

She stopped in front of the alarm console beside the front door of the showroom.

"The code is Tyler's birth year—not superoriginal, I know, but he insisted."

Jon watched as she punched four figures into the alarm console and explained the system.

"Cool, got it," he said.

"The lock is a little sticky. Sometimes you have to really force it."

"Sure."

"And we usually leave the showroom light on."

"Okay."

"Maybe I should leave you my number, in case you run into trouble."

It was on the tip of his tongue to tell her he had it covered, but she was already rummaging in her bag. He studied the neat part in her straight hair.

"Big night on the cards?" he asked. Maybe if they got to know each other a little she'd loosen up.

She glanced at him. "Not really, just dinner with my girlfriend."

He narrowed his eyes as the penny dropped. The no-frills clothes, the short hair, the lack of makeup, the whole not-available vibe—clearly, Ms. Wade batted for the other team. And based on the way she looked down her nose at him, she was one of those man-hating lesbians. The kind who thought the world would be a better place if men were cut out of the food chain altogether and replaced by lab technicians with turkey basters.

"Finally." She pulled a dog-eared business card from the depths of her purse. "My number's on the bottom. Call if you have issues with anything."

He tucked the card into the front pocket of his jeans. "I'm pretty sure I won't be needing it, but thanks anyway."

The expression on her face told him she had her doubts, but she didn't say anything. She moved toward the door and seemed surprised when he beat her there and held it open for her.

"Thanks," she muttered, giving him a distinctly ungrateful look.

He remembered what Tyler had said about her not liking people doing things for her that she could do for herself and suppressed a smile. Probably it made him a bad person, but for some reason he liked the idea of yanking her chain a little.

"See you tomorrow," she said, ducking past him into the warm night.

He waited until she'd reached her car and was safely inside. The moment he heard her engine start, he locked the door and returned to the workshop.

His footsteps echoed in the empty space. There

was no one waiting for him at home—if you could call a serviced apartment home. He could work here until the wee hours if he wanted to, and no one would miss him or care.

That was the way he liked it. No strings, no obligations. Nothing hard or demanding or restricting.

Just him—and the dozen or so monkeys on his back, of course.

CHAPTER TWO

GUILT NAGGED AT GABBY ALL through dinner with her old school-friend Shona. Jon had tried to be friendly, and she'd blown him off. He'd asked about her evening, opened the door for her. Then he'd watched until she was safely in her car. Even though those kinds of old-fashioned courtesies made her want to grind her teeth, she could appreciate the good manners behind them.

He was trying to be nice. And she'd been nothing but prickly and short.

Brushing her teeth before bed, Gabby tried to work out why he made her so bristly.

Sure, they'd gotten off on a bum note with the whole him-being-in-her-office thing, but she wasn't the sort of person to hold a grudge. And yes, she was worried that Tyler was taking on a staff member who was going to hold back the team rather than help them grow. But none of that was enough to explain the way she turned into Mother Superior every time she spoke to him.

She thought about the moment when he'd faced

her after she'd switched off the sander. She'd met his eyes and seen…nothing in their gray depths.

She paused, her mouth full of minty foam.

Maybe that was what it was. Jon was a whole lot of man—a commanding, demanding physical presence by sheer dint of the fact that he took up so much damned room—but when she looked at him she got…nothing. No sense of how he was feeling or what he was thinking. No hint of his mood or attitude. Just a contained, polite calm.

So what? Big deal if the guy doesn't go around advertising his emotions for all and sundry. He's a guy. That's generally what they do. If that's your big beef with him, you need to get over it, princess.

Gabby spit, then rinsed her mouth. Tomorrow was a new day. There was no reason why she couldn't start fresh with him. She'd take the time to chat with him, ask how he was settling in. She'd even insist on him using her computer again if he needed to check anything on the internet. Before long they'd be laughing and joking around the way she did with the other guys.

He was Tyler's brother, after all. It was impossible for her not to like him.

GABBY'S GOOD INTENTIONS turned to dust the next day when Jon didn't turn up until close to eleven o'clock. She was busy with her own work but she was very aware of his absence because she'd come in with the specific intention of starting over with him.

Initially, she thought he was simply running a little late, which was fine, since he'd stayed to finish the table last night. As the morning wore on, however, and he still didn't appear, she began to wonder if he was going to make history as the shortest-lived employee the company had ever had.

Then, just shy of eleven, Jon sauntered in. She took one look at him and knew exactly why he was late. The heavy eyes, the paleness—he'd had a *big night,* to use his own terminology. Probably been out to all hours, drinking and God knows what else. Then he'd slept it off and rolled into work as though he owned the place and answered to no one.

Gabby watched from her office as he exchanged a word with Dino, who was the senior on the workshop floor and didn't suffer fools gladly. She waited for him to let Jon know in no uncertain terms that the working day had started two and a half hours ago.

Dino said something. Jon replied. Dino laughed, the sound audible even over the whine of the table saw. She watched incredulously as he clapped Jon on the shoulder as though they'd been buddies for years. Dino was still chuckling as he crossed to the drill press.

As though he sensed her watching, Jon glanced at her, a big, no-holds-barred grin still on his face.

She blinked. He looked like a different man when he was smiling. Younger. A little dangerous.

Their eyes met and his smile sobered as he gave her a small acknowledging nod. Her own face felt frozen, but she forced herself to nod in reply. Then she swung in her chair and made a big deal out of being busy with her computer.

She told herself it was none of her business as she punched figures into the accounting software. If Dino was prepared to let the boss's unreliable brother get away with murder, it was no skin off her nose.

At lunchtime she walked around the corner and grabbed a sandwich. As she returned, she could see Jon through the window of the showroom. He was talking to a woman. Gabby frowned, taking in his body language: the way he was slouching oh, so casually against the counter; the almost-there smile on his face as he listened to something the woman was saying; the way his gaze traveled over her body in a slow, appreciative scan.

If he were in a bar, Gabby wouldn't hesitate for a second in assuming that he was hitting on the woman. But this was Tyler's showroom, and the woman was a customer. Jon was probably simply being friendly.

Gabby pushed the door open, stepping into the air-conditioned cool of the showroom.

"The thing about good design is that it's time-less. Ageless," Jon said. "It only gets better."

The woman was in her early forties, blonde and wearing a tight black dress. She flipped her hair over her shoulder as Jon gave her a loaded smile.

Gabby might not have had a date in a while, but she knew when a man was on the make—and he was definitely eyeing the blonde with carnal intent.

In his brother's showroom. At—she checked her watch—one thirty-five on a Tuesday afternoon.

Nice. Really classy.

Putting on her best professional smile, Gabby joined their cosy tête-á-tête.

"Hi. Hope you don't mind me interrupting. I'm Gabby." She offered the other woman her hand.

The blonde looked a little startled—no doubt she'd been so busy eating Jon up with her eyes she hadn't noticed Gabby approach.

"Hi. Fiona. Pleased to meet you."

Gabby turned to him, her smile still firmly in place. "Thanks, Jon. I'll take over from here."

For a moment she saw a flash of something

in his eyes—annoyance? Defiance?—then he straightened and gave Fiona a rueful shrug.

"Back to the grindstone."

Fiona laughed and flipped her hair again. "I'll keep in mind what you said."

"You do that."

Without looking at Gabby, he left the showroom.

"So, how can I help you...?" Gabby asked the other woman brightly.

Ten minutes later, Fiona was on her way with a handful of brochures and some preliminary pricing for the dining-room suite she was looking for. Gabby took a moment to gather her thoughts before heading to her office. Everything in her wanted to hunt Jon down and read him the riot act for behaving so unprofessionally. But he was Tyler's brother, and it was Tyler's business. If anyone was going to deal with Jon, it should be Tyler.

She entered the workshop, veering to the kitchen before hitting her office. She was rinsing a mug when she heard the heavy tread of someone entering. Her spine stiffened. Somehow she knew that it was Jon, but she refused to look to confirm it.

"She was into it, if that's what you're worried about," a deep voice said.

She turned to face him. "Excuse me?"

"Fiona. The blonde."

Gabby blinked, then shook her head. "Let me get this straight. It's your second day on the job, you walk in nearly three hours late, then you try to pick up one of our customers. And none of it is your fault?"

"That's not what I said."

"So you're not making excuses for treating our showroom like a pick-up bar?"

"*A pick-up bar?* Are you serious? We were having a *conversation.*"

"When it comes to your brother's company I'm usually pretty serious. I'm a little crazy like that, caring about him staying in business and whatnot."

He made a rude noise. "Lady, you need to lighten up."

"This isn't about me."

"Listen, I know you're all bent out of shape because I used your computer for a few seconds yesterday—"

"This isn't about you using my stupid computer. What do you think I am, a child or something?"

His gaze dropped to her chest for a telling beat. Never had she regretted being an A-cup so much in her life.

"I don't know. I can't think of another reason why you'd nearly blow a gasket because I was having a friendly chat with another consenting adult on my lunch break."

"She was a *customer*. She was looking for furniture, not a quickie in the parking lot."

"Personally I prefer a nice big bed and plenty of time, but don't let that get in the way of a good story."

To her everlasting chagrin, Gabby could feel heat stealing into her cheeks. "Stop trying to make this about me. You're the one who's taking advantage of Tyler, taking his job offer and then arriving late on your second day. How do you think it looks to the other guys, the boss's brother strolling in whenever he feels like it and—"

"I called Dino, told him I'd be in late and that I'd make up the time tonight."

Gabby was thrown for a second. "Well, good. At least someone knew where you were."

"What's wrong? Worried about me?"

"Hardly." She was fiercely hot now, her armpits prickling with self-conscious heat. It didn't help that he looked as cool as could be, as though he could barely bother to raise a sweat over her.

"You know what? Forget I said anything. Why I even felt the urge to explain is beyond me." He turned to go.

"Uh-uh. You don't get off that easy."

She raced around the table, barely making it to

the doorway in time to block his exit. He stopped short of plowing into her and she caught a whiff of male skin and spicy deodorant before he took a step backward.

"I want a promise from you that you won't talk to any of the customers again."

"What?"

"You heard me."

"Sweetheart, you have got to be the most uptight chick I have ever met in my life."

"My name is Gabby, thanks. And I want your word that you'll stay out of the showroom. If Dino's prepared to put up with you stuffing him around in the workshop that's his business. But Tyler and I handle sales and I won't have you screwing with our clients. Literally or figuratively."

Something fiery and dangerous flashed in his dark gray eyes. He grabbed her by the upper arms, forcibly picking her up and moving her to one side as though she were a piece of furniture. Then he was gone, and she was left gaping at his audacity.

"How *dare* you!" she said to the empty kitchen.

Good lord, she sounded like a Victorian maiden. An hysterical, outraged Victorian maiden on the verge of the vapors. Any second now she'd be reaching for her smelling salts or calling for her maid to burn some feathers.

How on earth had he managed to turn the

tables on her so effectively? He'd been utterly in the wrong, yet somehow she was left feeling like some uptight morals campaigner. He was the one who'd taken advantage of Tyler's generosity, not her. Jon was the one who should be feeling stupid and wrong and out of sorts.

You're an asshole, Jon Adamson.

Damn straight he was. That was why she'd been so prickly and bristly around him right from the start—her instincts had simply been ahead of the game, recognizing his essential asshole-ness way before he'd shown his true colors.

Which was great, except for one thing—she worked with him now. For the foreseeable future, she had to face him every day from nine to five.

Relax. He's a screwup. He'll mess up again. And next time Tyler will notice and then it will only be a matter of time.

She took a deep breath, then let it out.

Tyler was a good guy and a generous employer, but he was also an astute and passionate business-man. Once he realized his brother was deadwood, Jon would be gone.

It couldn't happen soon enough.

JON DIDN'T CONSIDER HIMSELF A tough guy to get along with. Sure, he wasn't a cuddly, let-me-be-your-instant-best-friend kind of guy, but he usually rubbed along okay with most people. He had a handful of good mates. He managed to end most of his romantic liaisons without tears and recriminations.

So why had Gabby taken such an instant and steadfast dislike to him?

He punched the table saw on and lined up his first cut, feeding the timber slowly into the blade.

He'd apologized for using her computer. He'd bitten his tongue last night when she'd been all bent out of shape about him locking up. He'd even sought her out to explain that she hadn't seen what she'd thought she'd seen when she'd come into the showroom. And she'd still looked at him as though she'd scraped him off her shoe.

It had to be the lesbian thing. Maybe she saw him as competition. Maybe she'd had a bad experience with a man that had tainted her view of his gender for all time. Whatever, he was done with worrying about her prickly sensibilities. From now on, it was every man—or woman—for himself.

You're the one who's taking advantage of Tyler, taking his job offer and then arriving late on your second day.

He frowned, shaking his head in an attempt to dislodge her words. As he'd explained to her, he'd called Dino, let him know he was running late. He'd been up half the night, unable to sleep, pacing the floor of his apartment and staring at late-night TV like a zombie. And when he'd finally fallen asleep in the early hours he'd been so out of it he'd slept through the alarm. But it wasn't as though he hadn't put in the hours yesterday—it had been nearly midnight when he left the workshop, bone weary and covered in sawdust—and it wasn't as though he wouldn't make up for the time today. As for taking advantage of Tyler... Jon's conscience was clear on that one, too. He and Tyler had an understanding, and it was none of Miss Prissy's business.

Jon lined up his next cut. Sawdust and wood chips flew as he ripped the length of the wood.

How do you think it looks to the other guys, the boss's brother strolling in whenever he feels like it?

He told himself to concentrate on the matter at hand, but Gabby's words continued to eat at him. He could tell himself she knew nothing and that her words held no weight. But the truth was that if he had an employee who'd turned up late on the second day of work, he wouldn't be too impressed, either. Not that he was Gabby's employee...but he could see her point. Considered objectively, it had probably looked bad. And it definitely didn't send a great message to the other staff members.

He swore under his breath, then hit the stop

button. Pulling the ear protectors from his head, he faced the inevitable: Gabby was right. But only about the late thing. He'd go to his grave defending his conversation with Fiona-the-blonde in the showroom. They'd been flirting, for Pete's sake—hardly a crime against nature. It wasn't as though he'd been about to club her over the head and drag her to his cave. They'd had a few laughs, eyed each other approvingly. Maybe, if things had warmed up, he'd have gotten her number. That's it.

Miss Prissy needed to get a life.

He glanced toward her office. She was visible through the open doorway, her head bent over her work. A small frown wrinkled her forehead. She was so *serious*. Did she never let her hair down? He tried to imagine it and couldn't. She was too stiff and distant and uptight.

She glanced up and he looked away before she caught him staring. God knew what she'd make of that. Sexual harassment, probably.

He smiled faintly. The idea of him trying to get it on with her was too absurd. She would probably kick him in the nuts then take photos of him writhing on the floor to show the rest of the sisterhood.

Dino walked past and gave him a questioning look. "You all right there, mate?"

Jon realized he was standing in the middle of the workshop with a piece of wood in his hands, staring at nothing. And that he'd wasted the past half hour thinking about Gabby Wade.

"All good," he assured the other man.

Then he collected the other pieces of timber and took them to where Carl was waiting.

GABBY LEFT WORK BEFORE SIX o'clock that night for the first time in months. Tyler and Ally had invited her for dinner to celebrate her birthday. Technically, it wasn't until the weekend but Ally and Tyler were hosting the firm's delayed Christmas party on Saturday night—they'd been so busy in the lead-up to Christmas that everyone had voted to postpone the party until a time when things were less hectic. Gabby would have been happy to combine the two events—or, better yet, forget her birthday altogether—but Ally had insisted they have a separate dinner to mark Gabby's special day.

Normally Tyler forgot her birthday, then made up for it by buying her something expensive a month or so later. Times had changed. He had Ally to remind him now.

Gabby parked close to their double-fronted Victorian home and fumbled in her bag for her lipstick. She found a roll of mints and two tampons, but no lipstick. Damn. Maybe she should have made the time to swing home and freshen up.

Who are you trying to impress, anyway? It's just Ally and Tyler.

Her hand stilled in her bag. It was a good question. Who *was* she trying to impress? Not Tyler anymore. That horse had well and truly bolted. As for Ally, right from the start she'd embraced Gabby has a friend.

Yet there was no denying the fact that Gabby found herself playing the comparison game whenever she spent any significant time with Tyler's wife. It was hard not to, given the superficial similarities between the two of them. They were both on the petite side, and they both had short, dark hair. Sure, Ally was much curvier than Gabby, and her hair was curly instead of dead straight, but it wasn't as though Tyler had gone off and married a six-foot-six redhead. Then there was the fact that both she and Ally were not exactly shy, retiring types…

Enough in common, really, to seed a host of unanswerable questions in Gabby's mind. But as she reminded herself regularly, Tyler had made his choice, and she was happy for him. Anything else was a waste of energy.

Which meant she didn't need to worry about lipstick. She was having dinner with two of her good friends. End of story.

Before she could examine her navel any more,

she got out of the car and made her way up the well-lit path to Tyler and Ally's porch. The door opened before she could knock and Ally greeted her with a hug. Dressed in an aqua dress with white embroidery around the hemline, she looked fresh and bright.

"I was beginning to think you were never going to show up," she said.

"Sorry. I got held up at work."

"As usual. Your boss is a slave driver."

"Don't look at me—it's the office manager who wields the whip," Tyler said as he joined them in the wide entrance hall. He kissed Gabby's cheek. "Happy early birthday."

Gabby laughed. "I can honestly say that's the first time I've heard those words pass your lips."

"What can I say? Forgetting dates is a guy thing."

Ally poked him in the ribs. "You're on increasingly thin ice with that one, mister. All the latest research is showing that there's precious little difference between the male and female brain."

Tyler captured her hand in one of his to save himself from further prodding.

"I kind of like the differences. Don't know about you," he said, smiling into his wife's face.

Gabby looked away. She could tell herself she was happy for Tyler until the cows came home, but there was no getting around the fact that seeing the way he looked at Ally made her chest ache.

Not once in three years had he ever looked at her in the same way. Not once.

Which is why he married her and not you, dufus.

"Something smells great," she said, sniffing appreciatively.

Ally hooked her arm through Gabby's. "I made us Moroccan meatballs with preserved lemons, pistachio couscous and orange-and-date salad."

"We're going through a Moroccan stage," he explained as they walked toward the open living space at the rear of the house.

"Well, you know me, anything that I didn't cook myself is manna from heaven," Gabby said.

"Good. Tyler was worried it might be too exotic for you."

Ally released Gabby's arm to pour wine into three of the four glasses on the counter.

"Here's to you," Ally said as she passed Gabby a glass.

"Yeah, happy birthday, Gab," Tyler said.

Gabby clinked glasses, distracted by the single flute still on the counter. It was possible, of course, that Tyler or Ally had simply put out one too many. She hoped like hell that was what had happened, because the alternative was that someone else was joining them for dinner. And since it was a small and cosy family affair, she had a horrible feeling she might know who that fourth person might be.

Right on cue, the doorbell rang. Gabby's stomach dipped with foreboding.

"I'll get it," Tyler said.

"We thought it might be nice to have Jon over, too," Ally explained as he disappeared to answer the door. "We've barely seen him since he's been back, because he was in Woodend so long. Now he's here, I've been bugging him to come for dinner every night, and finally he said yes."

Ally looked pleased. Gabby could only imagine how *she* looked. Constipated? Bilious? The last thing she wanted was to sit around a table making polite conversation with Tyler's knuckle-dragging brother.

"Wasn't sure what you guys were having, so I brought red and white," Jon said as he and Tyler appeared.

Jon's step faltered when he saw her standing there.

"Evening," she said, raising her glass.

For some reason his obvious discomfort made her feel better, made her feel less childish for being unhappy about *him* being here.

"Hi." Jon was frowning slightly as he put down the bottles of wine he'd brought.

"Finally I get you in my clutches. I'm determined to put some meat back on those bones, you know," Ally said, planting a kiss on his cheek and giving him a warm hug.

Jon hugged her as warmly, a faint smile on his face. Ally seemed very small in comparison to his big body. Gabby experienced an odd clench of... something as she watched them embrace.

Looking away, she swallowed a big mouthful of wine. Everybody loved Ally, it seemed. Even the arrogant, standoffish brother.

"Have some wine. We're toasting Gabby," Tyler said.

Jon's expression was unreadable as he accepted a drink.

"Gab, you know I'd be a mess without you. You're my right-hand woman. Hope this makes up for all the other birthdays I've forgotten," Tyler said.

Out of the corner of her eye, Gabby saw Jon tense as he registered the occasion. As she'd suspected, Ally hadn't told him tonight was her birthday dinner. In fact, given that small give-away hesitation when he'd first entered, Gabby was pretty damn sure he hadn't known she was going to be here. No doubt he would have come up with an ironclad excuse otherwise. Lord knew, she would have if she'd known.

"Happy birthday, Gabby," Ally echoed.

Some instinct made Gabby glance at Jon as she took a drink. She saw him lift his glass to his mouth, tilt it and wet his lips. But he didn't open his mouth. It was over in a split second, so fast she almost thought she'd imagined it, but she hadn't.

Jon had faked drinking a toast in her honor.

Wow. He must really dislike her.

She was surprised how much the realization stung. Then she gave herself a mental shake. She didn't care what he thought of her. The idea was laughable. Ludicrous. She'd met him only two days ago, and what she knew of him proclaimed him to be a screwup of the highest order—she should consider it a badge of honor that he didn't like her, not a slap in the face.

Tyler crossed to the sideboard to collect a small, neatly wrapped box. "From us."

Gabby took the box, very aware of the tall figure standing at the edge of her peripheral vision.

"This is awfully small for the company car I've been campaigning for."

"Next year," Tyler said.

Gabby tugged the pretty silver ribbon free and lifted the lid. Inside, a pair of stud earrings rested on a velvet cushion. Set with golden-brown gems, they sparkled in the overhead light.

"They're beautiful," Gabby breathed.

"They're golden beryls. I saw them and thought they were a match for your eyes," Ally said. "Tyler couldn't remember if your ears are pierced, but I was pretty sure you wore earrings to his birthday in August."

"My ears are pierced." Gabby touched one of the glittering stones, trying not to be hurt that Tyler couldn't remember. He'd been in her apartment, in her bedroom, hundreds of times. Had he really forgotten her messy jewelry box? And what about the time she'd freaked out over sucking up one of her favorite earrings in the vacuum cleaner? Had everything pre-Ally been consigned to the archives of his mind?

"If you don't like them, we won't be offended if you want to swap them for something else," Ally said.

Gabby realized she'd been silent for too long and she offered her hosts—her friends—a big smile.

"They're absolutely perfect. Gorgeous. In fact..."

She eased the earrings from the box. A few seconds later she let her hands fall to her sides and offered herself up to Ally and Tyler's scrutiny. "How do they look?"

"Just as I imagined," Ally said.

Gabby stepped forward to kiss her cheek in thanks. "Thanks for thinking of me."

Ally drew her into a hug, squeezing her tight. "It was my pleasure."

Gabby squeezed her back.

When Tyler had first introduced her to Ally, Gabby had been determined to like the woman who had made him so happy, even if it killed her. She'd been prepared to overlook anything, to be generous and accepting of any and all faults or shortcomings because Ally was Tyler's choice, the woman he loved.

The woman he wanted to spend the rest of his life with.

Then she'd met Ally and realized that it would be no hardship to like her. She was warm and generous, smart and funny. Easily one of the most thoughtful people Gabby knew—witness the beautiful earrings, chosen with care and consideration. Not too dangly or elaborate—because Gabby was not a fussy woman—and, apparently, a match for her eyes. Although Gabby was pretty sure it was a stretch to compare her ordinary brown eyes to the warm golden gems. It hadn't taken her long to understand why Tyler had fallen in love with Ally. She was very easy to love.

Tyler patted her on the shoulder fondly as she and Ally broke their embrace. Gabby gave him a wry look, then her gaze slid to where Jon was standing at a distance, watching them. Their eyes met for a moment before he glanced down at his still full wineglass.

"Okay, people. Make a beeline for the table, it's time for the feasting to begin," Ally said, waving them toward the dining table that occupied one corner of the room.

Gabby dutifully followed orders, but Jon lingered at the counter, arms crossed over his chest.

"That means you as well, my friend. The last thing I need is you hovering while I serve our meal," Ally said.

"Funny. I thought only men suffered from short person syndrome," Jon said.

"What's that supposed to mean?" Ally asked.

Jon looked at her, a smile quirking his mouth. "What do you think it means?"

"I think you're saying I'm bossy."

"Hey. If the shoe fits…" Jon said with a don't-blame-me shrug.

Ally laughed and gave him a shove. "Move, you big lug."

Gabby watched, fascinated, as Jon resisted Ally long enough to make her really work before finally deigning to shift from his position. There was a lazy, amused light in his eyes, not quite the same as the expression he'd had when he was chatting up the blonde in their showroom this afternoon, but certainly just as playful.

"Next to Gabby, please. Since I've already been labelled a dictator, I might as well have it the way I want it," Ally instructed.

Gabby gave a silent sigh. Great. Now she was going to have to rub shoulders with Captain Studly through three courses and coffee. Not exactly the birthday celebration she'd been hoping for. But there was precious little she could do about it.

Buckle up, it's going to be a bumpy night.

CHAPTER THREE

GABBY FIDDLED WITH THE STEM OF her wineglass as Jon hesitated for a telling second before pulling out the chair next to her.

Nice.

"Don't worry, I don't have cooties," she said as he sat.

"Good to know. Although I've never really been sure what they are."

"I think they're the equivalent of girl germs."

"Yeah? I've always been kind of partial to those."

Gabby flashed to the scene she'd witnessed this afternoon. "No kidding."

She realized immediately that he might take the comment the wrong way, but when she glanced at him askance he was smiling slightly.

Don't get too excited, but you may have had your first civil exchange with Jon Adamson.

Not quite a miracle, but close to it given their record. Which probably meant she should make an effort to extend the cease fire.

"So, um, how are you finding Melbourne after so long away?"

"Busy. The traffic is nuts. I don't remember it being this bad."

"You've been away ten years, haven't you? Melbourne's grown by about a million people in that time."

"That would explain it."

A small silence fell and they both glanced to where Ally and Tyler were serving the meal. To Gabby's admittedly inexpert eye, it looked as though they were still several minutes away from being rescued by their hosts.

Which meant more small talk was called for.

Over to you, buddy. I did my bit.

"So. It's your birthday, huh?" Jon finally said.

"Yep. Keeps coming around every year, whether I like it or not."

"Am I allowed to ask…?"

"Thirty-three. It's actually on Saturday, but since we're having the work Christmas party then, Ally wanted to do something tonight so I'd feel special."

"Sounds like Ally." There was a softness in his voice when he said the other woman's name.

"Yeah. She's pretty great."

Another silence.

My turn. Think of something. Anything.

But the only thought that popped into her head was that he would have a hell of a time buying a suit off the rack with his broad shoulders.

She took a breath to launch into a discussion about work, but he beat her to it.

"So, Dino was telling me you usually dress up for the Christmas party?"

She gave him a mental elephant stamp for coming up with such a nice, neutral topic. Even they couldn't go awry talking about this one.

"It's kind of become a tradition."

"What are you coming as this year?"

"I was thinking Rudolph. But I'm still toying with the idea of a Christmas tree."

"What about your girlfriend? Does she get into the whole dressing-up thing?"

Gabby frowned. "I'm sorry?"

She was vaguely aware of Tyler and Ally ferrying dishes to the table.

"Here we go," Ally said.

"Or aren't partners invited?" Jon asked, his questioning gaze going from Gabby to Ally to Tyler.

Partners. Girlfriend.

The words circled Gabby's brain like thought balloons. It took her a full five seconds to join the two together and jump to the only conclusion possible.

"I'm not a lesbian." It came out sounding a lot more high-pitched and defensive than she would have liked.

Ally's eyebrows rose as she stared at Jon. "You thought Gabby was gay?"

Tyler laughed. "Bloody hell. Where did you get that idea from?"

Jon's cheekbones were a dull red. "She mentioned her girlfriend, and I thought…" His gaze went to Gabby's hair, then dropped below her chin to her body. "I must have got the wrong end of the stick."

"*Girlfriend* as in a *friend* who happens to be a *girl*," Gabby said.

She didn't need a mirror to know she was bright red—she could feel the heat radiating off her skin. Although why she was embarrassed was beyond her—he was the one who had made a fool of himself.

"Sorry. My mistake," Jon said.

"No kidding," Gabby said. Talk about a lack of perception.

Tyler was still smiling.

"Tyler. It's not funny," Ally chided.

"I know. Sorry. It's just— Gabby as a lesbian… It boggles the mind."

"Can we let it drop?" Jon said. The glance he shot her was full of apology.

Great. First he outed her as a lesbian, now he felt sorry for her.

"This looks great, Ally," she said brightly, picking up her knife and fork. "You know, if you weren't married, I'd be tempted to nab you for myself."

Everyone laughed, including Jon. The knot in Gabby's stomach loosened a little.

"This reminds me of a letter I got last month for the column..." Ally said.

Gabby reached for her water glass as Ally launched into her story. Gabby nodded and laughed and made comments in all the right places, but all the while, behind her smile and her I-couldn't-care-less demeanor, her mind was whirring, obsessing over Jon's mistaken assumption.

She told herself that she didn't care what he thought, that being thought to be gay was not an insult, that some of her best friends were gay. She told herself that his lack of perception said a lot more about him than it did about her. She even got herself to the point where she half believed it—except she kept returning to that significant pause when he'd looked at her hair, then her body before apologizing for getting it wrong.

"Excuse me." She pushed back her chair and stood.

Hopefully enough time had passed that her leaving the table wouldn't be read as retreat. Right now she was beyond caring.

The bathroom door closed behind her with a soft click and she crossed the tile floor to stand in front of the full-length mirror mounted beside the old-fashioned tub.

She stared at the woman she saw reflected there, determined to prove to herself once and for all that Jon had his head up his backside.

The woman staring back at her had short, straight dark hair, with a crooked fringe and a pale face utterly devoid of makeup.

Heaps of women have short hair, her inner voice scoffed. *Audrey Tatou has short hair, and no one is calling her a lesbian.*

As for the no-makeup thing, well, she'd simply gotten out of the habit of it over the past few months. Admittedly, she looked a little...nondescript without it, but, again, it didn't make her gay.

She dropped her gaze to her body. Her T-shirt was old and stretched out, the fabric swamping her small breasts and bunching unattractively around her waist. Her jeans were cut for comfort rather than style, their fit loose and utilitarian. Her sneakers were old and scuffed, again chosen for comfort over appearance.

Gabby blinked, but it didn't change what the mirror was telling her. The voice in her head was suspiciously silent.

She looked like a boy.

Was it any wonder that Jon had made assumptions? Really?

She sat on the rim of the tub, feeling shaky. As though someone had pulled a veil from her eyes and forced her to see an unpalatable truth.

When had she stopped caring how she looked?

When had she stopped wearing makeup and going to the hairdresser instead of trimming her own hair with nail scissors? When had she stopped buying sexy underwear and high heels and pretty clothes?

When had she ceased to think of herself as an attractive, sexual being and slipped into this sexless, safe disguise?

She didn't know the exact date, but she could guess: the moment she'd given up on Tyler. Nearly four years, give or take. Four years of seeing him every day, convincing herself they were better friends than they had ever been lovers and that she'd done the smart thing—the only thing—in breaking off their relationship.

She laughed suddenly as a bitter irony hit her: she'd broken up with Tyler to protect herself, but he was the one who had moved on. He'd found love, while Gabby, apparently, had been marking time.

A wellspring of emotion tightened the back of her throat. She pressed her fingers against her eyelids. If she started crying, she'd never stop. And there was no way she was going to hide in the bathroom and cry at her own birthday party while her ex and his new wife fretted about her on the other side of the door.

No. Freaking. Way.

She took an unsteady breath, then another. She stood and shook out her hands.

"Come on, princess. Get it together."

She tried out a smile in the mirror. It looked more like a grimace than a smile, but it would have to do.

Then she threw back her shoulders, straightened her spine and opened the bathroom door.

She had a birthday party to survive, after all.

Jon shook his head as Tyler offered to refill his wineglass, his brother only belatedly noticing that Jon hadn't finished his first glass yet.

"Driving," Jon said at Tyler's enquiring look.

Tyler didn't say anything, but Jon guessed from the dawning understanding in his brother's eyes that they would be having a conversation about his abstinence in the near future.

Great. Exactly what he wanted. Not.

He glanced toward the hall for the second time in as many minutes, very aware that Gabby had been gone for a long time. Judging by their casual demeanors, neither Tyler nor Ally seemed to find her extended absence unusual but they were still in the honeymoon phase of their marriage, totally wrapped up in one another. They probably wouldn't notice if Jon jumped on the table and started doing the chicken dance.

It was possible he wouldn't have noticed Gabby's absence, either, had he not been sitting next to her. He'd felt her tense when he'd asked about her girlfriend. And even though she'd brushed off his assumption and made a joke about it, he'd felt her continuing tension. She'd practically vibrated with it, like a plucked harp string.

He'd hurt her feelings. Unintentionally, but the result was the same. He might be a lot of things, and she might be a pain in the ass, but if he could take back the moment, he would.

He was about to suggest Ally go in search of her absent guest when Gabby returned. Jon studied her face as she sat. She was wearing a polite social smile but he could see the unhappiness behind her eyes.

Damn.

He was going to have to apologize. Not that he hadn't already done so, but clearly he was going to have to try again.

He reached for his glass, his fingers closing around the stem. Only when he was carrying the wine to his mouth did he register what he was doing. He reversed the action without drinking.

Two months. That was how long he'd sentenced himself to abstinence. Not because he truly believed he had a drinking problem, more to prove to himself that he could stop if he wanted to.

It occurred to him that a guy who didn't have a drinking problem should be finding it a hell of a lot easier to go without than he had the past few days. Certainly he probably shouldn't keep catching himself fantasizing about grabbing a six-pack on the way home from work, or imagining the warm creep of alcohol stealing over his body and numbing his mind.

"So, Jon, what's this mysterious apartment you're staying in like? Tyler tells me it's around the corner from the workshop," Ally said, drawing his thoughts back to the moment.

"It's a serviced apartment. Nothing mysterious about it that I can see," he said.

"Great. Then I guess the coast is clear for Tyler

and I to come over for dinner one night soon." Ally had a mischievous twinkle in her eye.

He was well aware that his sister-in-law was quietly campaigning for a closer relationship between him and his brother. It was never going to happen, for a variety of reasons, but Ally would realize that soon enough on her own without him pointing it out to her.

"Sure. As long as you like take-out pizza."

"You're as bad as Gabby," Tyler said. "I swear I was never that pathetic when I was single."

"Isn't there a rule about not dissing a person on their birthday?" Gabby said.

"No. And even if there was, it's not until Saturday, so I'm in the clear," Tyler said.

"I can cook," Gabby said.

"Ditto," Jon said, because he figured he owed it to her to provide backup.

"Microwaving frozen meals doesn't count," Ally said.

"Toast does," Jon said. There was an echo, and he realized Gabby had said the same thing simultaneously.

She glanced at him, disconcerted. He offered her a faint smile. Not too big, since he didn't want to push his luck.

Her gaze became frosty.

He was still in her black books, then. It figured.

She hadn't liked him much before he'd got her sexuality wrong—she would probably go home and burn an effigy of him in her yard after tonight's events.

Ally served lemon cheesecake for dessert—Gabby's favorite, apparently—and they all watched as Gabby dutifully blew out the single candle. They moved to the couches while Tyler prepared coffees with their shiny new espresso machine.

Jon's gaze kept drifting to the wall clock, trying to calculate when it would be acceptable for him to leave. Immediately after coffee? Or would that mark him as the crassest of social boors?

He jiggled his leg impatiently, willing Tyler to hurry. Once the coffee was ready, Jon gulped his down while it was still too hot and earned himself a burned tongue for his troubles. Finally he decided he must be in the clear and made his excuses.

It wasn't until he was on the porch, the door closed behind him that he remembered he'd planned to apologize to Gabby again.

He turned, raising his hand to knock, but lowered it without doing so. The least he could do was apologize in private, save Gabby a rehashing of what had obviously been an embarrassing moment.

He'd have to find a few minutes alone with her at work tomorrow. No doubt she'd find some way to give him a hard time. But he'd do the right thing because, contrary to what she obviously believed, he wasn't a bad guy.

IT WAS NEARLY MIDNIGHT BY THE time Gabby let herself into her apartment. She threw her bag onto the couch and checked her answering machine— nothing—then walked to her bedroom and into the ensuite.

Flicking on the light, she gave herself a moment to adjust to the sudden brightness before beginning her nightly ritual. First, she washed her face, then patted it dry and smoothed a lightly scented moisturizer onto her face, neck and shoulders. She switched to almond-scented body lotion for her arms, hands and legs, working it in with long, smooth strokes.

At least you didn't give up everything. Apparently, you still care if your skin is nice.

Her hands stilled on her calf. Somehow, she'd managed to keep a lid on her emotions. But now she was in the safety of her own home and it was time to come clean with herself.

More than time—about four years overdue, in fact.

She straightened, and for the second time that

night she stared at her own image in the mirror, trying to understand herself.

Was she still in love with Tyler? Was that what all this was about? Had she been kidding herself for years when all along she'd been holding a candle, pining, hoping?

Dear God. Please don't let me be that woman. Please don't let me be that pathetic.

She didn't want it to be true. But the facts were pretty damned convincing. She'd gone on exactly one date since she'd broken up with Tyler. One date in four years. And it wasn't through lack of invitations, either. She'd had her share of admirers in those first few years of being single again. She couldn't remember what excuses she'd come up with for not accepting any of the offers to see a movie or go out for dinner. She simply hadn't been interested, and eventually the offers had dried up.

If she was being honest, she'd have to admit she hadn't really noticed or cared. She'd been too busy organizing Tyler's business—whipping it into shape when she first came on board then doing all she could to help lift him to the next level in subsequent years. Too busy recasting herself as Tyler's faithful sidekick, the sexless, tireless little buddy who never let him down.

What did you think was going to happen—that he'd admire your skill with a balance sheet so much that he'd finally fall all the way in love with you?

Because, of course, Tyler had never loved her the way she'd loved him.

It still hurt, even after all these years. She turned her back on her reflection, unwilling to play witness to her own unhappiness. Which pretty much answered the big question, didn't it?

She brushed her teeth, staring at the tile wall. Once she was finished, she walked into the bedroom and stripped to her underwear. Kicking her clothes into the corner, she crawled beneath the covers.

The sheets were cool against her skin and she shivered as she waited for them to warm, legs drawn up, arms pulled tightly to her chest.

On nights such as these, she used to make Tyler spoon her from behind, the heat of his body like a furnace against her back. She'd loved feeling his warm breath on the nape of her neck, loved having one of his strong arms wrapped around her. Tyler had always moved in his sleep, however—he'd liked to spread out, to have his own space. Nine times out of ten she'd woken to find their positions reversed, him curling away from her while she clung to his back, her body molded to his.

Chasing him, needing him, even in her sleep.

She made a distressed sound and burrowed

deeper into the pillow. It didn't stop the tears from coming. Four years' worth, pushed down deep.

The truth was, she'd never allowed herself to grieve for Tyler. She'd been too busy being tough. Moving on. Assuring him there were no hard feelings and that they'd still be a part of each other's lives. She'd convinced herself that she'd done all her grieving beforehand, before she'd made the painful, wrenching decision to call things off between them. She'd been so sure she had it all together, that she was on top of it.

More fool her.

Her pillow was getting wet. She rolled onto her back. The sound of her sobs seemed very loud in her quiet bedroom. Tears streamed from the corners of her eyes down her temples into her hair. She pressed her palms to her sternum and pushed, willing the ache to go away.

She didn't want to still love Tyler. She didn't want to be this weak and tragic.

Dear God, if Mom could see me now, she'd kick my backside into the middle of next week.

The thought prompted a hiccuping laugh. Gabby sniffed noisily, then sat up and wiped at her eyes with the backs of her hands.

She'd been raised by a fiercely independent woman who'd prided herself on never needing anyone—men being at the very top of that list. Divorced from Gabby's father when Gabby was only two years old and her sister, Angela, barely one, Rachel Wade had thrown herself into single motherhood like an Amazonian warrior. She'd taught herself how to change fuses, tap washers and car tires and had hammered into her daughters from the moment they were old enough to understand that they always had to stand on their own two feet and that no one could ever make them unhappy unless they allowed it.

Nice in theory, but often not so great in practice, as Gabby and her sister had discovered many times over the years.

Fortunately for Gabby, her mother was halfway around the world at present, living her dream of working and traveling through Europe.

Still, the thought of her mother was enough to make Gabby reach for the box of tissues. She blew her nose, mopped her eyes dry. Then she switched pillows and lay down and tried to go to sleep.

There wasn't much else she could do, after all. She'd been in love before—Billy Harrison when she was seventeen, Gareth Devenish when she was in her early twenties. Neither of them had been as important in her life as Tyler was, but both experiences had taught her that there was no willing away a broken heart. She would simply have to wait the pain out.

It's been four years. How long do you freaking want?

A good question. A scary one, too, because she'd already wasted four years longing for something she could never have.

She fell asleep late and woke early. The first thing she did was walk to her wardrobe and throw the doors open. She had to dig deep to get past jeans and yet more jeans, but after a few minutes she pulled out her black leather miniskirt and her stiletto ankle boots. A rummage in her chest of drawers produced the tight orange tank that through some mysterious trick of design managed to give her cleavage. In the shower, she shaved her legs and her armpits, washed and conditioned and exfoliated. Then she smoothed on body lotion and pulled out her make-up bag. Twenty minutes later she inspected herself in the mirror on the back of her bedroom door.

She'd always had good legs, and her backside was a nice shape, neat and round and perky. The boots and the skirt she'd chosen made the most of her two best assets, while the tank and push-up bra worked their magic upstairs.

Jon was going to eat his words when he saw her this morning. He was going to take one look at her in this outfit and realize how wrong he'd been about her. He was going to—

Gabby froze in the act of spritzing on her most expensive perfume as it occurred to her that, as well as all those other things, he was going to know that she'd done all this—the legs, the hair, the makeup, the clothes—for him. To prove something to him. Because she cared what he thought.

"Damn it."

Annoyed with herself, Gabby stripped. Dressed only in her underwear, she pushed hangers out of the way until finally, at the back of the wardrobe, she found what she was looking for—a pair of shapeless cargo pants she kept for really dirty work. The top shelf yielded the box with her Doc Martens boots, a relic from her teen years. She was stumped for a moment with regard to the top, but then inspiration struck and she grinned. Throwing herself across the bed, she grabbed the phone from the nightstand and dialed.

"Jen, it's Gabby. Sorry it's so early, but I need to borrow something…"

No way was she going to let Jon think that she cared what he thought or said. No. Way.

JON WOKE BATHED IN SWEAT, HIS heart racing. It took a full five seconds to work out where he was and that he'd been dreaming.

He let out a sigh and lifted a hand to his face. His skin felt clammy and cold. Throwing back the covers, he stood and walked out of the bedroom and into the apartment's living space. He poured coffee into a fresh filter and turned on the coffee machine.

Hard to work out what was worse—suffering broken sleep from the nightmares that had become his almost nightly companions since he'd given up drinking or waking with a thundering hangover.

This morning's dream had been a doozy—his father storming up the hallway of their family home toward him, the thick leather belt he favored for beatings clutched in one hand. Tyler's whimpers of fear from behind him. No sign of his mother, although Jon knew she should be there, that she should be the one standing between them and the monster bearing down on them. The almost overwhelming urge to run had gripped him. The need to abandon Tyler and run, run, run to save himself. And then, finally, he'd been hit with the dawning, horrible knowledge that there was no escape, that there was nothing he could do to save himself or his brother.

Really restful stuff. The kind of stuff that made a guy want to spring out of bed whistling a tune, ready to head out into the day to rub shoulders with his fellow man.

The carafe was full. He grabbed a cup, poured coffee, stirred in sugar. Mug in hand, he wandered over to the sliding doors that led out onto his tiny balcony. He glanced at the redbrick wall opposite, then changed his mind about going outside. The lack of view hadn't bothered him when he'd taken the place, but the looming wall that filled every window was starting to get on his nerves.

No one's forcing you to stay. Book a ticket, get on a plane. Go find someplace with no memories, no ties. No expectations.

It was what he'd wind up doing eventually, he was sure. But he wasn't ready to go. Not yet.

He wasn't sure what was holding him back. But soon enough he'd get over whatever it was, pack his meager belongings and head off to a new start somewhere.

Downing the last of his coffee, he dumped the mug in the sink and went to shower. It was early, but he might as well be at work as here.

Half an hour later, he pulled into the parking lot at T.A. Furniture Designs. Belatedly it occurred to him that he'd left the key in his jeans from yesterday—then he spotted the red car parked close to the building.

Gabby. It figured she'd be the first in. If there was an employee equivalent of teacher's pet, she was it.

Still, it would give him a chance to apologize to her again without the risk of the guys overhearing. He'd get it out of the way, then he and Gabby could go back to pistols at ten paces or whatever it was they did whenever they were in the same room.

He locked his truck and strode to the entrance. He pressed the doorbell that had been provided for after-hours visitors and waited. When no one came after a couple of minutes, he knocked and tried the bell again.

A few seconds later the workshop door swung open and Gabby walked through. The good-natured smile on her face faded when she recognized him through the glass. His gaze took in first her T-shirt, then her baggy combat fatigues and finally her chunky punk rocker boots as she strode toward him. Lastly, he focused on her hair, which had been parted to one side and gelled into a shiny brown helmet of asexual hair.

She unlocked the door and pulled it open. "Exactly how long do you think it takes to walk from the back room to the front door?"

His gaze dipped to the image of k.d. lang printed across her chest. "Nice T-shirt."

He wasn't stupid—he knew a challenge when he saw one—and he couldn't hide the smile curving his lips a moment longer.

"What's so funny?"

He patted her on the shoulder as he moved past her. "I'm flattered you went to so much trouble for me. I didn't realize you cared."

He heard her quick intake of breath.

"Please. I know you think you're the center of the universe and God's gift to women, but you're not the center of my world, Jon Adamson. Maybe it's time to get over yourself."

He waited while she finished her little speech. Then he grabbed the price tag that was still dangling from her collar, tugging it free.

"Must have been hard to find that T-shirt on such short notice. Like I said, it's nice to know you care."

He dropped the tag into her hand. He'd delivered the perfect exit line and the script called for him to walk away now. But he couldn't resist hanging around to see her reaction. Maybe it made him a little twisted, but he was starting to enjoy these sparring sessions.

She looked at the tag in her hand, then slowly raised her gaze to his. He was all set to savor his victory, but she shifted slightly and a shaft of sunlight hit her face, catching her eyes and glinting off the earrings that Tyler and Ally had given her.

He blinked.

Ally was way off base—Gabby's eyes were far richer than the gemstones sparkling at her ears.

He didn't even have a name for the warm golden tone of her irises. Cognac? Honey? Amber? None of them seemed adequate. Set off by long, dark lashes, they were hands down, no questions asked, the most arresting, beautiful eyes he'd ever gazed into. No mineral composite dug out of the ground was ever going to do them justice.

The silence stretched between them. Jon realized he was staring, but couldn't make himself stop.

"I suppose you think you're pretty clever," she said.

"No."

For the life of him he couldn't think of anything else to say. Then she stepped out of the sunlight and his brain came back online.

"I want to apologize," he said. "For last night. For the whole gay/lesbian thing."

Her mouth tightened. "You already said sorry. It was a misunderstanding. I get it."

He looked at k.d. lang again. "Do you?"

She pulled her keys from the lock and dropped them into the pocket of her baggy pants.

"You done? Because I've got work to do." She turned on her heel. He grabbed her elbow. She stilled, then narrowed those incredible eyes.

How had he not noticed them before? He must have been blind.

"I really am sorry, Gabby. I know we didn't exactly get off on the right foot, but I didn't mean to embarrass or hurt you last night."

He felt her stiffen. She shook off his hand.

"I wasn't embarrassed. And you certainly didn't hurt me. I barely know you. Why would I care what you think of me?"

She was so damned prickly. He bet the word *gracious* wasn't even in her vocabulary.

"You know, I have no idea. Just like I have no idea why I even bothered to apologize again. You go ahead and enjoy your indignation. I'm sure it's very satisfying." He walked away from her.

"Fine. I accept your apology," she called after him.

"Good. Great." He pushed through the swinging door with more verve than strictly necessary.

The door swung sharply back, cutting off anything she might have been about to say. He stood in the silent workshop for a long beat, trying to rein in his temper.

What was it about her that pissed him off so much? Even when he tried to be nice they wound up fighting. She took everything he said the wrong way, even his apologies.

He simply didn't get it.

The door opened and Gabby entered. She didn't

look at him as she marched toward her office. He watched her straight spine, then he shrugged.

So what if she didn't like him? He wasn't one of those people who had to have everyone love him. He was a big boy. He could live with her animosity. It wasn't as though it was forever, after all. A few months from now, he'd be somewhere else and she'd be nothing but a fading memory, notable only for her defensiveness and fantastic eyes.

He turned his back on her. He had work to do.

CHAPTER FOUR

GABBY FELT LIKE AN IDIOT. She'd been so determined to show Jon that she didn't give two hoots what he thought of her. Then she'd put so much time and energy into dressing to meet his mistaken assumptions that she'd done the exact opposite. She might as well have stuck with the miniskirt and stilettos.

She glanced at the k.d. lang T-shirt. She'd had to drive twenty minutes out of her way to pick it up this morning before coming to work. Just so she could thumb her nose at Tyler's brother.

God, she was dumb.

But that was fairly well established after last night's self-revelation.

What had she said to him? *I barely know you. Why would I care what you think of me?*

It should have been true. She wished it was. But she had only to look in the mirror to know what a big fat lie it was. She'd spent *hours* this morning caring about what Jon thought of her. And for the life of her she didn't understand why.

The beginning of a headache pulsed behind

her left eyebrow. She pulled her in-tray close and grabbed a stack of invoices. She needed to stop gnawing on this stuff. It was doing her head in—literally.

It took some serious willpower, but gradually she lost herself in her work. The rest of the team straggled in, until finally she heard Tyler's deep voice as he called out a greeting to the crew.

Her stomach tensed and she put down her pen.

Any minute now he would stick his head through the door and say hello. A dart of panic raced up her spine.

Relax. It's a day like any other. He'll say hi, and you'll say hi back, and the world will keep spinning. The same as it did yesterday, the same as it will tomorrow.

The only difference was, yesterday she hadn't acknowledged that she was still in love with Tyler. Seeing him this morning, looking into his face with all those feelings of grief and rejection so close to the surface… It was going to be hard. Damned hard.

"Morning, Gab. Anything I need to know about?" Tyler asked from the doorway.

She took a moment to compose herself before facing him. Tyler must never know how she felt. Ever.

"All good here, chief," she said, a bright smile on her face.

"Bloody hell. What have you done to your hair?"

She blinked. "Excuse me?"

"It looks like a helmet. Or that snap-on plastic hair they have for Lego figurines," Tyler said, moving closer to get a better look.

For a moment she didn't know what he was talking about, then she remembered she'd pulled out all the stops for Jon this morning, including gluing her hair down with gel and creating a ruthlessly straight side part.

"Is that hair gel?" Tyler asked.

"I'm trying something different."

"Like what? Sculptural hair? I could carve this stuff." He tapped her hair experimentally.

Gabby pushed her chair back out of his reach. "I'm going to go out on a limb here and guess you have no idea how rude you're being right now."

If this were truly a new look she was experimenting with, she would be utterly crushed by his reaction. As it was, she was mildly offended. It didn't look *that* bad. In fact, before she'd scrubbed off her makeup this morning she'd thought she looked a bit like one of the models in that Robert Palmer "Addicted to Love" video.

"Sorry. It's just— I guess you took me by surprise."

"Next time I try something different I'll make sure to run it past you in advance."

Tyler wisely shifted the subject to a work matter. They talked for a few more minutes, then he gave her hair one last bemused look before heading for the kitchen to make his coffee.

She kneaded her forehead with her fingers after he'd left, painfully aware that the conversation was the sort of exchange a brother might have with his kid sister. Vaguely insulting and comfortably familiar. If ever there had been any doubt in her mind about where she stood in his life—and there wasn't—that conversation would have killed it stone dead.

She was Tyler's friend. No doubt if Ally had come along sooner in his life that was all she would ever have been.

The phone rang, providing a welcome circuit breaker for her thoughts. It was only as she was reaching for the receiver that it hit her that despite having known her for only three days, Jon had taken one look at her this morning and understood exactly why she was dressed like a drag king. Not so Tyler, who had known her for years.

She wasn't sure what the realization meant, but like everything to do with Jon, it made her uneasy.

AFTER TYLER'S REACTION, SHE should have known the rest of the crew wouldn't be able to resist offering their unsolicited opinions on her new hairstyle. By midmorning she'd pretty much resigned herself to a day of taking it on the chin. Every time she passed through the shop they hit her with another question. Dino wanted to know when she'd joined the army. Paul asked if they should call her Gabe from now on. Kelly kept calling her Che and asking when the revolution would begin.

They were her friends and they were funny and she couldn't help but laugh, even though she was acutely aware of Jon taking it all in, his dark gray eyes not giving anything away as usual. She wondered idly if he'd had to practice to perfect that opaque, emotionless expression. Maybe he'd taken the Sphinx as his model. Or one of those impassive stone heads on Easter Island.

It was pie day at the local pub on Wednesdays— a favorite with the boys—and Dino ducked into her office before lunch to persuade her to join them.

"Can't this week, sorry. Gotta get this stuff into the mail or we'll miss another billing cycle," she said, gesturing toward the pile of invoices on her desk. Getting their clients to pay in a timely manner was the bane of her existence.

"I'll have two pies, in solidarity," Dino promised.

"You're a trouper. I'm touched."

The workshop was silent when she exited her office in search of a stray invoice a short while later. As usual, there were several pieces in production, each at various stages of completion. A still-rough dining table in spotted gum. A hall table in plantation mahogany. A sideboard in rich red gum. But it was the small, delicate drum table sitting in the corner that drew her eye. She veered off course to inspect it.

Made from aged French oak, it was one of Tyler's new designs, based on a client brief. The legs were curved and sensuous, the top simple but beautiful, the clean design allowing the grain of the wood to take center stage. She rested a hand on the smooth surface, unable to keep the smile from her face. She had zero creative ability herself, but she could appreciate it in others and she'd always admired Tyler's ability to coax the best from a piece of wood.

"Pretty sexy, isn't it?"

She glanced over her shoulder as Tyler approached. "It's beautiful. The Lintons are going to be over the moon."

"They should be. Jon's put in a lot of hours making this design work."

Gabby couldn't hide her surprise. "Jon did this? I thought he was just a builder?"

"Nothing *just* about any of Jon's stuff. He and his partner in Canada built artisan houses, one-offs for people who could afford to pay for the best. Some of their places would blow your mind."

Tyler crouched and inspected the legs more closely. "I thought I was going to have to go back to the drawing board on this one. Once Jon started on the legs he realized there was no support at the stress point. I was ready to scrap the whole thing and start again, but Jon was sure he could do something. He used three interlocking dowels here to support the join. Managed to hide it, too. Pretty clever, huh?"

Tyler touched the point where the three legs intertwined in a seamless join. Gabby found herself crouching beside him to inspect it. As Tyler had noted, it was smooth and flawless, the work of a master.

"Yeah. Clever."

Tyler pushed to his feet. "With a bit of luck he'll hang around for a while. I could use his help with all those designs we'll be prototyping for the new collection."

Gabby was slower getting to her feet. "I've been meaning to talk to you about that. I'm doing payroll this afternoon. You didn't mention how you want me to handle Jon's wages…?"

"Right."

She remembered his reticence on the subject when he'd first announced Jon was joining the business.

"Look, if you want to handle it yourself, that's fine. I'll email the payroll file to you."

Tyler rubbed the back of his neck. "Yeah. That's probably not necessary, since Jon is still refusing to take a wage."

"What?"

But she knew she'd heard correctly.

"I argued until I was blue in the face, but it was the only way he'd take the job."

Gabby flashed to the self-righteous little speech she'd delivered after the incident with the blonde in the showroom. *You're the one who's taking advantage of Tyler.*

She closed her eyes briefly. "I wish you'd told me this earlier."

"Jon's a private guy."

"You know he was here at seven-thirty this morning? And that he'll probably be the last to leave tonight?"

Tyler gestured impatiently. "What can I do? Shove the money down his throat? As far as I'm concerned, it's enough that he's here. The rest can wait."

There was an undercurrent to his words, a frustrated determination. He wanted his brother here, in Melbourne. Close.

It was on the tip of her tongue to ask what was really going on, but she swallowed the question. It wasn't only because she suspected Tyler would be reluctant to answer. She'd seen the way Jon held himself apart, the way he watched the world from behind those eyes. It might seem odd given the tenor of their relationship, but it felt disrespectful to be digging into his personal business behind his back.

"It could get awkward if the other guys find out about this," she said.

"Let's worry about it when it happens."

Gabby studied Tyler a moment. "If he stays longer than a few weeks, you have to revisit this. You know that, right?"

"You sound like Ally."

"Which means we're both right."

"I wouldn't get too hot and bothered about it. He probably won't hang around long enough for it to be a problem."

Gabby was unsettled as she returned to her office. It had all been much simpler when she thought she knew exactly who and what Jon was—before she knew he had it in him to apologize and that he was working for free and that he could bring beauty into the world with his clever hands.

Much, much simpler.

JON STAYED PAST QUITTING TIME again that night. He was working on another prototype for Tyler, but Dino was also waiting on the drawers for a partners desk and he didn't want to let either man down. He had no idea what time it was when he decided he'd done enough for the day and switched off the sander. He brushed the sawdust from his forearms and pulled his phone from his back pocket to check the time. Nearly eight. Right on cue, his stomach rumbled.

He glanced toward Gabby's office. Sure enough, the light was still on. No surprises there—it probably would have killed her to leave without fully briefing him on the alarm system again and giving him a hard time of some description.

He swept the floor and put away tools, and only when he'd run out of things to do did he approach Gabby's office. She wasn't behind her desk, however, and he went in search of her. Light spilling from the open doorway of a room at the rear of the building drew his attention. He stopped when he reached the threshold, frowning at the sight of Gabby on a tall ladder, burrowing through an archive box that was balanced at the very top of a long metal shelving unit. The remaining walls in the small room were lined with similar shelves, all of them loaded with filing boxes and folders.

"That must be some pretty urgent paperwork you're after," he said.

She started, clutching the side of the ladder to prevent herself from falling.

He stepped forward. "Sorry. I didn't mean to scare you."

"I'm fine. And you didn't scare me. You just took me by surprise."

"There's a difference?" he asked, reaching out to brace the ladder.

She twisted to look down at him.

"Yes." She frowned. "What are you doing?"

"Steadying the ladder."

"It's not going anywhere."

"Now it isn't."

She sighed heavily. "This is one of those male chivalry things, right? Like opening car doors?"

"You have a problem with me making sure your ladder doesn't overbalance?"

"I've climbed this hundreds of times. It's not going to overbalance. So if you wouldn't mind…" She waved him away with an imperious shooing motion.

"You really have a problem with me holding the ladder steady for you?" he asked incredulously.

"I have a problem with what it represents. If I were Dino, would you be standing there worrying about me?"

"Dino probably wouldn't need the ladder to reach the top shelf."

"That doesn't answer my question."

"If he was up that high, I probably would," he lied.

"Liar."

"Fine. Have it your way." He took a step backward, holding his hands wide to show her she was on her own. "My humble apologies—again—for being courteous."

"Courteous. Right. How would you like it if I implied you were incapable of climbing something as simple as a ladder? Or opening a door? Or changing a lightbulb? Are you telling me you wouldn't find that even vaguely insulting?"

Was there no end to this woman's stubbornness?

"Try not to burn your bra while you're up there," he muttered. "It'll set off the smoke alarm."

"If you're trying to be derogatory, at least get your facts straight. Contrary to popular belief, no bras were ever burned as part of the feminist movement."

He rolled his eyes. "I stand corrected."

"What's wrong, afraid to really think about it? Afraid it will mess with your world order if you acknowledge that I'm perfectly capable of climbing a ladder on my own?"

He frowned. "I was being courteous. Considerate. It was what my mother taught me to do."

She'd taught him a bunch of other things, too, of course. That he'd deserved every blow his father aimed at him. That he was ungrateful, selfish, no good. That he was destined for failure, along with his brother. That he was a disappointment and the cause of so much of her unhappiness.

"I bet your mother told you pornography was bad, too, and that women belonged on a pedestal," she said.

She was right on the money, but he wasn't going to let her know that.

"You telling me you think pornography is *good?*"

"Not all of it. There's some good stuff around, but a lot it is frankly laughable. At the end of the day, it's all about taste. So basically as long as it's consensual, I don't have a problem with it. I've got bigger things to worry about than sex between consenting adults."

There was a long silence as he grappled with the idea of a porn-loving Gabby Wade.

"What's wrong, cat got your tongue?" She was enjoying herself, her eyes bright with challenge.

"I'm wondering what bigger things than sex between consenting adults you have on your mind."

"Touché."

"At last."

She was smiling as she started down the ladder. "I guess every dog has his day. If he waits long enough."

"I've always been a patient man."

She glanced over her shoulder to give him a dry look—which was probably why she fumbled the next rung. She wasn't far from the ground. She probably wouldn't have hurt herself if he'd stood back and let it happen. She might even have recovered her balance.

He didn't give her a chance. He reached up to support her lower back, his other hand making a grab for the side of the ladder. That hand gripped cool metal. The other grabbed a handful of feminine backside.

A minor miscalculation.

They both stilled. He knew he should let go and take a step backward, putting some distance between them. Knew he was about to get the feminist tongue-lashing of a lifetime. But he was too busy registering the warm resilient shape of her in the palm of his hand to do much more than stand there like a dodo.

Who knew that Gabby Wade had been hiding

a sweet, tight little butt beneath all that baggy khaki? A truly perfect handful.

She cleared her throat. "Would you mind unhanding my ass?"

"Sure. Of course." But it took a real act of will to make himself uncurl his fingers and step away.

She finished descending the ladder and made a big show of dusting her hands down the front of her khakis before meeting his eye.

"Thank you. For the rescue, not the grope."

"It was an accident."

"I know. I just wanted to be clear."

She grabbed a sheaf of papers from one of the lower shelves and turned for the door. He waited till she was gone before mouthing an obscenity.

This morning, she'd been an irritant, a thorn in his side. Then she'd walked into a beam of sunlight and he'd discovered the depths in her eyes.

And now he knew she had a fantastic ass.

She's still got a mouth that won't quit and more attitude than a mall full of teenagers.

Both of which should have more than neutralized the power of those eyes and that ass. But today he'd also discovered that she had a sense of humor. The guys had ragged her mercilessly over her terrible hairstyle and her army boots and she'd copped it on the chin and laughed along.

All of which led him to an almost inescapable

conclusion: she wasn't quite the unmitigated pain in the rear he'd first imagined her to be. Instead, she was shaping up to be almost…fascinating.

Dude, you need to get out more. When was the last time you got laid?

It was a good question. Well over two months ago, by his calculations, back when he'd been wrestling with the ghosts of childhoods past in Woodend. Clearly he was overdue for a little horizontal action if he was starting to eye his brother's scary office manager with carnal intent.

As for the idea of actually making a move on her…

He laughed out loud. As if that was ever going to happen. He might be horny, but he wasn't deluded. Gabby would shred him verbally then stomp all over him with her hobnailed boots if he even looked at her funny.

Shaking his head at the craziness of his own thoughts, he followed Gabby.

GABBY COULD HEAR HER HEARTBEAT thumping in her ears as she marched to her office. She wanted to pretend it was because she'd set such a brisk pace returning from the archive room, but she wasn't that good a liar.

Her heart was beating like a tom-tom because Jon had touched her ass. Not just touched, *grasped.* In a very male, very possessive, very intent way. She could still feel the heat of his hand burning through the seat of her khakis. Worse, she could still feel the answering heat that had washed through her.

It had been a long time since a man had touched her intimately. Years, in fact, for reasons she'd spent the night sobbing over. And yet she'd gone up in flames the moment Jon's hand had curled around her.

It had taken every ounce of self-control she possessed to tell him oh, so coolly to unhand her then look him in the eye and chastise him for groping her. What she'd really wanted to do was grab him by his shirtfront and shake him and demand to know why, after all these years, he had to be the one who reminded her that sex had once been a very welcome and needful part of her life.

Because that was what he'd done with a single touch. A bare five seconds of contact. Long enough to tilt her world off its axis.

I don't even like him.

But she was wise enough in the ways of the world to understand that sometimes it wasn't about liking the other person. Sometimes it was about pure animal attraction. And apparently, whether she liked it or not, the animal in her was definitely attracted to the animal in him.

She could hear Jon's footsteps and she pulled her keyboard close and started typing. Just in case he thought she'd been sitting here brooding over what had happened between them.

She watched in her peripheral vision as he stopped in the doorway and crossed his arms over his chest, propping his hip against the frame. Waiting for her to acknowledge him.

She made him wait a long time before she glanced up. "Sorry. I didn't see you there. I thought maybe you'd gone home," she fibbed.

He let a beat pass. She had the distinct impression he could see through her, down to the fact that she was struggling to look him in the eye without blushing like a Catholic schoolgirl.

"How much longer do you think you'll be?"

"About another half hour. Why?"

"Just checking." He pushed himself away from the doorway and disappeared into the workshop.

She stared at the place he'd been standing, going over what he'd said in her mind. Then she went looking for him.

He'd pulled a stool up to the corner workbench he'd made his own over the past few days and was poring over a set of blueprints.

"Listen, Jon, you don't need to hang around because of me."

He raised his eyebrows and immediately she felt stupid.

"I mean, I lock up on my own all the time. So you don't need to feel obliged to escort me to my car or anything."

"Okay."

It was the sort of frustrating nonanswer she should have expected from him and it left her with exactly nowhere to go. She shifted her weight from one foot to the other.

"Well," she said.

Turning on her heel, she went to her office. She spent the next twenty minutes trying to concentrate and failing miserably. Despite what Jon had said, she couldn't get past the feeling that the only reason he was still hanging around was because of her. She hated the notion that he felt he had some misguided obligation to play bodyguard to her, but she suspected it was exactly the sort of Me-Tarzan-You-Jane value he subscribed to.

She'd been working late for years, ever since Tyler had first employed her. Not once in all that time had she required the services of a security escort—and she didn't want one now. But how was she supposed to get rid of a man who refused to admit he'd cast himself in the role of gallant knight?

When she'd typed the wrong figures into a

spreadsheet three times in a row, Gabby realized she was both too tired and too distracted to keep working. She saved the file and shut down her computer, then switched on the answering machine and grabbed her bag.

Jon was still at his bench, his head propped on his hand as he studied the blueprints. It wasn't until she was only a few feet away that she saw his eyes were closed. She remembered that, like her, he'd started early this morning. She reached out a hand to rouse him, only to find herself hesitating.

He looked oddly boyish with his eyes closed. His dark lashes fanned across his cheeks, and there was something supremely innocent and unguarded in his expression. Perhaps it was the softness around his mouth, or maybe it was because he wasn't barricading himself away behind those impenetrable eyes of his. Whatever it was, it made her pause for a heartbeat before she finally rested her hand on his shoulder.

"Jon," she said softly.

His eyes snapped open.

"You were asleep."

"Man. I only closed my eyes for a second." He looked sheepish.

She realized her hand was still on his shoulder. She dropped it to her side and took a step backward. "I'm heading off now. Do you want me to go over the alarm for you again?"

"It's Tyler's birth year, right?"

"That's right."

"Then I'm good." He gave her a small smile and she could suddenly see how tired he was.

"You should go home, too," she said before she could stop herself. It was none of her business what he did. She wasn't his mother, or—God forbid—his wife.

"Yeah, I should." He stood and stretched. "I'll walk you out."

The hem of his T-shirt rode up as he arched his back and she caught a flash of hard male belly. She looked away, disconcerted. The last thing she needed was to know what Jon's belly looked like.

They walked to the showroom in silence. Gabby unlocked the door, remembering how she'd had to let him in this morning and how they'd squabbled like children after he'd apologized. She glanced at him and saw that he was watching her, a faint smile lurking around his mouth, and she knew exactly what he was thinking.

"One for the road?" she asked.

"What the hell. What do you want to argue about? Freedom of speech? Animal cruelty? Politics?"

"They're all pretty tempting."

"We could always skip straight to the insults."

"Now, that's really tempting."

His eyes glinted with appreciation. He crossed his arms over his chest. "Go for it. I'll give you a free shot."

She eyed him for a moment, then shook her head. "You know what? It's been a long day. I'm going to pass."

"Chicken."

"Maybe. Good night, Jon."

She slipped past him to the parking lot. As he had last time, he lingered until she was in her car and had started the engine. Then, and only then, did he lift his hand in farewell.

As she drove home, she wondered how much longer he intended to work. Then she remembered that she'd been convinced he'd hung around only because he didn't want her to lock up on her own.

That was the thing with Jon—she never could find her feet with him. She had no idea where the truth lay—if he was a misguided chivalrous knight determined to minister to a reluctant damsel who definitely wasn't in distress, or if he was simply a man who was in no rush to go home.

She flexed her hand on the steering wheel, remembering the firmness of his shoulder when she'd woken him.

It was the first time she'd touched him voluntarily. She wondered why that felt so significant. Then she shrugged it off. She was hungry and tired. She'd stopped thinking straight hours ago.

Her apartment smelled stuffy when she let herself in. The light on the answering machine stared at her like an unblinking eye, signaling that she had no messages. There was dust on the windowsills and a vase of dead flowers on the corner table.

She stared at them, wondering how long they'd been all wilted and shriveled and unnoticed. Two weeks? Three? She honestly couldn't remember.

She walked slowly into her bedroom and stared at the mess she'd left this morning. The scrunched up tissues from her crying jag, the discarded clothes, her abandoned towel.

It occurred to her that Jon wasn't the only person who wasn't rushing home at the end of the day.

"Gabriel Wade, you need to get a life."

Even though she was only talking to herself, her words had the ring of resounding truth.

CHAPTER FIVE

JON WORKED LATE THE FOLLOWING two nights. Both times he manufactured reasons to hang around after the work Dino had assigned him was completed while waiting for Gabby to finish for the day.

He was well aware that Gabby would spit nails if she learned he was staying because of her. But it was beyond him to walk away and leave her alone in a dark building in the middle of an industrial neighborhood. Tyler might be fine with it. Jon was not.

It wasn't as though he had anywhere better to be, and there was an odd sort of comfort in knowing another human being was only a few feet away. Even if he and Gabby barely exchanged half a dozen words once everyone else had gone home, hearing her at her computer and move papers around on her desk was far better company than sitting in his apartment staring at bad TV.

It probably said something about both his social skills and current mental state that finding a more attractive third option was beyond him.

Saturday brought a new challenge—his first full day in months with no work on hand to distract him. When he'd been in Woodend, there had always been something to do, no matter what the time of day or week. But he was a wage slave now—even if he wasn't technically taking a wage—which meant his weekends were his own.

Yippee.

He tried to sleep in, but by 7:30 he was wide awake, staring at the ceiling. He cleaned the apartment and did his laundry. It didn't take nearly long enough. The apartment was a shoebox, and after months of working on the house, most of the clothes he'd brought with him from Canada had been more or less trashed. His current wardrobe consisted of several pairs of new jeans and a handful of T-shirts in either black or white. One load of washing and he was done.

Which meant by 10:00 he was at loose ends again. He walked to the corner store to buy a newspaper, but by the time he'd read the damned thing from cover to cover he was ready to throw something off the balcony.

He needed to do something. Frame a wall or rip up a floor or sand a table. Without the distraction of hard labour, his thoughts inevitably drifted to the past. He didn't want to go there. But what he wanted didn't seem to be holding much sway with his psyche these days.

He'd thought he'd left it all behind when he'd left Australia. Thought he'd consigned all the beatings and abuse and fear to the dark corners, never to see the light of day. He'd made a life for himself in Toronto, built a business. No one had known the truth about him, where and what he'd come from. He'd been free to become whoever he wanted to be.

Then, out of the blue, Tyler had called to say their father had cancer and it had all come rushing back.

The pain. The shame. The failure and guilt and anger. All the crap Jon thought he'd walked away from. All the memories.

His chair scraped across the floor as he stood abruptly and grabbed his car keys. What he really wanted to do was drive to the liquor store and load up on beer and spirits. Instead, he drove to the local school and ran lap after lap around the football field. Anything to stop his churning thoughts.

He ran till he was dripping with sweat, till his muscles ached and his lungs burned. Then he stretched out on the grass and stared at the sky while the sweat cooled on his body and his heart rate returned to normal.

For the first time all week he felt calm, his body

relaxed. And all he'd had to do to get here was almost kill himself.

After ten minutes, the sound of voices approaching made him sit up. Two women were circling the field, each with a small white dog straining on the end of a leash. One of the women was tall with red hair and legs up to her armpits. The other was small and petite with short dark hair.

His eyes narrowed as he honed in on the shorter woman. Surely it wasn't…? What were the odds, given all the football fields in all the suburbs of Melbourne?

He glanced at himself. His T-shirt was soaked with sweat, his shorts equally drenched. He ran a hand over his hair, smoothing it down. Then he caught himself. What the hell did he care how he looked, even if it was Gabby?

Especially if it was Gabby.

The women were getting closer with every second. The smaller woman threw back her head and laughed. He looked away.

It wasn't Gabby. Gabby's laugh was low and earthy. This woman's was high, a little nervous.

He waited until the women had passed him before pushing to his feet and dusting the grass off his backside.

He should have known it wasn't Gabby the moment he'd spotted the fluffy dog. No way would she be caught dead with a designer pooch. If she had a dog, it'd be something big and scary and substantial like a Rottweiler or a Doberman or an Irish wolfhound. A big dog to match her big attitude. It hit him suddenly that he was disappointed that it hadn't been her.

Which means you really are a perverse SOB.

He thought about it as he crossed the field. It wasn't about those eyes of hers or the cute little behind he'd inadvertently discovered. It was simply that when he was with her, he wasn't thinking about anything or anyone else. Including himself. She sharpened his focus, kept him on his toes.

So, yeah, he was a little disappointed it hadn't been her.

Not a big deal.

Palming his car keys, he got in his truck and headed home.

GABBY WINCED A LITTLE AS SHE pulled on her underwear that evening. She'd paid a visit to the salon today and had the works—pedicure, bikini wax, facial, haircut. It was her birthday, and she'd figured she deserved a little pampering. After that, she'd met her sister for a late lunch and some shopping. She pulled the red dress she'd bought as part of her birthday splash-out over her head and wriggled until she'd tugged it down her body. The hem hit her at midthigh. Looking at herself in the mirror in her bedroom without the encouraging salesgirl at her side and all the bright lights and loud music of the store to lull her into a false sense of wonderfulness, she couldn't help wondering if maybe, perhaps, the dress was on the short side. She was thirty-three, after all, not twenty-three.

After a long moment she shrugged. What the hell. It was only the company Christmas party. While Tyler always invited a few suppliers and clients and some of the guys often brought friends, it was unlikely that there would be many hot prospects there tonight. Still, it would be a good way to dip her toe into the dating waters. She could polish up her rusty flirting skills and ease herself into things. Once she was feeling a little more solid, she would phone one of her party-loving friends—Shona, or maybe Dee, or maybe both— and hit the clubs. Or wherever it was that women went to meet men these days. She honestly had no idea, which was sad in and of itself given how long it had been since she broke up with Tyler.

She slipped her black ankle boots on. Then she did her makeup. A touch of blush to highlight her cheekbones. Two shades of golden-brown eye shadow, black kohl. A deep berry-colored lipstick to match her nails and toenails. She finished with a spray of her favorite Dolce & Gabbana perfume and stood back. Her shapeless helmet of hair had been transformed into a tousled, sexy gamine style thanks to the attentions of a very expensive hairdresser. Her eyes looked big and mysterious, her mouth shiny and red.

She reached for the Santa hat she'd bought, a token nod toward her usual practice of dressing up for the Christmas party, then decided against it. You didn't spend two hundred bucks on a cut and color only to hide it under a hat. The world would have to live with the fact that this year, Gabby Wade was going to be the life of the party in a different way.

Brave words.

She wasn't feeling quite as brave as she inched out of her car half an hour later. Amazing the things you could forget, such as how hard it was to get out of a car without disgracing yourself when you were wearing a short skirt. Finally, she managed to haul herself to her feet, tugging the hem of her skirt down and smoothing it over her hips. One of her heels sank into the lawn and she held on to the car door while she tugged herself free.

A very elegant start to the evening.

It's practice, remember? This is a trial run.

That didn't stop the butterflies from doing an aerial show in her stomach as she click-clacked her way up the garden path. There was no way people weren't going to notice her change of appearance. They were going to comment, and Dino and the crew were going to make jokes. And Jon was going to look at her and—

She stopped in the middle of climbing the porch stairs.

Jon was going to look at her and…what? Stare? Drool? Laugh?

She didn't want any of those reactions from him. She didn't want anything from him at all.

A car door slamming announced the arrival of more guests and she stepped onto the porch and hit the doorbell. Ally opened the door wearing a flowing white halter-neck dress.

"Gabby! Wow. You look fabulous. You're going to cause a riot in that dress." Ally gave Gabby a frank once over. "Turn around so I can check all of you out."

Gabby dutifully turned in a circle.

"Check out that little caboose of yours. I think I'm going to have to stand out of the way so I don't get crushed beneath the stampede when the guys see you."

"Hardly," Gabby said, half-grateful, half-embarrassed by her friend's assessment.

"I have a feeling this is going to be a good party."

They walked together into the open living space

at the rear of the house. The room was already crowded. Dino, Kelly and Carl were hanging around the kitchen counter, helping themselves to the chips and dips. To Gabby's everlasting chagrin, they all stopped and stared the moment they saw her.

"Hubba hubba. Come and sit on Santa's knee, Gabby baby," Dino said with a comic leer.

"Could have given us a bit of warning, Gab. Heart's not what it used to be," Kelly said.

Carl simply stuck two fingers in his mouth and wolf-whistled so loudly Gabby was amazed the windows didn't shatter.

Ally laughed, delighted. "What did I tell you?"

Gabby made a disparaging noise but she could feel herself blushing as people looked over, clearly wondering what all the fuss was about.

This is what you wanted, wasn't it? To remind everyone that you're a woman?

"What would you like to drink? Champagne? Beer? White wine?" Ally asked.

"Um, champagne would be great."

Gabby let her gaze drift around the room, smiling as she caught the eye of one of their major clients and lifting a hand to wave to Dino's wife, Lucia. Then Lucia shifted and Gabby found herself locking gazes with Jon.

He stood near the window, a bottle of beer in

hand. He gave her a leisurely head to toe. She fought the urge to suck in her tummy or jut out a hip or tug down her hem. When he'd finished his perusal, he lifted his beer and took a long, slow pull. As usual, his dark eyes gave nothing away.

Yet somehow she felt she knew exactly what he was thinking: that her skirt was too short, her shoes too high, her makeup too heavy.

Well, too bad, buddy, because I didn't dress like this for you. I dressed like this for me.

She turned her shoulder on him. Screw him. He was the last person she wanted to impress.

Ally returned with a glass of champagne and Gabby took a gulping swallow. Bubbles hit the back of her throat and a few seconds later she felt the warmth of alcohol spreading through her empty stomach.

Ally was right. This was going to be a great party.

Tilting her head, she drained the rest of her drink and went in search of another.

JON WATCHED GABBY CROSS THE room in her stiletto boots, her hips and ass swaying provocatively with every step.

He wasn't the only man watching, just as he was sure he wasn't the only man wondering if her slim, finely muscled legs were as smooth and firm as they looked.

So much for her dressing as either a reindeer or a Christmas tree.

He swallowed another mouthful of apple juice. He'd made a deal with himself that he'd endure the party for another hour. But maybe now he'd stick around a little longer.

In case Gabby had any other surprises up her sleeve.

Ally and Tyler had asked him to come early so he could help Tyler rearrange some furniture—Ally was redecorating for the fourth time since he'd known her—and he'd been left to kick his heels for half an hour while his hosts had slipped off to "shower" before the guests arrived. As Jon had expected, neither Ally nor Tyler had been ready in time to greet the first wave of guests and it had been left to Jon to play host, directing people to the bar on the patio and taking their coats and handbags into the guest room.

At least it had given him something to do. Once Tyler had emerged from the master suite looking both sheepish and a little smug, Jon had been demoted to the role of guest and the real torture had kicked in.

He wasn't a party person at the best of times, but the prospect of enduring several hours of polite chit chat with a group of people he barely knew without the benefit of a few beers under his belt seemed like a refined form of punishment.

He'd been sober for ten days. Ten long, hard days. By now, he'd figured the whole abstinence thing should have been getting easier. It was simply a matter of discipline, right? And yet he'd cruised past the bar more times than he cared to count this evening, his gaze lingering on the bottles of beer spilling out of the ice tubs, his mind handing him excuse after excuse to grab one of those icy-cold bottles.

It was a party, after all. A special occasion. He could start his cold turkey thing again tomorrow.

And everyone else was drinking. He'd be out of step with the social rhythm if he remained stone-cold sober.

And so on.

Each time he'd kept walking, helping himself instead to one of the sparkling apple juices Ally had bought for him.

"In case you're driving tonight," she'd said when he'd first arrived. "I figured they'd be a change from water."

No point pretending that he hadn't been offended by her considerate gesture. He'd felt coddled, patronized. As though everybody was bending out of shape to accommodate his perceived weakness.

Careful with drink around Jon. He can't control himself.

Only the knowledge that the past ten days had been far, far harder than he'd imagined had stopped him from letting her know what she could do with her apple juice.

Now, he crossed the room to dump the empty bottle in the bin, then worked his way through the crowd until he was stepping out onto the patio.

Gabby was on the lawn, her red dress drawing his eye like a flare. She was talking with Ally and a bunch of young guys he didn't recognize. To a man they were all grinning like idiots, their chests puffed out as they checked her out with varying degrees of subtlety. As he watched, Gabby laughed at something one of them said, then gulped from her champagne glass.

She was really knocking back the drinks. If she didn't pace herself, she'd be messy drunk within the hour.

Check out Sir Drinkalot. Policing other people's consumption when he can barely get a grip on his own.

What Gabby did was none of his business. Just as it was none of his business that every man in the group with her was wondering what it was going to take to get her into bed tonight.

Common sense told him to go inside and forget

about her. Instead, he crossed to the barbecue where Tyler was holding the fort. Jon remained there for the next half hour, ostensibly making small talk and trading jokes with his brother and a few of the other guys, but in reality keeping tabs on Gabby.

For a little person, she sure could drink. In the time he watched her she threw back two glasses of champagne before moving onto beer. By the time Tyler was piling the buffet table high with burgers and sausages, she was well on her way to oblivion.

Jon reminded himself that he'd just met her, and that they were hardly bosom buddies—for all he knew, this might be a typical Saturday night for her. Still, he loaded up a plate with meat and salad and a couple pieces of bread, grabbed a knife and fork and napkin, and made his way to where she was still holding court.

"Gabby," he said from behind her.

She turned, her eyes widening when she saw him. He thrust the plate into her hands.

"Ally told me to bring this to you," he lied.

She blinked, frowned, then pursed her lips as though she was about to object.

He should have known—nothing to do with this woman was ever easy.

"By the way, happy birthday. It's tonight, right?"

He surprised them both by leaning forward and planting a kiss on her cheek.

She smelled of something floral and fruity and she jerked a little away from him as he withdrew.

"That's right," she said warily.

"Have a good one," he said, raising his apple juice in toast.

Then he headed to the barbecue, his good deed done for the night.

He could feel her following him with her eyes and he kept his face carefully blank as he rejoined his brother.

"What was that all about?" Tyler asked.

"Just making sure she gets something to eat."

"Don't worry, Gabby never passes up a free feed. I have no idea where she puts it, but she eats more than almost anyone I know."

"Except for the times she skips dinner because she's working late for you."

Tyler frowned, then glanced at her. "She's eased back a lot on the overtime."

"Mate, she worked late almost every night this week."

"I guess I need to talk to her again."

"Like that's going to make a difference."

Tyler gave him a sour look. "You got a better idea, have you?"

"Yeah—hire her an assistant. Or outsource

some of the work. She's working from dawn to dusk, which means there's too much to do for one person. Talking to her isn't going to make a difference. She's the kind of person who works until the job is done."

"She won't like that, either, you know."

"Because she's a control freak. Tough. She's killing herself putting in so much time."

Tyler didn't look happy, but Jon figured it was more about the conversation he was going to have to have with Gabby in the near future than the money he'd spend to hire her an assistant. From what Jon had seen, the business could more than afford to take on extra administration staff, and Tyler didn't strike him as being the stingy type.

Ally joined them, encouraging them to abandon their post at the barbecue to come mingle with the guests more. Jon left Tyler in her clutches and filled a plate for himself at the buffet. He found a chair in a quiet corner of the garden and sat, balancing his plate on his knee.

Every time he glanced up he caught sight of Gabby. It was that red dress of hers. Plus she always seemed to be laughing. She had yet another beer and he watched her make short work of it as she flirted and talked with her circle of admirers. So much for trying to slow her down with some food.

She's hardly your responsibility, mate.

The thought was enough to get him on his feet. All his life he'd dodged relationships and held people at arm's length in order to remain unencumbered. He didn't want to have someone else's well-being on his conscience. Didn't want the burden of worrying about their happiness—he had enough trouble keeping his own head above water without worrying about anyone else.

Given he was such a seasoned expert at avoiding personal entanglements, it was more than mildly baffling to him that he seemed to be unable to stop himself from watching over the office manager. First he felt compelled to play bodyguard to her, now he'd appointed himself her moral guardian.

The irony was that she was the last person to welcome his concern. She had attitude to spare, and then some. He was willing to bet that she'd fight to the death rather than admit she needed anyone.

So why was he hovering like a fretful nanny?

He walked inside. Maybe he'd go home after all. There was nothing for him here except temptation and aggravation.

"Just the man I'm looking for. Come help me get the extra wineglasses out of the hall cupboard." It was Ally in full hostess mode.

He allowed himself to be hauled off. He'd go after he'd helped Ally out. Definitely.

GABBY LAUGHED AT SOMETHING ONE of the guys— Vaughn? Or maybe it was Dane?—had said, then lifted her beer to her mouth for a swig. She overestimated the distance between her hand and mouth, however, and the rim of the bottle hit her front teeth with an audible click.

"Oops!" she said, laughing even harder.

God, this was a good party. The best Christmas party Tyler had ever thrown, hands down. Probably that was Ally's touch. She made everything better. She was that kind of person. Warm and friendly and fun. That was probably why everyone was having such a good time.

Because of Ally.

Against her will, her gaze picked Tyler and Ally out of the crowd. They were standing near the bar, heads close together as they talked. He laughed at something she said, then lifted a hand and rested it on the nape of her neck. She kept talking, and all the while his thumb caressed her gently, lovingly.

The way he looked at her, the way he held her— as though she was the most precious thing in the world to him. As though she was a wonder. A miracle.

Envy and sadness twisted inside Gabby. She

hated herself for coveting Ally's happiness, for being unable to look away. There was no point to it, only pain.

A swell of music washed over the yard. Gabby allowed it to distract her. A couple of women had claimed the space to the left of the French doors as an impromptu dance floor and cranked up the stereo. Already more people were joining them, moving with varying degrees of skill and grace.

"Dancing. I love dancing," she said to no one in particular.

Dumping her almost empty beer bottle, she turned to the nearest man and grabbed his hand. "Dane. Do you dance? Please tell me you dance."

"Vaughn. And yeah, I'll dance with you." He said it in a way that implied he'd be happy to do a lot more than dance, too.

She smiled at him, enjoying the attention. *This* was what she'd been denying herself for the past few years. Male admiration. The sense that she was desirable. The sense that she meant something to someone.

To anyone.

"Let's go dance, then." Hooking her finger into one of his belt loops, she led him to the dance floor.

A couple of the other guys joined them and pretty soon she was surrounded. She had no idea who half of these people were. Vaughn—Dane?—was one of Kelly's friends. At least, she thought so. Most of them were younger than her, in their early twenties.

"You rock, Gabby," Dane said as he danced close behind her. "You've got the moves."

His hand brushed her hip, then the side of her thigh, then his hips were pressing against her backside, moving with her in time to the beat.

She could go home with him tonight if she wanted to. He was attractive in a young sort of way—blond hair, blue eyes, surfer-guy good looks. His body was lean and boyish, not yet fully developed, but no doubt he'd be an enthusiastic lover.

She tried to imagine kissing him, letting him touch her, but the notion left her cold. She'd never really been into blonds. But that didn't mean she should rule him out all together. She'd decided it was time to get a life, hadn't she? And Dane—Vaughn?—seemed like a good way to kick-start her social life. Definitely he seemed like a good way to create new memories to replace the old ones she'd been picking over like Miss Havisham for the past four years. Even if it was for only one night.

She deserved a little fun, didn't she? A little passion. A little attention.

The song changed to a classic dance track. The

area became even more crowded. Closing her eyes, Gabby gave herself over to the music for a few beats, letting the mindless joy of the moment wash over her.

She was alive. She felt good. She was sexy and desirable and fun.

She could do this. She really could. She could get over Tyler.

Then she opened her eyes and caught a glimpse of a severe, expressionless face through a gap in the crowd. For a split second her gaze locked with Jon's. He stood near the French doors, a bottle of beer in his hand as he watched.

A devil prompted her to slip through the crowd toward him.

"Come on, Stonehenge. Loosen up and dance with me."

She grabbed his arm and attempted to pull him toward the gyrating throng. His arm was hard with muscle, his skin very warm. It was like trying to move a mountain and he didn't budge an inch.

"I don't dance."

"Now, there's a big surprise." She released her grip. "Do you ever do anything fun?"

He looked at her silently for a long beat. "I have my moments."

"Whatever that means." Because she wanted to get a rise out of him, she plucked the beer from his hand and took a swig. Sweet bubbles flooded her palate. She pulled a face.

"What is this?" She peered at the label. "Sparkling apple juice?"

What was he doing drinking apple juice?

"If you're thirsty, I can get you some water."

"You can get me some champagne."

He frowned. She crossed her arms over her chest and imitated both his stance and his frown.

"Should have known you'd be a difficult drunk," he said.

"I'm not drunk," she protested. "Yet."

She poked him in the chest with her finger to emphasize her point, then turned on her heel and sashayed to the dance floor. She knew without a doubt that he watched her backside the entire way and she put a little extra wiggle into it. Just to really annoy him.

She slipped into the middle of the action and only glanced at him when she was sure enough time had passed.

He was still standing there. Watching her. Disapproving.

He'd felt as solid as a rock when she'd poked him. A big, warm, hard rock.

"There you are. Thought I'd lost you," Dane said.

She shifted her attention to the younger, happier

man grinning at her and wondered why she'd even bothered to talk to Jon. What did she care if he obviously didn't know how to have a good time? It was nothing to do with her.

She danced to song after song till she was damp with sweat and her calves and thighs ached. She danced with men and women, to hard rock and techno and a club beat. She drank the beers her newfound friends brought her and closed her eyes and raised her arms in the air and moved as though her life depended on it.

For all she knew, it might. Crazier things had happened, and this was the first day of the rest of her life, after all. No matter what happened, she was going to make it count.

GABBY WAS, AS JON'S YOUNGER self would have phrased it, off her face. Not quite falling-down drunk, but pretty damned close.

Someone should do something. Step in and force-feed her some bread or water. Or at least cut her off before she did something really stupid, such as go home with one of the guys who'd been sniffing around her all night.

Jon looked around, but as usual Tyler and Ally were lost in one another, cuddled close together on one of the garden seats. A nuclear bomb could detonate a foot away and they'd be blind to it.

The music switched abruptly to a heartfelt ballad. The dance floor thinned predictably as James Blunt crooned about how beautiful someone was. Gabby looked annoyed, he couldn't help noticing. Then the blond kid who had been practically humping her leg earlier pulled her close and started swaying with her. She looked as though she was about to protest, but she subsided as another couple joined them. Jon smiled at the chagrined, slightly self-conscious expression on his brother's face as Ally stepped into his arms. Like Jon, his brother had never been a big dancer. But clearly he was prepared to make certain sacrifices to please Ally.

If the expression on his brother's face was any indication, there was little he wouldn't do for her. Leap tall buildings. Split the atom. Fly to the moon.

Jon almost felt embarrassed by the raw devotion in his brother's eyes as he looked into his new wife's face. A little bit of dignity wouldn't go astray. There was no need for the whole world to know how utterly besotted the poor bastard was.

And yet… It was hard to be truly condemning. Tyler looked happy. Happier than Jon had ever seen him. That could only be a good thing.

He was about to cruise the dessert offerings when he caught sight of Gabby again. She was still with the leg humper, her arms looped loosely around his neck. She was watching Tyler and Ally over his shoulder and the misery and desperation on her face was so palpable it stopped him cold.

He followed her sight line to his brother, then returned his gaze to her. Suddenly it him like a freight train.

The unhappiness he'd sensed in her at her birthday party on Tuesday night.

Her almost zealous dedication to Tyler's business.

The "not available" signal she broadcast.

The look in her eyes right now.

She was in love with Tyler.

Desperately in love, if her expression was anything to go by.

Jon looked away. He felt as though he'd seen something he shouldn't have. Something intensely private and personal.

A million questions crossed his mind. How long had this been going on? Did Tyler know? Did Ally?

He looked at Gabby again. Unless he missed his guess, she was seconds from tears.

He scanned the crowd uneasily. He wasn't the only one watching the dancers. Any minute now someone else would see what he had and make the same connection.

He acted before he could think it through. Gabby was a grown woman, more than capable of looking after herself in ordinary circumstances—but tonight was an exception. She'd consumed enough alcohol to fell a horse, and consequently her guard was down. He knew without a doubt that she would be humiliated if she knew her secret was out.

He was there in two strides. He slipped past another couple, then tapped Leg Humper on the shoulder. "My turn."

The guy looked as though he was going to argue the point, but Jon simply stepped between him and Gabby and pulled her into his arms.

"Hey!" she protested.

"Don't worry, this is hurting me more than it's hurting you."

He half danced, half walked her to the edge of the dance floor. Once they were clear of everyone, he let her go.

"You want to sit down? A glass of water?"

"I want to dance. Which was what I was doing until you came along."

"You looked like you needed a break to me," he said quietly.

She shot him a searching, disconcerted look. He held her gaze and she glanced away.

"I was fine. I was having a good time."

"Were you?"

Her chin came up. Some of the desolation had left her eyes. "Yes, I was. I know you probably found the signs hard to recognize."

"Let me get you some water," he said again. He wasn't going to get any sense out of her tonight. She was too far gone.

"I can look after myself."

She walked away from him, weaving slightly. She made it to the bar where she said something to the bartender. Jon frowned as he watched her accept a glass of champagne. Sober, Gabby was a pain in the ass. Drunk, she was hell on wheels and the most stubborn person he'd ever had the misfortune to know.

Sighing, he headed her way. She was about to sip her drink when he plucked the flute from her hand. Her expression of comic astonishment would have made him laugh under any other circumstances.

"Give that back." She sounded exactly like a thwarted child.

"Time to take it easy."

Her eyes widened with outrage. "Excuse me? Who are you to tell me what to do?"

"I'm doing you a favor. Trust me."

"I don't want you to do me a favor. I don't want anything from you. Except my drink."

Her hand shot out so quickly she'd grabbed the champagne from his grasp before he had a chance to react. Tilting her head, she gulped the entire contents in one big swallow.

The look she gave him as she lowered the glass was pure triumphant defiance.

"That's your last one," he said, taking the glass and handing it to the eavesdropping barman. "No more for Ms. Wade, okay?"

Predictably, Gabby turned pink with outrage as she registered his words.

"Who the hell do you think you are? You're not the boss of me. You're not even close to being the boss of me. I'll do what I like when I like and—"

She paused, a peculiar look passing over her face. She pressed a hand to her stomach.

"Ugh. I don't feel so good."

She'd barely got the words out before she bent over and threw up.

All over his boots.

CHAPTER SIX

GABBY SCOOPED ANOTHER HANDFUL of water from
the running tap and sluiced it over her face. Cold
water ran down her neck and onto her chest. She
blinked, then repeated the action.

The towel Ally had given Gabby was soft
against her skin as she blotted her face dry. Her
bra was wet from all the water she'd splashed
around, and she blotted it with the towel, also,
before reaching for the T-shirt Ally had loaned her.
She was a little smaller, but it was a decent fit, as
were the pair of gray track suit pants, although she
had to roll the cuffs a couple of times to stop them
dragging on the ground. She wondered vaguely
if that meant she was shorter than Ally or if Ally
had to roll the pants, too.

Gabby stood in the center of the bathroom for a
moment, looking for something else to delay the
moment when she had to exit and face her humili-
ation.

Her sexy red dress was in the corner, a sodden
pool of damp, funky-smelling fabric. Tyler had
taken her shoes someplace to clean them.

She closed her eyes. Much of the evening was still a blur but the moment where she'd thrown up all over herself and Jon was etched in her memory, like acid on stone.

Of all the men in all the parties in all the world, why did it have to be his boots she'd tossed her cookies on?

At least the nausea was gone. She'd thrown up twice in front of the bar, then Jon had calmly man-handled her to a distant corner of the garden where she'd thrown up a third time. After it had become clear that the urge to purge had passed, Ally had taken over, leading her inside to clean up.

Even though she was feeling markedly less muzzy than she had been, Gabby was still drunk enough to have lost track of time. How long had she been locked in here? An hour? Twenty minutes? She honestly had no idea.

The only way to find out was to gird her loins, open the door and face the music.

The hall was silent when she emerged. She padded on bare feet into the living area. Empty.

Which meant what remained of the party was probably outside—if it wasn't over entirely. With the exception of high school parties, she couldn't remember a single event that had been enhanced by one of the guests heaving spectacularly in the middle of festivities. Was it any wonder that people had run for the hills?

Gabby shuffled on reluctant feet toward the French doors. Sure enough, Tyler and Ally were out there, talking quietly as they collected empty beer bottles and glasses.

"Hey," she said sheepishly.

They both turned to face her.

"Gabby. How are you feeling? I was about to come check on you," Ally said with a sympathetic smile.

"Better."

Tyler was trying to hide a grin, without much success.

"Don't start," Gabby said. "I'm already going to get it from the guys on Monday."

"I had to tip the barman, he was so traumatized."

Gabby winced. "I'm really sorry. I have no idea what happened."

Tyler laughed outright. "Don't you?"

Ally gave him a dark look. "Don't laugh at her when she's feeling sick."

"Do you want a hand cleaning up?" Gabby asked, because she figured it was better than telling more lies.

She knew exactly what had happened—she'd

drunk like a fish because she was in love with a man she could never have.

"We're fine. It's mostly glasses," Ally said. "We'll do the rest tomorrow."

"Then I'll call a cab and get out of your hair." Making a hasty escape smacked of cowardice, but Gabby figured there would be plenty of time to dwell on her foolhardy behavior tomorrow. Then, of course, there was Monday, when the full repercussions would come home to roost.

She figured it would take her about a month to live this night down. Certainly Dino and the guys would give her hell for at least that long.

"Give me a sec to find my keys and I'll drive you," Tyler said.

"No." Gabby held up her hand.

Both Ally and Tyler stared at her and she realized she'd sounded a little too urgent. But the last thing she wanted was to be stuck in a car alone with Tyler when she was feeling this stupid and vulnerable and sorry for herself.

"I mean, you've already had to clean up after me. Which, again, I'm really sorry for. I'll grab a cab, and you guys can go to bed. I'll be fine."

"It's not a problem," he said.

"I'd really prefer to get a cab."

"Gabby. Relax. I don't mind." He was like the Terminator, unstoppable. Determined to do his duty.

"I'll take her," a deep voice said.

As one, they turned to find Jon standing in the doorway. He was wearing a pair of faded jeans that she recognized as Tyler's instead of the newer pair he'd arrived in, and his boots looked damp.

Great. Apparently, she'd hurled on his jeans as well as his boots. This evening just kept getting better and better.

"Perfect," Ally said. "Gabby's place in Brunswick is pretty much on your way to Thornbury."

Gabby tried to find the words to protest, but Jon already had his keys in hand. Short of throwing a genuine tantrum, there was no way she could avoid having him drive her. Another good deed for him to rack up for the night.

"I'll grab a bag for your things," Ally said, scooting past her into the house.

A few minutes later, Gabby was walking toward a black truck, a shopping bag containing her ruined dress and shoes banging against her calves.

Jon opened the door for her. She hesitated before getting in.

"Look, I can call a cab. I'm sure you don't want—"

"Get in, Gabby." He sounded long-suffering. Like a worn-out parent.

Muttering under her breath, she climbed in.

"Where are your shoes?" Jon asked, apparently noticing her bare feet for the first time.

"They're ruined. And Ally's are a size too small."

He shut the door without commenting. She waited until he'd circled the truck and climbed in before speaking.

"I want you to know I appreciate this. It's kind of you to go out of your way when you must be tired." Not to mention pissed with her for yacking on his boots.

"You might want to hold off on the thanks."

She gave him a searching look. What on earth was that supposed to mean? It was on the tip of her tongue to ask, but at the last minute she decided against it. Almost every conversation she'd ever had with Jon had deteriorated into a fight and she was hardly in top form right now. Far better to let it slide and live to fight another day.

Jon put the truck in gear and pulled onto the road. She clutched her clammy bundle and willed time and space to fold so she could be home that much faster.

"Where am I going?"

"Um, Perry Street. It's off Barkly Street."

"Which side of Sydney Road?"

"The Carlton side."

He nodded and the ride passed in uncomfortable

silence. Three times she started to apologize but never got past the point of forming the words in her mind. There was something about his expression that put her off. He looked…forbidding.

Not that she was scared of him or intimidated by him. He might be bigger than her, but she was more than his match.

"We need to take the next left," she said as they drove along the busy café section of Sydney Road. "Perry's the second street on the right."

He followed her instructions and within moments they stopped in front of her apartment block.

"This is me," she said, and she could hear the relief in her own voice. "I'm really sorry about your boots and your, um, jeans. I'll cover the dry cleaning if you let me know what I owe you." She hesitated, then forced herself to finish. "And thanks for looking out for me tonight. You know, the water and the food and whatnot. I guess if I'd listened to you I wouldn't be sitting here in Ally's clothes right now." She threw a self-deprecating smile his way and reached for the door handle.

"It's not going to go anywhere. You know that, right?" he said. "Tyler likes you, but he loves Ally."

Her fingers tightened around the door handle. She wanted to tell him that she had no idea what he was talking about, but she didn't think she could pull it off. All she could pull off, apparently, was a bunny-in-car-headlights stare.

"And he's not the type to cheat, even if he wasn't head over heels." Jon didn't sound condemning. He was simply stating a fact. Yet she was still offended.

"You think I would do that to Tyler? To Ally?"

He shrugged. "People do strange things when they think they're in love."

"Think? I only *think* I'm in love with Tyler, do I?"

"You can never really know someone from the outside looking in. Hell of a lot of crushes have died through familiarity."

From the outside looking in? Crushes?

He doesn't know. He has no idea Tyler used to be mine.

The realization hit her like a slap. But why would he know? He'd been in Canada for over a decade. And before their father's illness had changed things, she'd never known Tyler to contact his brother. They hadn't known the finer details of each other's life, and she couldn't imagine a circumstance where her history with Tyler would have come up in conversation between the two brothers in recent weeks. Men simply didn't talk that way, especially men like Jon and Tyler Adamson.

For some reason, the idea that Jon thought she was the kind of silly, shallow woman who convinced herself she was in love with a man without ever really understanding or knowing him made her blood boil. She wasn't a little kid—she was a woman, with a woman's understanding of the world. Which was why she had bloody well broken up with Tyler in the first place—because she understood herself and him too well to let things grind on any longer.

"You have no idea what you're talking about."

"I saw your face tonight."

She'd guessed as much. Most of the evening was an inchoate blur, but she could remember the ache she'd felt watching Ally and Tyler slow dance together. And Gabby could remember the way Jon had looked at her after he hauled her off the dance floor. Apparently, her poker face needed some serious work.

"You still don't know what you're talking about." She opened the door and swung her legs out of the car. Strong fingers wrapped around her forearm.

"I'm saying this as a friend. Don't waste your time chasing a fantasy."

"We're not friends, and you are so far off base

it's not funny. Tyler and I went out for three years. We practically lived together," she said. "So maybe you should get your facts straight before you start handing out advice people didn't ask for."

She tugged her arm free and slid out of the truck. She slammed the door, then marched up the path and into her apartment building. In some well-hidden, still-sober corner of her brain she noted that Jon didn't drive away until she'd let herself into the secure foyer of her building.

He was such a freaking Good Samaritan.

She stepped into the elevator, fuming at his presumption. Then she caught a glimpse of herself in the polished steel doors—panda eyes, wet hair, someone else's clothes—and her shoulders sagged as all her outrage drained away, leaving her with nothing but shame and embarrassment.

She'd made a fool of herself. She'd behaved like a silly adolescent, flirted with all the wrong people and ignored good advice when it was offered. Then she'd compounded all of the above by getting maudlin and pathetic over Tyler and been so obvious about it that his brother—of all people—had guessed her dirty, sad little secret.

So much for getting a life.

She let herself into her apartment and walked straight to the kitchen. She poured herself a big glass of water, then crossed to the living room. She sat on the couch, knees drawn to her chest, and forced herself to drink all the water, even though she didn't really want it.

Tomorrow was not going to be pretty, on many levels.

She let her head drop back. She was tired and her feet hurt and she felt like the biggest idiot alive. Worse, she was now hugely indebted to Jon, who was the keeper of her secret.

It occurred to her that she should probably be worried that a man she barely knew was privy to her most personal feelings. If he told Tyler or Ally, Gabby's friendship with them would never be the same.

But she wasn't worried. Not even a little bit. Embarrassed, yes. Mortified and angry with herself, too. But not worried.

She pondered the notion for a few minutes, her alcohol-soaked brain moving slowly. She couldn't come up with a solid answer. All she knew was that in some odd, crazy way, she trusted Jon. He was an honorable man, and she knew without asking that he would consider telling anyone her secret a huge breach of trust.

You're really, really drunk.

There was no denying that. Struggling to her feet, she made her way to her bedroom. Between flashbacks to the party and the conversation with Jon, it was a long time before she fell asleep.

GABBY AND TYLER HAD BEEN lovers. Not just lovers, they'd been in a long-term relationship. Three years, she had said.

It felt wrong. Really wrong. And for the life of him Jon couldn't work out why. Tyler had obviously had a life before Ally. Gabby was a grown woman. Big deal if they'd been together.

But Jon couldn't stop chewing it over as he drove home, to the point where he snatched up the phone and called his brother the moment he hit the apartment. It was late, but he was confident Tyler would still be up. And if he wasn't, tough. This was important.

"What's up?" Tyler asked the moment he answered the phone.

"You never told me you'd gone out with Gabby."

There was a small pause. "It never came up."

"You didn't think it was worth mentioning?" He sounded angry, Jon realized. He *was* angry.

"Actually, no. What's going on?"

"How long ago did you break up?"

"I guess it's coming up to four years now."

"Why did it end?"

"You want to tell me why I'm under the hot lights at one in the morning?"

"Why did you break up with her?"

"I didn't end it, she did."

Jon frowned at the wall. Gabby had ended things with Tyler? Yet she was still in love with him. It didn't make sense. "You must have done something."

"Thanks for the vote of confidence."

"Gabby wouldn't have broken up with you without a good reason."

There was a long pause. "What's going on? Did something happen between you two tonight?"

"No."

"Then I don't get it. Why the third degree?"

"She said something, that's all. I was surprised."

"It's not a big deal. It wasn't working between us, she pulled the pin. I met Ally and realized Gabby had been right."

He sounded so matter-of-fact. And yet Gabby was eating her heart out over him.

"Jon. Hello?"

"Yeah. I'm still here."

"Is something going on between you and Gabby? Ally mentioned that she thought there was a bit of a vibe between you two—"

"Nothing's going on. And there's definitely no vibe."

"Right. So why are we having this conversation?"

Jon rubbed the bridge of his nose. "Sorry. I couldn't sleep. I'll see you on Monday."

Tyler sighed heavily. "You know, the sky's not gonna fall if you talk to me. Life as we know it isn't going to end."

"There's nothing to talk about. I was curious, that's all."

"Sure. Whatever you say. See you Monday." Tyler sounded weary.

Jon put down the phone. Calling Tyler had been a mistake. In fact, Jon was beginning to think that coming to Melbourne and taking the job offer had been a mistake, too. Every time he hung out with Tyler, every time they talked, it set up unrealistic expectations. Tyler was so loved-up courtesy of Ally that he couldn't see that it was too late for them to be the kind of brothers who pulled together through the hard times. It had never been that way, and it was crazy to think it could be that way now.

All through their childhood they'd fought their own battles, kept their own counsel. Other brothers might have bonded over the shared experience of a brutal childhood. But not them. And they'd continued the pattern into adult life. The moment he'd been old enough to legally leave home, Jon had bailed and hadn't looked back. Even though he'd known his absence would mean Tyler would bear the brunt of their father's anger, Jon had saved his own skin first. Tyler had left a couple of years later, and after that the only time they had seen each other had been on Mother's Day when they'd both made the annual obligatory guilt visit to Woodend. He'd flown to Canada the day after their mother had been buried and had barely exchanged a handful of emails and phone calls with Tyler over the next decade.

The truth was, Jon knew his ex-business partner better than he knew his own brother. He'd spent more time with him, shared more jokes, shared more of himself than he'd ever shared with Tyler.

Despite the lateness of the hour, Jon flicked on the TV. He knew himself well enough to know he wasn't even close to being ready to sleep yet. His mind was too busy. Gabby, his brother, Gabby *with* his brother, the fact that even now he wanted a beer so badly his mouth watered…

You're a freakin' basket case, you know that?

He turned up the volume on the TV. Anything to drown out this thoughts.

GABBY MADE SURE SHE WAS THE first person in the office on Monday. At least that way she could spare herself the walk of shame past all the men in the workshop. It would be bad enough as it was.

A hot day had been forecast so she'd dressed

accordingly in a black wrap skirt and yellow tank. Despite the fact that she'd had half a pack of aspirin and several liters of water yesterday, she was still feeling gritty-eyed and tired as she dropped into her chair and turned on her computer.

Apparently, she was really out of practice with being a party animal. Fancy that.

She'd been working for an hour when she heard the first arrival. She braced herself. If it was Jon, she would have to look into his eyes and know that he was the keeper of her most personal secret. If it was anyone else, she would have to live through the first of what was sure to be many recaps of her behavior Saturday night.

She saw Dino's balding head and relaxed a little. Of the two options, she definitely preferred teasing to self-conscious squirming. Dino sauntered over to her office, his jeans hitched too high as usual.

"Yo, Gabby. How are you doing?"

"Good, thanks. How 'bout you?"

He nodded, a cheerful smile on his middle-aged face. Innocent as the day he was born.

Gabby wasn't fooled for a minute.

"Yeah, I'm good, thanks. Except… Ooh. Wait a minute. I don't feel so good…" A full minute of wretching noises ensued before Dino finally bent forward and let a pizza-shaped piece of plastic vomit fall onto the floor.

He immediately collapsed, laughing. She waited until he'd calmed down a little before smiling benignly at him.

"You done?"

"For the moment. You mind if I take that back?" He pointed to the plastic vomit. "I want to do it again when the boys get in."

"Of course you do." She gestured gracefully toward the plastic vomit. "Help yourself."

Still chuckling, he stooped to collect his prop. "Oh, and Lucia said to remind you about our anniversary party. Not this Sunday but the next, at the Burvale, one o'clock."

"Got the invitation on my fridge," she assured him.

He gave her a thumbs-up and disappeared into the shop to work up more pranks.

By lunchtime she'd collected three fake vomits and a can of pea-and-ham soup. The guys had laughed until they'd cried and she'd listened to them describe her moment of glory many times—complete with sound effects, naturally. Everyone, it seemed, had something to say about her party trick—except Jon. He worked quietly on the latest prototype Tyler had given him to finesse and only looked up from his tools a couple of times when Paul and Kelly were being particularly boisterous. Even then Jon glanced at her briefly as though assessing how she was taking it before resuming his work.

Generally speaking, she loved working in a predominantly male environment, but it was a long day and a real test of her sense of humor. She was more than a little relieved when the shop emptied at five o'clock. Even Jon left on time, which meant she'd be able to work in peace this evening. It felt like a small blessing.

She celebrated by stretching her legs and making herself a cup of coffee. She was pouring in the water when she heard movement in the workshop. She walked to the door of the staffroom. Sure enough, it was Jon.

"I thought you'd gone," she said before she could stop herself.

"I was giving Carl a lift home. His son borrowed his car today."

"Right."

Damn. So much for her peace and quiet. She returned to her office. She could hear Jon moving around as she saved the sales report she'd been working on. Now that it was only the two of them, she couldn't stop thinking about what he'd said to her on Saturday night and the way he'd looked at her when he'd said it. For some reason, that moment in the archive room popped into her head. The warm, firm grip of his hand on her backside.

That long, sticky pause between him grabbing her and her telling him to unhand her.

She shook her head to dislodge the memory. She was here to work, not to brood over Tyler's difficult brother. She wrote up another six invoices, then printed them off and folded them into envelopes. She was searching her desk for stamps when she glanced up and realized Jon was standing in the doorway.

"Hi," she said warily.

"I'm going to grab a pizza. You want anything?"

"I'm fine, thanks."

No way was she sitting through an awkward meal with him. Or even a nonawkward one. The less time she spent with him, the better.

He turned to go.

"I don't know if Tyler told you, but there's no rush on that campaign table you're working on," she said, before he could slip off. "So there's really no need for you to put in all these long hours."

Because, really, her life would be a lot easier if she could go back to the good old days when she'd had the place to herself after hours. This arrangement was way too…intimate for her peace of mind.

"Sure."

He left, and she mulled over what he'd said. Or, more accurately, what he hadn't said. Last week she'd been suspicious that he was hanging around at work out of some misguided notion that she needed protecting. She was getting that sense again tonight, by the bucketload. Sure, he'd denied it when she confronted him, but that didn't mean she hadn't been right.

By the time she heard Jon returning with the pizza she'd worked up a righteous head of steam on the subject. She was a grown woman. She lived her own life, made her own decisions. She didn't need or want some random man appointing himself her protector. In the back of her mind, a small part of her observed that it was almost a relief to have a reason to be angry with him again.

Throwing down her pen, she rounded the desk and strode out to confront him. A wary look came over his face and his steps slowed.

"I want an honest answer," she said. "Do you have work you need to do tonight or not?"

He shrugged. "There's always work to do."

A beautiful nonanswer. He was a master of the art form.

"Okay. Let me ask this another way so we can both be absolutely clear. Are you hanging around on purpose out of some stupid idea that I need help locking up?"

He put the pizza on the workbench. "Does it matter?"

"Uh, yeah, it does. In one scenario, you're here for a legitimate reason. In the other, you're acting like a patronizing chauvinist."

His eyes narrowed. "So thinking it's dangerous for you to be here alone in the dark and walk across a badly lit parking lot makes me a chauvinist?"

"No, assuming I can't take care of myself makes you a chauvinist. I know you'll find it hard to believe, but I stayed here on my own for years—*years*—before you. I don't need you to babysit me."

"Did you see the glass in the street the other day? Someone's car was broken into."

"So?"

"So what if you were leaving when that was happening?"

"I'd call the cops."

"Great. They'd arrive in time to draw the chalk outline."

"I'm not stupid, Jon. I park my car as close to the door as possible. I always make sure I'm locked in. And I might be small, but I can look after myself."

She grabbed his pizza from the workbench and shoved it at him. "Eat your pizza at home. Your services are not required here, Sir Galahad."

He took the box, but his eyes flashed dangerously. She'd seen that look in his eye one other time—when he'd picked her up and bodily moved her out of the way. A thrill of something that was almost fear raced down her spine. She swiveled on her heel and marched to her office. After a short pause, she heard Jon following her. She ignored him, even though all the little hairs on the back of her neck were standing on end. Only when she was safely on her own turf did she deign to turn and acknowledge his presence.

"Still here?" she asked coolly.

"Show me." He was all belligerent male, his eyes turbulent, his body tense as he moved toward her.

"I beg your pardon?"

"Prove it. Prove to me you can take care of yourself and you won't hear another peep out of me."

Her jaw dropped open. "You are unbelievable. I don't have to prove anything to you."

"You're the one with all the big talk. What have you done? A self-defense course? A bit of tai chi or something?"

She gave him a scathing look.

"Go home, Jon. Before you really piss me off."

"Lady, you have no idea."

He moved closer, crowding her. Every instinct screamed at her to back off, but she refused to play his game.

"I'm not scared of you."

"I'm not the one you need to worry about."

He was so close now she could feel his warmth. His chest brushed her folded arms. She had to tilt her head to maintain eye contact with him, he was so much taller than her.

"What next? Are we going to have a stare-off?" she asked. "Or maybe we could see who can hold their breath the longest?"

He responded by moving closer again, so close that his thighs were pressed against hers, his whole body looming over her. Even though she was determined not to be intimidated, she couldn't stop herself from arching away from him a little. She felt the desk against the back of her thighs and realized she really was cornered.

"Wow. Impressive." She hated the fact that her voice rose slightly on the final word. She flat-out refused to be intimidated by him. "You've proven you're bigger than me. I bet if we got a tape measure your dick would be bigger than mine, too. Is that enough superiority for you for one night?"

He planted a hand either side of her on the desk, effectively boxing her in.

"I know you've got a tongue in your head, but that's not going to stop someone who wants to hurt you. Show me how you can look after yourself, Gabby," he said, his voice low and dangerous.

Their faces were inches apart. She could see the individual whiskers of his five o'clock shadow, could smell his skin and his deodorant.

"I'm not playing games with you."

His body was hot and hard against hers, six foot plus of solid, angry male.

"Aren't you?"

There was something in his eyes that made her shiver all the way to the soles of her feet.

"Back off or I'll give you a head start on singing soprano."

Before he could respond, she ducked under his arm and darted to her left. She barely made it two steps before he was on her, slamming her into the wall. She struck out blindly with her right arm but he grabbed it before it contacted, pinning it to the wall beside her head. She used her knee, but he deflected it with his leg. She fisted her left hand and drove it into where she hoped his solar plexus was, keeping her thumb tucked on the outside the way she'd been taught. He grunted, then he had her left arm, too, and she was pinned by his body weight and his grip on her arms.

They were both panting, their chests heaving as they glared at each other.

"Is that it?" Jon demanded. "That all you've got?"

He released her left arm, sliding his hand boldly

down her body to grab her backside. His hand spread wide, he hoisted her higher up the wall. His hips pressed into hers, and she could feel the hard length of his erection pressing against her stomach. Something primitive and utterly instinctual exploded inside her.

"Not even close." She fisted her hand in his T-shirt and leaned forward, sinking her teeth into the thick cord of muscle where his neck met his shoulder.

He stilled. She tasted salt and skin and her head was full of the smell and feel of him. So big and hard and strong. She pressed her tongue against him, tentatively at first, then more brazenly.

Slowly she relaxed her jaw. Lips replaced teeth as she explored his neck with hungry open-mouthed kisses. The hand on her backside tensed, then relaxed, and then Jon's hips were grinding into hers and both of his hands were on her backside, as well, lifting and angling her, encouraging her to wrap her legs around his hips. She locked her ankles behind his back and moaned against his throat as she felt his erection pressing against her where she needed it most.

"Gabby," Jon said, his voice pure gravel.

His mouth found her ear, then the sensitive skin beneath it. She pulled him closer. He kissed his way across her cheekbone until finally their mouths met, a fiery clash of lips and teeth and tongues as they tried to devour each other.

She slid a hand down his chest to find the hem of his T-shirt. His belly muscles tensed as she smoothed her palm upward until she was cupping one smooth pec in her hand. Jon angled her head back, intensifying their kiss. She found his nipple with her thumb and rubbed it before pinching it firmly. He jerked against her, then suddenly the wall was gone from behind her. He dropped her on the desk, still kissing her, and she swept her arm blindly to clear the surface, pushing papers over the edge with reckless abandon.

He broke their kiss, stared at her. For the first time since she'd known him everything he was feeling was in his eyes for her to see—need and desire and demand. Maintaining the eye contact, she used her elbows to crawl backward until she was lying fully across the desk. She reached for the hem of her tank top and yanked it over her head. He did the same with his T-shirt. She eyed his chest and belly, excitement surging inside her. She snapped open the front closure on her bra and let it slide down her arms.

Jon's eyes roamed from one peak to the other before he put a knee on the desk and climbed on top of her. Her legs fell open in welcome. He ducked his head and pulled a nipple into his mouth, his tongue laving her roughly before sucking firmly. The pleasure was exquisite, sharp and sweet, and she arched, grabbing his head and hanging on for dear life.

He suckled her till it almost hurt, then soothed her with his tongue before switching his attention to her other breast and starting all over again. She moved restlessly, her hands running over his shoulders and back and belly, her hips rubbing against his. He was so big, so overwhelming, but she didn't feel overpowered. She felt powerful. Sexy. Desired.

He blazed a second trail across her body with his hand, cupping her breast, pinching her nipple, gliding down her rib cage to her belly. She trembled as his hand smoothed over her skirt then beneath it to her wide-spread thighs.

"Please," she pleaded brokenly.

She didn't even know what she was asking for, but Jon seemed to understand. He slid his hand onto her mound, cupping her quivering sex in his palm, exerting just the right amount of pressure. She started to pant, her fingers digging into him.

He replaced his hand with a single, knowing finger as he traced the seam of her sex through her underwear. She jerked against him when he found the right spot and she felt him smile against her breast. Then his thumb was rubbing her and she forgot to breath.

It was so good. So intense. She felt like a teenager again, as though she was discovering all of this for the first time. Her first kiss, her first caress, her first taste of true desire.

Except she was a women, not an inexperienced girl, and she knew exactly what she wanted.

Her frantic hands found the waistband of Jon's jeans and tugged at the stud there. He slipped a finger beneath the elastic on her underwear and made an approving sound when he felt how wet and ready she was. She almost came off the desk when he slid a finger inside her. She clenched her thighs around his hips and moaned as he stroked her again and again. Tension built inside her, an ache that demanded satisfaction. She renewed her assault on his jeans, tugging the zip down and reaching into his boxers for his erection. Her hand closed around him and she gave a little moan of approval. He was incredibly hard, and so long and thick she wanted to cry.

He slid a second finger into her, his thumb hitting her sweet spot every time he withdrew.

She shivered and twisted beneath him, craving so much more.

"You," she whispered. "I want you."

She pushed at the waistband of his jeans again,

and he took the hint and pushed them the rest of the way down, his mouth never leaving her breasts. She levered her hips up and slid off her panties, tugging at the tie on her skirt to free herself. Jon lifted his head from her breasts to finish kicking off his jeans. She stared at his erection as he tore open the foil packet he took from his pocket. He was every bit as big and beautiful as she'd imagined. More so. Her gaze traveled hungrily over his powerful thighs and the defined ridges of his belly. She'd never seen a man like him.

He smoothed on the condom, his movements slow and very deliberate. He surveyed her when he'd finished, his gaze traveling over her breasts and belly before zeroing in on the heart of her. She bit her lip as he smoothed a hand up her thigh, using his thumb to tease her intimate folds, watching his own actions and her reaction with a focused, knowing intent.

His gaze found hers. Neither of them broke the contact as, at last, he pushed forward, probing her entrance with his erection. Then he flexed his hips and she closed her eyes to savor the slow, thick slide as he came inside her for the first time.

She gripped him with her thighs, her hands, her inner muscles. He felt so good. So right.

He muttered something under his breath—

possibly *unbelievable,* she wasn't sure—then he started to move with deep, controlled strokes.

She lost track of time. The world contracted to the feel of him inside her, to the suction of his mouth on her breasts, to the knowing caress of his thumb just above where they were joined. She smoothed her hands over his body, reveling in the sheer strength of his shoulders, squeezing his firm, round ass in her hands, digging her fingers into the muscles of his back, wrapping a leg around his hips to encourage him deeper.

Jon made a guttural noise and abandoned her breasts to kiss her, his hand framing her jaw as his tongue slid against hers, his teeth nipping at her lips before he plunged deep to claim her.

She tensed as her climax swept toward her, holding her breath. Her back arched and she closed her eyes tightly.

"Yes. Come for me, Gabby," he whispered near her ear. "Come for me."

Her climax seemed to last forever, a never ending wave of pleasure. He wrung every last drop from her with small, nudging thrusts, barely withdrawing before grinding himself into her again. Finally, the pleasure waned, and she opened her eyes to find Jon watching her, a triumphant glint in his eye.

He ducked his head to kiss her, then he began

to move inside her once more, his thrusts increasingly urgent. His upper lip curled back from his teeth, his jaw clenched. His body tensed, every muscle solid. He drove himself deep inside her one last time, pressing his cheek against hers, his breath harsh in her ear as he shuddered out his own climax.

She felt the tremors in his body, felt him ride the wave of pleasure.

He let his weight rest on her for a moment afterward. She could feel his heart hammering, could feel the dampness of sweat where his body pressed against hers—chest, belly, thighs. Then he pushed himself up, withdrawing from her as he rolled to the side.

She blinked at the ceiling, feeling utterly drained and more than a little dazed. Her heart was pounding in her ears, her sex throbbing with the intensity of their lovemaking. Her brain was foggy, overwhelmed with sensation.

She'd never experienced anything like it. She felt…subsumed. As though she'd lost a piece of herself.

He stood and she watched as he stooped to put on his jeans. It wasn't until he looked at her that she came fully down to earth. He'd retreated behind his guard again, giving away nothing, and she was suddenly acutely aware that she was sprawled on her desk, naked, while he was mostly dressed.

"Won't be a moment," he said.

He left her office. She assumed it was to dispose of the condom. She slid off the desk. She didn't bother trying to pull her bra on, instead scooping her tank top from the floor and turned it right side out with not-quite-steady hands. She was knotting the tie on her wrap skirt when Jon returned.

Her gaze gravitated to the angry red mark on his left shoulder, a perfect imprint of her bite. Never in her life had she deliberately hurt anyone, and definitely not during sex.

She looked away from the evidence of her own out of control need. She crouched and began to collect the paperwork she'd pushed off her desk. After a few seconds he joined her.

"It's fine. I've got it," she said tightly.

He kept working and she clenched her jaw.

Five minutes. Five minutes and this will be over with, she promised herself.

Finally, they'd collected the last of the papers. She stood. Jon followed suit. He placed his pile of on her desk and she put hers beside it.

"Gabby."

He hadn't put on his T-shirt yet and she couldn't look at him, couldn't stand the sight of the mark she'd put on his shoulder.

"I don't want to talk about it," she said.

He was silent for a long moment and she could feel him looking at her.

"I need to know if you're okay. Did I hurt you?"

Her gaze flew to his face. "No. Of course not."

He was the one with the mark on his shoulder, not her.

He studied her face. "Okay."

He turned to collect his T-shirt from where he'd thrown it over her chair and her throat tightened when she saw his back. Welts criss-crossed his shoulders and lower back, more evidence of how crazy she'd been.

She glanced down at her hands. Her nails weren't even that long.

"I think you should go." She desperately needed to be alone. Any second now she was going to lose it, and the last thing she wanted was for Jon to witness it.

He took a long time to answer. "If that's what you want."

"It is."

He didn't say anything more, simply turned and left. She listened to the sound of him walking through the workshop. She heard the exterior door open, then close. Then and only then did she let out the breath she'd been holding.

She was in shock. There was no other way to

phrase it. Never in her life had she experienced anything so intense, so all consuming. She had literally been beyond control. She'd goaded Jon, then she'd fought him and hurt him before she'd finally admitted what she really wanted from him.

And not once—not for a second—had she thought about Tyler. It had all been about Jon. His body. The way he looked at her. How much he infuriated her. The things he said to her. The way he challenged her.

She didn't understand herself. The night of her birthday dinner she'd been convinced she still loved Tyler. The pain in her chest had been real. Her grief had been real. Her tears had been real.

And yet less than a week later she'd had knock-down, drag-out sex with his brother. On her desk. At work.

She sank into her chair and pressed her hands to her face.

She was so confused. She felt as though she'd been careening from one disaster to the next since she'd met Jon. He'd thrown her off balance from that first day and she'd never recovered her equilibrium. He'd forced her to take an honest look at herself…at her life. She'd revealed her secrets to him. And now she'd had sex with him.

She remained there for long minutes, her thoughts whirling, her stomach churning. The press of a growing headache finally forced her to move. She collected her bag, turned off the light. Feeling ridiculously fragile for a woman who had tried to take a chunk out of a man's shoulder, she did a circuit of the building, flicking off lights and checking that the machinery was all shut down. She punched the code into the keypad, then slipped out the door with the ease of long practice. It was only when she turned to walk to her car that she realized there was a second car in the parking lot.

Jon's black truck was in the far corner. The windows were dark, but she could feel him watching her. After a small hesitation she walked to her hatchback. She got in, started the engine. She turned her lights on, but didn't pull out. After a few seconds, Jon's lights came on and he drove away.

He'd waited for her. Even though she'd told him to go. Even though this whole thing had started over her refusing to allow him to take responsibility for her.

He'd sat in the dark to ensure she was safe.

She didn't know whether to laugh or cry, to be angry or touched. Apparently she was all about not knowing these days. Apparently that was her thing.

She drove home, thoughts still churning. She

didn't bother turning any lights on when she let herself into her apartment, walking straight to her ensuite. She turned the shower on while she shed her clothes, then stepped beneath the spray.

Needles of hot water pricked her skin. She reached for the soap and washed her breasts and belly and finally between her legs, trying to ignore the residual sensation there. It wasn't until she stepped out and flicked on the overhead light to locate her toothbrush that she saw her body in the mirror. She gasped, her hands going to her chest.

A red suck mark marred her left breast, and another marked the skin beneath her ear on the right. Her face was pink from whisker burn, and when she turned she saw five small, distinct bruises across her backside where Jon had lifted her against him.

She should have been shocked, but she wasn't. Instead, something inside her relaxed. What had happened—whatever it was—had been mutual. They'd both been caught up and crazy.

She wasn't sure why it made her feel better, but it did. Which went to show how messed up she really was.

CHAPTER SEVEN

JON PICKED UP THE PHONE, THEN put it down. He paced to the balcony, then back to the kitchen counter. Picked up the phone. Looked at the keypad. Put it down again.

He'd been caught in the same loop since he'd arrived home. He couldn't call Gabby—she didn't want to talk to him—but he couldn't stop thinking about her, about what had happened.

Even if she did take his call, he had no idea what he would say to her.

Sorry for assaulting you and throwing you on your desk and having dirty, rough sex with you?

Yeah, that would fix everything.

He dragged his hand over his face.

He'd never treated a women that way in his life. Had never so much as lifted a finger in anger. The lessons of his childhood were far too deeply ingrained for him to ever want to watch someone weaker than himself cower in fear.

And yet he'd tried to intimidate Gabby. All five-foot-nothing of her. He'd been so angry—furious—at her refusal to be smart about her safety that he'd lost it. She was all lip and attitude—and she wouldn't stand a chance against anyone out to hurt her. Yet she stubbornly refused to believe it.

The thought of her trying to fend off some desperate junkie or opportunistic hood made his blood run cold.

He'd gone into her office with the intention of showing her how vulnerable she was, to prove to her that being feisty and mouthy was no defence against superior strength. But she hadn't backed down. She'd stood her ground, glaring defiance at him with those golden-brown eyes of hers and refusing to so much as flinch. He'd pushed and pushed until he was so close he could feel the adrenaline vibrating through her body—and the excitement.

Her pupils had been dilated, her breathing shallow. Her body had been hot against his as he'd pressed her against the desk.

Then she'd tried to slip away from him and things had gotten really crazy.

He grit his teeth as he remembered the way he'd slammed her against the wall and pinned her there with his body weight.

You're a real freaking hero, you know that?

He'd hurt her. He'd bullied her and manhandled her and then he'd rubbed his freaking erection against her and—

Jon punched the wall. Hard. The plaster cracked but didn't give. He shook his hand out. The anger drained away as abruptly as it had flooded him and he sank onto the couch.

He dropped his head into his hands.

Images flashed across his mind's eye, but the one that stuck was the look on her face when she'd told him to go. She hadn't even been able to look him in the eye, she'd wanted him gone so much.

And why wouldn't she? He'd behaved like an animal. Like Robert Adamson's son.

"Jesus."

He shot to his feet. He didn't want it to be true. Didn't want to be the man he'd undeniably been tonight.

Angry. Out of control. A slave to his passions.

He grabbed his keys and headed for the door. Everything in him wanted to drive over to Gabby's and beg her to forgive him. But there was nothing he could say that would take back what had happened and she'd copped enough of his crap for one night.

The lights were still on at Tyler and Ally's place. He strode up the path and waited tensely for someone to answer the door. He heard footsteps, then a short pause and the rattle of a door chain being disengaged. The door swung open.

It was Ally, dressed in bright pajamas, a pair of reading glasses on the end of her nose.

"Jon," she said. Her welcoming smile faded as she took in his tense posture. "Is everything okay?"

"Is Tyler around?"

Her brow wrinkled with concern. "I'm sorry, but he's helping a mate pick up a fridge or something. He should be back soon, though."

Damn.

He glanced toward his truck, trying to think. He didn't want to be in his apartment. And he was afraid to go to the pub.

"Come in," Ally said, her hand closing around his forearm. "Wait for him."

He didn't want to wait, but he didn't know what else to do so he let Ally lead him into the house.

"I'll make you a coffee." She didn't release his arm, almost as though she was afraid he'd run off if she did. "Or maybe you'd like a hot chocolate?"

"What I'd really like is a bottle of Scotch."

She smiled sympathetically. "Yeah. I know that feeling."

She pushed him toward the couch and crossed to the kitchen to put the kettle on. He sat on the edge of the seat and looked at his hands. He had no idea why he'd come here. Gabby was like family to Tyler and Ally; the moment his brother heard what had happened he'd punch Jon's lights out.

Maybe that was why he was here—to cop to a little of what he'd dished out tonight. To get a little of what he deserved.

Ally returned and sat at the other end of the couch.

"Have you eaten? Do you want some cheese and crackers? Or I could make you a sandwich?"

"I'm fine. Thanks." He examined his hands, rubbing the thumb of his left hand over the newly bruised knuckles of his right.

"Listen, Jon, if you want to wait for Tyler in peace and quiet, I can disappear. I've got some edits to do on my column, it's not a problem."

"I don't want to keep you from your work."

"That's not what I was saying." She sighed. "You Adamson men. I swear, it's like pulling teeth getting you to talk about anything."

He glanced at her, then at his hands. He didn't want to talk to her about this. It was too ugly. *He* was too ugly.

"Something happened with Gabby tonight," he said, surprising himself as well as Ally.

"What sort of something are we talking about? A conversation? A fight? The opposite of a fight?"

He shifted uncomfortably.

"Both," he eventually said.

"A fight? And the opposite of a fight?"

He sighed, ran a hand over his head. He might as well get this over with. Cut to the part where she stared at him in horror.

"I've been working late so I can be around when Gabby locks up. I knew she wouldn't be too keen on anyone looking out for her, so I've been making up excuses. Well, apparently I suck as an actor because she called me on it tonight and sent me home."

"Sounds like Gabby," Ally said with a small smile. "But I'm willing to bet you didn't go home, right?"

He shot her a look. "Why do you say that?"

"Don't take this the wrong way, but stubbornness runs in the Adamson blood. And you've got that whole older-brother-protective-thing going on. A pretty deadly combination."

He frowned. Obviously Tyler hadn't told her how he'd bailed on him when they were in their teens. Hardly the actions of the protective older brother she was painting him as.

"You know what that neighborhood is like. Smashed glass in the gutters, syringes. Once all the factories close for the night, there's no one around. It's dangerous. I couldn't leave her there on her own."

"So you guys had it out, huh?"

"I told her I'd go if she could prove to me she could take care of herself."

"I bet that went down well."

"She told me to go to hell. So I decided I was going to show her why she was wrong. I backed her up against the desk—"

He shot to his feet. No way could he describe what had happened next. It was too personal. Too visceral. Too shameful.

Ally simply waited. He stood in front of the couch, head lowered, one hand rubbing the back of his neck. He told himself he should go, but instead he found himself talking again.

"She wouldn't back down. We…we fought. Physically, I mean." It was hard to push the words past the tightness in his throat. "She tried to get away from me, I slammed her into the wall. Then we— Then things changed."

"This is the opposite of fighting bit, right?"

He looked at her. She didn't look even slightly appalled by what he'd told her. "Yeah."

"Well, then. Tyler owes me fifty bucks."

Jon stared at her. He'd confessed to throwing a ninety-pound woman against the wall, to fighting her physically, and Ally was pleased that she'd won a bet?

"I could have really hurt her."

"*Did* you hurt her?"

"I pushed her against the wall."

"I bet that would have really pissed Gabby off."

He thought about the way she'd bitten him. "It did."

Ally patted the couch. "Sit. You're giving me a crick in my neck."

He sat.

"You're giving yourself a hard time because things got physical with Gabby, right?"

Wasn't it obvious?

"I could have hurt her," he said again.

"But you didn't, Jon."

"Things were out of control."

"Right." Ally nodded. "That's important for you, isn't it? Being in control?"

Wasn't it to everyone? As far as he was concerned, taking responsibility for your own actions was the most basic requirement of adulthood.

"Typically the children of abusive parents go two ways," Ally said thoughtfully. "Some of them become abusers themselves, perpetuating the misery. And the others do everything in their power to break the cycle. It constantly amazes me that you and Tyler are the people you are, given what you came from. That even though you were given so little love and compassion, you're both good, good men."

He shifted uneasily. "This isn't anything to do with any of that."

Ally spoke very gently. "I think it is, Jon. I think it's everything to do with why you're upset tonight."

He checked his watch. "I should let you get to bed. It's getting late." He stood.

Ally looked up at him ruefully. "Pushed you too far, huh?"

"It's late."

Ally stood. "Can't tempt you with some ice cream?"

"Thanks, but I'm not really an ice cream fan."

"Huh. Interesting. Gabby's not mad about it, either."

Jon collected his keys and phone from the coffee table. "Don't turn this into some big romance, Ally. Gabby and I... Even if she doesn't hate my guts after tonight, there are a lot of reasons why nothing's ever going to happen between us."

Starting with the fact that Gabby still had feelings for his brother.

"What's your favorite thing about her?"

The question was so unexpected he responded without thinking. "She never quits fighting her corner, even when a smart person would stop. And she's mouthy."

Ally's smile was smug. "I like those things about her, too. Plus she has an awesome ass."

She shocked a laugh out of him. They walked to the front door in an oddly companionable silence. He opened the door before pausing to say goodbye.

"Thanks. And sorry if I messed with your work schedule."

He leaned close and kissed her on the cheek. He was about to turn and exit when Ally's hand caught his wrist.

"Jon. You can come here anytime, okay? Day or night. Whatever. Tyler and I are both here for you. If you want to talk or not talk. Even if you just want to hang out. Okay?"

She stood on her toes and embraced him. He patted her back awkwardly. She sank onto her heels and gave him a wry look.

"One of these days you're going to hug me properly, you know."

He looked down at his car keys. "I do appreciate it, Ally," he said quietly.

"I know. Off you go. I won't make you any more uncomfortable."

He descended the steps and started up the path. Halfway to the gate, he pivoted on his heel.

"Don't forget to put the chain back on," he said.

"I won't, big brother."

He hesitated. He felt as though he was perpetuating a fraud, letting Ally assume he was the typical kind of big brother, the kind who took responsibility and looked out for his siblings. But tonight wasn't the night to straighten her out.

His brain was less busy as he drove home. Despite how quickly he'd bailed when Ally had brought up his father, the stuff she'd said about self-control being important to him had struck a chord. It was true that he'd always been careful to govern his passions. He never ate too much, never acted in the heat of anger, never let himself get too swept up with a woman. For many years his one vice had been cigarettes, but despite a short relapse recently he'd managed to kick the habit.

In fact, there were only two areas where he'd ever really lost control: with drink, and with Gabby. He was coming to grips with his drinking, but Gabby... No matter what he did, he didn't seem to be able to keep a lid on himself when she was around. She pushed him in so many ways. And tonight she'd pushed him to the edge and over.

Then stay away from her. It's that easy.

A pretty simple solution. He'd been making noises about moving on for a while now, but maybe it was time to put words into actions.

One thing was for sure, Gabby would be glad to see the back of him.

GABBY WOKE WITH A SINGLE IMAGE from the previous night etched in her mind: Jon's face when he'd returned to her office and she'd refused to talk to him. He'd looked...*shaken* was the only word she could come up with. Maybe even stricken.

At the time, she'd been so busy trying to protect herself that she hadn't thought about him. She'd let him inside her body, run her hands and mouth all over his, yet she hadn't considered his reaction.

There was an argument to be made that Jon had most likely been more than happy to escape so lightly from a potentially awkward situation. The fun bit was over; he'd had his thrills. What more could he want?

A lot of guys—most guys—would have been skipping all the way to their cars, thrilled to have avoided a postcoital debrief.

But Jon wasn't most guys. He had a fierce sense of duty and he always did the right thing. Always. He'd given in to Ally's cajoling and come to dinner, even though the whole deal had clearly not been his cup of tea. He'd apologized to Gabby about the whole lesbian thing—twice. He'd made up excuses so he could watch over her while she locked up. He'd tried to step in when she was heading for trouble at the Christmas party. He'd been painstaking in his attention to detail in the work he'd done for Tyler.

Jon was a good man. An honorable man. Overbearing at times. Arrogant in his own unique I-know-best way. But he had a good heart, and he'd been decent to her on numerous occasions. Some might even say he'd been kind.

She owed him an apology, and she owed him a conversation. She had no idea what that conversation would consist of. No doubt it would end with them disagreeing. So be it. It had to be done.

She lay in bed girding her loins for a full ten minutes after her alarm went off, then she rolled out of bed and marched into the bathroom.

She gasped when she saw the hickey on her neck in the cold light of day. Last night, the evidence that Jon had been as lost in their mutual passion as she'd been had been comforting. This morning, not so much.

The mark on her breast she could live with—no one was going to see that—but she'd already survived a solid day of being pilloried for her performance at the Christmas party. The thought of enduring another round of teasing and questions and innuendo over the scarlet mark on her neck was enough to make her want to write a letter of resignation on the spot.

Which meant the hickey had to go. The last time she'd had to employ hickey camouflaging techniques had been the first year of high school.

She had a vague memory of something to do with toothpaste, but she figured that a scarf tied in a jaunty little bow and some cover-up stick was probably the better bet.

She experimented for twenty minutes with the only summer-weight scarf she owned before she was satisfied she could hide the incriminating mark. Red with white dots, it made her look a little like Maryanne off *Gilligan's Island,* but it wasn't as though she had much choice. She was tweaking her scarf for the fourth time when she caught sight of her alarm clock and made a grab for her keys and headed for the door. She was almost certain that her office still needed a bit more work before it could pass as a place of business again instead of a makeshift bordello, which meant she needed to be the first one in.

Half an hour later, her office was back to its pre-desk-sex state and she was watching the clock, waiting for Jon to arrive for the day so she could do what had to be done.

Her foot jiggled beneath the desk and she glanced up every time she heard the showroom door open. Carl was in first, then Dino. Finally, the door to the showroom swung open and she was rewarded with the sight of Jon's broad shoulders and dark head. Nerves tightened her belly. Her palms got sweaty.

Time to woman up, princess.

She stood, twitching her scarf a little more to the right. In the workshop, Jon hung his jacket over the back of the stool at his workbench and began to set up for the day. She stared at his shoulders, impossibly wide under a white T-shirt, then let her gaze drop to his backside. She'd never truly allowed herself to appreciate it before, but it was great. Really, really great.

A rush of sense-memories washed over her— the rasp of his beard on her breasts, the slide of his fingers between her legs, the resilient firmness of his muscles beneath her hands.

She plucked at the front of her T-shirt, trying to dissipate some of the heat. She was not approaching Jon the morning after their ill-advised liaison with glowing cheeks. That was not going to happen.

She fanned her top a few more times, then plunged into the fray.

Her legs felt shaky as she rounded her desk. She concentrated on putting one foot in front of the other. Through some malicious trick of psychological chicanery, the distance to her doorway seemed to stretch to eternity.

Get it done and over with, you big scaredy cat.

Jon was frowning at some brass cabinet fittings when she reached his side.

"Jon. Hi. Um, would you have a minute to spare?"

He put down the hinge he'd been examining and looked at her. A muscle twitched in his jaw. "Sure. When did you have in mind?"

"Now. If you're free, that is?"

"I'm free."

"Well, then." Feeling supremely uncomfortable, she turned to lead him back to her office and nearly tripped over her own feet. Out of the corner of her eye she saw him reach out a hand to steady her—only to hesitate at the last moment.

He didn't want to touch her.

Something small and sharp twisted in her chest.

"I'm fine," she said, even though he hadn't asked.

She waited until he'd entered her office before she shut the door behind her. Anyone passing would wonder why—she never closed her door—but she wasn't taking any chances with anyone overhearing what she had to say.

She faced him. He was standing in the center of the room, and she knew him well enough now to know that he was far from comfortable. Good. She'd gotten herself so worked up she felt sick—it was nice to know she wasn't alone.

"I wanted to apologize for last night."

Jon went very still. His gaze slid to the desk.

"Not for the sex," she clarified hastily. "For afterward. When you came back and I said I didn't want to talk. That's the part I'm sorry for. Not the other bit."

The other bit?

She winced mentally. She was such an idiot. And she'd even rehearsed this in bed less than an hour ago.

He shifted his weight. "Okay."

She took a breath. "Also, I wanted to ask how your shoulder is."

Impossible to stop herself from blushing now.

"It's fine."

"Are you sure? Because it looked pretty raw last night."

"It's fine."

She'd never seen him look more serious.

"Well, good." Her hands found each other at her waist and she clasped them together. "That was… That's not something that's ever happened for me before. I'm not really sure what happened—"

"I do. I pushed you. I backed you into a corner."

She could hear the self-condemnation in his voice, the judgment.

"You didn't push me anywhere. I gave as good as I got."

"No." His voice was very tight, utterly certain.

She studied him, noting the signs of tiredness in his face, the tension around his mouth.

He'd been giving himself a hard time over this, she realized. Convincing himself that he'd been responsible for what happened. In all her obsessive analyses of what had occurred last night—and there had been many as she lay awake into the small hours—the notion that he might think the sex had been anything but a meeting of equals had not even crossed her mind.

"There were two people in this office last night, Jon, not one. And you didn't do anything to me that I didn't do to you."

"Except one of us is six foot two."

"You're the one with the injuries, not me. And please don't even start to tell me that the sex was all your idea or something ridiculous like that. I wanted it. I enjoyed it. Okay?"

He frowned.

"If I'd wanted you to stop last night you would have stopped. At any point."

"How do you know that?"

She could hear the uncertainty in his voice.

"Because I wasn't scared. Not once. Not even a little bit. And you knew that. If I'd called a halt, if you'd seen I was scared, you would have stopped."

"You have a lot of faith in me."

"You've earned it."

His frown deepened. He looked so uneasy and unhappy. This was a really big deal for him.

"Okay. Fine," she said. "I get that you're a man of action, that words aren't your thing. So if what it takes is a rematch, let's get down to it."

She reached for the hem of her T-shirt.

"Whoa," Jon said, taking a step forward, one hand extended. "Aren't you forgetting something?"

He glanced toward the glass panel in the door. He looked so scandalized she almost smiled. Given what they'd done on her desk, the prospect of the guys seeing her in her bra seemed pretty tame.

"Here's a deal for you—you stop blaming yourself for something we both took part in, and I'll keep my T-shirt on."

That got a small smile out of him. "Do you ever not play hardball?"

"Absolutely—when I figure my opponent isn't up to it. So, what's it going to be, Jon?" She tugged her T-shirt up a couple of inches, displaying her belly to him. "Am I going to traumatize the guys for life or are you going to admit it takes two to tango?"

That shocked a laugh out of him. She could tell he still didn't quite believe she'd go through with it. She arched an eyebrow.

"Well? What's your answer?" She lifted her

T-shirt some more, exposing the lower half of her bra.

"Gabby. Come on." He shot a worried look toward the window, then took a step forward and grabbed the hem of her T-shirt, tugging it down and holding it there.

They were standing very close, his body almost brushing hers, his hand warm on her belly. She looked into his eyes.

"That fight was an excuse for us to both do what we wanted to do. You know that, right?" she said.

He looked at his feet, his lashes brushing his cheeks. She was reminded of the night she'd caught him sleeping at his workbench. He'd looked so vulnerable then.

He was vulnerable now, too.

She had a sudden flash of insight, a moment of intuitive connection, as she studied his down-turned face. Last year, she'd stood on the sidelines as Tyler struggled through his father's final days. He'd never said anything directly, but she'd understood that there had been a lot of unhappiness in his childhood. Violence, maybe, or some other form of abuse. It hit her now that a man who'd grown up in an angry, violent household might find it difficult to put last night into its proper perspective. In fact, such a man might find it almost impossible to forgive himself for letting his passions get away from him.

It was just a guess, but it felt right. A wave of compassion washed over her and the urge to comfort him was so strong she didn't even try to deny it. She wrapped her arms around him and lay her cheek against his chest.

"It's okay, Jon."

He tensed, his body as unyielding and unbending as concrete. She refused to let go. She knew he was stubborn—it took one to know one, after all—but he had to let go of the crazy idea that he was responsible. She felt his rib cage expand as he breathed in, then all of a sudden his arms came around her and he pulled her more tightly to his chest. She felt his cheek press against the top of her head, could hear the unsteady thump of his heart beneath her ear as he held her.

There was an intensity, almost a desperation to his embrace that touched something deep inside her. Maybe she was being fanciful, but she had the feeling that Jon had experienced precious few moments of compassion and acceptance in his life.

The thought brought the unexpected heat of tears to her eyes.

"You'd better get that," Jon murmured.

"What?"

His arms loosened and he stepped backward. She realized her phone was ringing.

"Right," she said. "The phone."

She moved to her desk and lifted the receiver.

"Gabby Wade speaking," she said.

"Gabby, it's Brandon Sinclair from Vibe Interiors," a voice said in her ear.

"Hi, Brandon, how are you?" She assumed her best professional voice.

Movement caught the corner of her eye and she turned to see Jon heading for the door. She stared at him as Brandon explained why he was calling. For the first time it struck her that being a big man, a powerful man, brought with it its own expectations and prejudices. It was all too easy to assume that a man who looked as solid and unassailable as Jon did never had any doubts or fears. But he was flesh and blood, with all the usual weaknesses and foibles that came with being human.

"So I was wondering if you guys thought you could meet those deadlines," Brandon was saying in her ear.

She blinked and dragged herself back to the here and now.

"Sorry, Brandon, I was just calling up your file on the computer," she fibbed. "What were those dates again?"

CHAPTER EIGHT

JON KEPT HIS HEAD DOWN FOR most of the morning, not participating in the chat between the guys, pretending an absorption in his work that, for once, he didn't feel.

Gabby had floored him with her apology. And that stunt with her T-shirt…

He'd told Ally that one of the things he most admired about Gabby was her willingness to fight her corner even when a smart person would concede defeat. She'd been pretty damned convincing, boldly telling him that he hadn't scared her, that she trusted him, that their fight had simply been an excuse they'd both used to get close.

But the thing he really couldn't get out of his head was the way she'd wrapped her arms around him, so easily and naturally and forgivingly. He'd always thought of her as a small woman, petite and delicate despite her large personality, but her arms had been strong and sure. When she'd rested her head on his chest he'd been powerless to stop himself from returning her embrace.

It was such a small, trusting gesture. More than

anything she'd said it had proved to him that she wasn't afraid of him. That he hadn't stepped over the line with her last night.

He'd never been comfortable with physical affection. There hadn't been a lot of it in the Adamson household and as an adult, sex was the only time he felt comfortable getting physically close to another human being. It had always seemed to him that hugs and kisses and casual caresses came with strings attached, and he didn't want to be forced into the position of disappointing anyone's expectations.

Gabby's embrace hadn't felt as though it had strings attached to it. He hadn't felt as though she wanted anything from him; she'd simply offered him comfort.

It had scared him how much he'd wanted to accept it, how good she'd felt.

Letting her go had been one of the hardest things he'd done in a long time.

"Mate, Tyler wants you."

He looked up to find Paul by his workbench, gesturing to where Tyler was standing at the top of the stairs. It was evident from Tyler's bemused, slightly frustrated expression that he'd been trying to get Jon's attention for some time.

"Right. Thanks." Dusting off his hands, he started up the stairs to the mezzanine.

"You had your ears tested lately?" Tyler asked good-naturedly.

"I was concentrating." Jon could just imagine his brother's reaction if he told him that he'd been thinking about a hug, of all things.

Tyler gestured for him to precede him into his office and Jon dropped into the chair opposite the desk. To his surprise, Tyler sat beside him rather than behind the desk.

Jon was instantly wary, remembering the conversation with Ally last night. Only an idiot would expect spouses to keep secrets from one another.

"I wanted to talk to you about your salary."

His shoulders relaxed a notch. This wasn't about Gabby, then.

"I don't have one. Remember?"

"As if I could forget. I've had Gabby in my ear every five seconds telling me I need to pay you."

This was news to him. "I didn't realize she knew."

"Mate, there's not much she doesn't know about this business."

"Right."

"I know we talked about this being a temporary role while you worked out what you will do next. But I wanted to ask how you've been finding it."

"If you're asking if I like the work, the answer's yes."

"Does that mean you'd consider sticking around?"

Jon looked at his watch, fiddling with the strap as he tried to work out what to say. Last night, he'd more or less made the decision it was time to move on. He'd planned to ask Tyler for access to a computer to look for airfares. After his conversation with Gabby this morning, some of the urgency had gone out of the decision.

He figured he could give his brother a few more weeks, maybe a month, tops. Anything longer was only delaying the inevitable. As much as he admired what his brother had built up here, he didn't have it in him to be anyone's employee anymore, not after years of being his own boss. He might be floating at the moment, but long-term he wanted to be running his own business again.

"How long do you need me for?"

"How about thirty years, depending on when you want to retire?" Tyler asked.

Jon's first impulse was to laugh—then he saw the bound document in Tyler's hands.

"These are the company records for the past four years." Tyler leaned forward and collected another document from his desk. "These are our profit projections for the next five years."

Jon looked at the proffered documents but didn't take them from his brother's hands.

"I appreciate the offer. But like I told you in

Woodend, I'm not looking to settle here. I'm happy to fill a gap or take up the slack for you till you find someone permanent, but I'm not interested in a long-term job."

"I'm not offering you a job. I want you to buy into the business. Become my partner."

Whoa.

Jon stared at his brother, his mind a complete blank.

"I know it's out of the blue. And you don't need to make a decision right now, but I want you to think about it," Tyler said. "I figure we could do a fifty-fifty split, because I know I wouldn't be interested in anything else if the shoe was on the other foot, but the details are negotiable."

He offered the paperwork to Jon again. He took it and stared down at the glossy cover.

He didn't know what to say. Not for a second had he imagined that his brother would be willing to share something that was obviously so close to his heart. Tyler had built this business from scratch, poured his sweat, blood and tears into it, and now he was riding what Jon suspected was the very beginning of a massive wave of success. And he was inviting Jon along for the ride.

It was incredibly generous. Especially given their long estrangement.

"I wasn't expecting this," he finally said.

"Yeah, I got that." Tyler leaned back in his chair, apparently completely relaxed about the outcome of their discussion. Only the telltale jiggling of his foot gave away that this meant anything to him.

"How would you see this working?"

"Until recently, I've been splitting my time between design, production and sales. Gabby's been stepping into sales more, and doing a bloody good job of it, so I feel we're covered there. The workshop still needs a lot of my time. Dino's prepared to step up to a certain point, but he doesn't want more responsibility or hours than he already has, and none of the other guys has the initiative to make a good production manager. Every time there's a problem, I get dragged away from design work—and let's face it, nothing gets made if I don't design it first."

Jon could see his brother's problem. Essentially, there was only one of Tyler, but there were a number of areas where his skill, passion and commitment were required to keep the business driving forward.

"I'm a builder. I haven't done this kind of thing before."

"You've run a construction team. You've made some incredibly ambitious plans a reality. That place you built in the Laurentians was freaking amazing. The way you had to sink those concrete supports into the mountainside to support that cantilevered roof..."

Jon stared at his brother. He had no idea that Tyler was familiar with his Canadian builds. Then he thought about the times he'd looked Tyler up on the internet over the years. He'd told himself he was simply making sure Tyler was still alive, but he'd been pleased to see Tyler's growing success.

Tyler moved to the edge of his seat. "Look, I know the work won't be as challenging for you here, but there are still lots of areas for us to branch out into. High-end bespoke kitchens, for starters."

It was on the tip of Jon's tongue to assure his brother that he'd gotten a lot of satisfaction out of the pieces he'd built since he'd come on board, but he didn't want to mislead him or get his hopes up. It was a good offer—a great one—but that didn't mean it was an offer he would accept.

He flipped open the cover on the financial report, scanning a few lines while he tried to word the question in his mind. Finally he realized there was no polite way to say it.

"Why?" he asked, meeting and holding Tyler's gaze.

"I told you. I need a partner to make the next step forward."

"You could find a production manager if you

looked hard enough. You could even offer him a smaller cut of the business if you wanted him to have an investment."

"It wouldn't be the same. You're my brother."

"So, what? Blood is thicker than water? We both know that's bullshit."

Tyler's gaze was steady. "I don't think it is."

Jon couldn't maintain the eye contact. He fought the urge to remind his brother of all the times he'd let him down in the past. But that would mean getting into a bunch of stuff he had no intention of exhuming. "Can I have some time to think about it?"

"Take all the time you need."

Jon stood, reports in hand. He turned to leave, then paused. "Does Gabby know about this?"

Had she known about this when she spoke to him this morning? Was that little speech about keeping him around?

"I haven't spoken to her yet. I figured I should sound you out first."

He was relieved, and he realized it was because he'd wanted this morning to have been about him and Gabby alone.

"I'd better get back to it," he said.

He glanced at the reports in his hand on the way down the stairs. He still couldn't quite believe that his brother was prepared to put so much trust in him. To share his future.

Gabby was talking to Dino about a delivery. Jon studied her profile, wondering how she was going to feel when she learned about Tyler's offer.

Happy? Uncomfortable? Indifferent? He asked himself how he'd feel, being tied to a business that included her.

Gabby laughed at something Dino said then gave him a little encouraging punch on the arm. Smile firmly in place, she headed for her office and it hit him that he could think of worse fates than having to see Gabby every day.

GABBY WAITED NERVOUSLY TO SEE what would happen when quitting time came around that night. One by one the rest of the crew cleaned up their workstations and said their goodbyes, heading home to their partners and families. By five-thirty it was down to her and Tyler and Jon.

She eyed Jon's back as he bent over the campaign desk he'd been working on the past couple of days. She knew it was pointless to try to convince him that he didn't need to hang around for her. For whatever reason, he had a real thing about her being alone here at night. She didn't know any way of getting him to respect her wishes on the subject, short of seeing him off the premises at gunpoint—and even then he'd probably wait in his truck the way he had last night.

She was about to head to the archive room to get rid of some files when Ally breezed into the workshop. Gabby listened to her greet Jon with fond familiarity before she appeared in the doorway of Gabby's office, a big smile on her face.

"I've come to rescue you."

"I wasn't aware that I needed rescuing."

"I have it on good authority that you're being held captive by paperwork. I've got lighter fluid and a box of matches and I'm going to blow you out of this gulag."

Gabby laughed. "The spirit is willing, but the in-tray says otherwise."

Ally looked at the overflowing tray suspiciously.

"Is there anything in there that can't wait? A cure for baldness? A miracle weight loss treatment?"

"No, but—"

"Then you're coming out for dinner."

"Ally—"

"No buts. This is the one and only time I will ever exert my authority as wife of the boss. You deserve a break, Gabby. Plus I have a voucher from the newspaper for a meal for four at a swanky restaurant in North Fitzroy."

Gabby's gaze slid over Ally's shoulder to where

Jon was packing up his things. He met her gaze and she knew without asking that he was the fourth member of their party.

Twenty-four hours ago she would have faked an appendicitis attack to avoid dinner with Jon.

Ally settled into her guest chair. "The table's booked for six-thirty."

Gabby checked her watch and saw it was nearly ten past six. It would take them at least fifteen minutes to get to North Fitzroy in rush hour traffic. Which meant she needed to hustle if she was going to make herself presentable.

"Pass me my bag," she said.

It took her a couple of minutes closeted in the ladies' room to put on some lipstick, tidy up her eye makeup and tweak her hickey camouflage. Once she was as presentable as she was going to get, she shouldered her handbag and left the bathroom.

Jon and Tyler had joined Ally in her office.

"Okay. I'm ready to go," Gabby said.

"Cool. Let's hit the road," Tyler said.

After a brief discussion in which Tyler and Ally suggested they all go in their car and Gabby insisted on driving herself, they started out for the restaurant in a two-car convoy. Traffic was predictably busy and Gabby spent most of the stop-start drive tailing Tyler's truck, staring at the back of Jon's head through the rear window.

She still couldn't quite believe that she was about to voluntarily have dinner with Jon. After what had happened between them last night, they should have been putting as much distance between them as possible. But the whole world had shifted after their conversation this morning. North was south, east was west, and she no longer knew which way was up or down. She felt as though she was seeing him for the first time. She'd made so many assumptions about him. She'd thought he was arrogant and distant, an overdeveloped knuckle-dragger. He wasn't any of those things. He was very private, and he held himself to a high standard, and he had a fierce sense of duty. He was also, she suspected, a pussycat under all those muscles.

To be fair, he'd made some screwy assumptions about her, too. Apparently neither of them had taken the time to stop and consider before judging and jumping to conclusions about the other.

Ahead of her, Tyler stuck a hand out the window and pointed toward the group of cafés they were approaching. She took this to mean that they'd arrived at their destination and started trawling for a parking spot. She found one ten car-lengths ahead of Tyler and fed change into the meter. The others were waiting for her in front of the restaurant as she approached, Tyler and Ally standing arm in arm, Jon a little off to one side. It struck her that he often stood to one side that way, slightly removed—as though he wasn't quite sure where he belonged. Or maybe it was more that he wasn't sure he'd be welcome.

"Okay, before we go in, I have some ground rules for the evening," Ally said. "No matter what, we all order three courses, and we all stuff ourselves. I get about one perk every five years from those cheapskates at the newspaper, and we are milking this sucker."

"Aye-aye, sir," Gabby said.

"Your word is our command," Jon said.

Their table was in front of a huge floor-to-ceiling window that had been softened with a sheer curtain in a hazy shade of bronze. The lighting was low, the tablecloth a crisp white, the chairs all upholstered in bright jewel tones. Not surprisingly, Gabby found herself sitting next to Jon. Equally not surprising, his arm brushed hers once they'd shoehorned themselves into their seats.

"Sorry. There's not a lot of room," Jon said.

"It's okay," she said.

"Right. Let's do this," Ally said after the waiter had left them with their menus. "Remember, three courses." She fixed them each with a stern eye. "No shirking."

"Are we allowed doggy bags?" Tyler asked.

"As if you'll have trouble fitting three courses in," his wife said.

"Gabby can help me if I struggle," Tyler said.

Gabby kicked him under the table.

"Hey!"

"Oh, I'm sorry. Was that your leg I kicked? I was aiming for something higher."

Out of the corner of her eye she saw Jon smile.

Ally was studying the menu with a small frown.

"Hmm. The ravioli looks nice. But I wonder if pecorino is classed as a soft white cheese."

Gabby shrugged. "Sorry. My expertise is limited to tasty versus cheddar."

"We can ask the waiter," Tyler said.

"It's all right. I'll have the crab cakes. Oh, damn." Ally frowned.

"What?" Gabby asked.

Ally darted a look at Tyler. He was watching her indulgently, a small smile on his face.

"Off you go," he said.

"You don't mind?"

"It's totally up to you."

Gabby exchanged a sideways glance with Jon. He quirked an eyebrow. Clearly, he had no idea what was going on, either.

Ally placed both hands flat on the table and took a deep breath. "I'm pregnant. About seven weeks, we think. Which means no seafood and no soft white cheeses and no sushi and no champagne—"

"Wow. That's fantastic news. Congratulations. I know my math should be better, but when are you due?" Gabby waited for the inevitable twinge of jealousy. After all, if she and Tyler had made it as a couple, she might be the one announcing a pregnancy.

But all she felt was genuine happiness for her friends.

Interesting.

"We think mid-October, but the doctor's going to confirm that at my twelve-week scan," Ally said.

"Great news," Jon said.

Ally looked so excited Gabby couldn't resist reaching across to squeeze her hand. "You guys are going to be great parents." She looked to Tyler, smiling.

He smiled back. She'd honestly never seen him look happier.

It wasn't until she released Ally's hand that she registered the tension in Jon's body. She glanced at him curiously. He was smiling, but one of his hands was busy fiddling with his wineglass, twisting it round and round on the table in endless circles on the tablecloth.

Gabby looked to Tyler to see if he noticed his brother's odd reaction, but he was focused on Ally.

"I guess that means you're going to be an uncle, then," Gabby said to Jon.

He glanced at her, and for a split second she saw a terrible bleakness in his eyes. Then he blinked and it was gone.

"Yeah. Better sharpen up my footy skills."

"I think I can teach my own kid how to kick a footy," Tyler said.

"Sure you can. But if you want him to be any good at it…" Jon trailed off suggestively.

Tyler laughed and gave his brother a challenging look. "Are you saying I can't play footy?"

Jon paused for the exact right amount of time before focusing on Ally. "I think pecorino is sheep's cheese, Ally. There's a glossary at the end of the menu."

Tyler grinned. "Too scared to say it, mate?"

"Not scared, no," Jon said. "But I figured you wouldn't want me to embarrass you in front of your wife by talking about the time you kicked a goal for the visiting team."

"I was seven!"

Gabby listened to the two men banter. She'd never seen Jon like this, relaxed and easy. Tyler seemed delighted by his brother's playfulness, too, and for a moment she could see the boys they'd once been as they battled for supremacy.

The waiter's arrival ended the football discussion—if it could be called that—and they all dutifully ordered three courses.

When it came time to order drinks, Tyler opened the wine list and glanced at Gabby.

"Red or white?"

"I don't care. What's everyone else feel like?" She glanced at Ally, then Jon.

"I can only have a sip or two, so I don't think my vote counts," Ally said.

Jon shook his head. "Nothing for me." He turned to the waiter. "I'll have some mineral water, thanks."

"Let's grab a bottle of red, Gab. That way we can kid ourselves it's good for us," Tyler said.

"Sure," she said distractedly.

She was too busy remembering the apple juice Jon had been drinking at the party to pay much attention to what Tyler ordered. She didn't think it was a coincidence that Jon hadn't drunk then and that he wasn't drinking again tonight, especially since he wasn't driving.

She knew a couple of people who didn't drink. One had a parent who was an alcoholic. The other *was* an alcoholic. She glanced at Jon's profile.

He was listening to Ally, but he turned his head slightly and met her gaze and she knew that he knew exactly what she was thinking. He waited until Ally had finished her story and Tyler was speaking before leaning toward Gabby.

"I'm taking it easy for a while," he said quietly.

"Okay."

He lifted an eyebrow. "That's it? Okay?"

"What else is there to say?"

He stared at her intently for a beat. "Just when I think I've got you pegged..." he murmured, almost to himself.

"Ditto, buddy. Ditto."

He smiled and she couldn't help smiling in response. When she tuned into what was happening on the other side of the table, she saw Ally was watching them with bright, curious eyes.

Gabby steeled herself for the inevitable inquisition. Ally wasn't the kind of person who pulled her punches or thought twice about asking embarrassing questions.

But Ally simply reached for her water glass and took a sip before commenting on the painting hanging on the far wall. Gabby slowly relaxed. She made a mental note to avoid going to the bathroom tonight if she possibly could. No way did she want to risk being cornered by Ally and being badgered into answering questions about Jon. Not when she had no clue what the answers were.

The rest of the meal passed smoothly. Jon talked about a build he did in Canada where the client had wanted to incorporate a living tree into the design, and Ally shared the juiciest morsels from her latest round of letters. Tyler tried to get Gabby to fill him in on her mother's latest exploits, but Gabby staunchly refused.

"You want to laugh at her," she said.

"I would never laugh at your mother. She's way too scary," Tyler said.

"Gabby has a scary mother? Now, that surprises me," Jon said, deadpan.

Gabby gave him a look. "Careful."

"I said I was surprised," Jon said, playing innocent.

"My mother is simply very protective of her independence," Gabby said.

"Gabby. Come on. She hasn't had a boyfriend for thirty years. That's not protective, that's a declaration of war," Tyler said.

"I want to meet her," Ally said. "She sounds awesome."

"She is," Gabby said firmly.

Tyler made eye contact with Jon and mouthed the word *scary* again.

Only the arrival of their coffees prevented

Gabby from kicking him for a second time. By the time they'd finished those and a plate of complimentary chocolates, it was nearly eleven.

"I'd better get going. Got to get in early to take care of all the paperwork I didn't do tonight," Gabby said, shooting Ally a smile.

"I've been meaning to talk to you about that. I think it's time we hired someone to help out with the admin," Tyler said.

"Not yet. We said we'd review it later in the year, remember?" she said dismissively.

"You need help now, Gabby," Tyler said.

"I don't think—"

She blinked in surprise as Jon pressed his fingers to her lips.

"Listen to the boss," he said. "You work too hard. You need help."

She blinked again, more than a little astonished by what he'd said and the way he'd said it. As though he cared. As though he liked her.

"Well. There's not much I can say to that, is there?" Flustered, she grabbed her bag. "Thank you for a great meal."

Jon started to stand. She pointed a finger at him.

"Don't even think about walking me to my car."

He met her determined gaze. She tilted her head to one side, silently daring him. He resumed his seat. Gabby was aware of Tyler and Ally exchanging amused glances.

"Thanks for sharing your perk with me, Ally. I'll see the rest of you tomorrow."

She gave them a little wave and headed for the door. She half expected Jon to follow her despite what she'd said and debated with herself whether she would make a scene or not. She glanced over her shoulder when she reached the front door, but he was still seated at the table.

Huh.

You are the world's biggest freaking hypocrite, Gabby Wade.

It was true, she was, because there was no denying she was a little disappointed Jon had given in so easily—not because she needed his self-appointed security services, but because she'd been looking forward to the tussle of wills with him.

Which officially made her a sick puppy.

She was so preoccupied with her own twisted thoughts that she didn't realize it had started raining until she stepped out into the night. The road was shiny-wet, the air full of the smell of rain on hot concrete. She glanced toward her car, then tucked her bag firmly under her arm and broke into a run.

She was only feet from her car, fumbling to

activate the keyless entry, when she noticed her
hatchback was listing to one side. Her steps slowed
and she did a quick circuit of the car. She groaned
when she saw that the passenger side rear tire was
completely flat.

"Shit."

She stood in the rain for a moment, contemplat-
ing her bad luck. Then she opened the passenger
door and tossed her purse inside before opening
the trunk to haul out the spare.

Sometimes being an independent woman and
her mother's daughter sucked, but someone had
to do it.

CHAPTER NINE

JON WATCHED GABBY UNTIL SHE disappeared through the door. He told himself they were in a busy café area with good street lighting, and that her car was barely a minute's walk away.

And, as she had told him on more than one occasion, she could take care of herself.

He focused his attention on the table to find Ally and Tyler watching him with identical knowing smiles.

"Nothing's going on," he said instantly.

"We can tell," Tyler said as he pushed himself to his feet. "I'll go get the car."

Ally frowned. "Why on earth would you do that?"

"It's raining," Jon said.

"Well, then I guess we'll get wet." She stood.

"I'll get the car. You two wait here," Tyler said firmly, pressing her back into her seat.

"Tyler. Don't be ridiculous," Ally said.

Tyler kissed her firmly on the mouth. "Stay here."

Ally harrumphed with frustration and Jon hid a smile as his brother headed for the door.

"I'm pregnant, not water-soluble," Ally grumbled. "He is so not treating me like this through the whole pregnancy. I'll go nuts."

"Good luck with that."

She gave him an assessing look. "How are things with you and Gabby?"

"Okay." Jon should have known she wouldn't let it slide.

"I'm going to need a little more than that."

"We talked this morning." He figured he owed her something, since she'd listened last night.

"And?"

"She said she's fine. She said she was just as responsible for what happened as I was."

"That's my girl."

He checked his watch. Ally grinned.

"Enjoying being my captive audience?"

"What do you think?"

He frowned as he saw Tyler entering, a disgruntled expression on his face. His hair and the shoulders of his shirt were wet with rain.

"What's up?" Jon asked as Tyler strode to their table.

"Gabby's got a flat tire. She's being difficult about letting me change it, so I wanted to let you guys know I may be a few minutes with the car."

He sounded supremely frustrated as he turned to go.

Jon was pushing back his chair to join him when Ally spoke.

"If she wants to change the tire, let her do it."

Jon turned to stare at her, aware that his brother was doing the same thing beside him.

"It's dark, it's raining," Tyler said.

"She's got to jack up the car, loosen the nuts. Then she has to lift the spare. You ever tried to lift a tire?" Jon said.

"Can she do it on her own? Is it physically possible?"

"Probably," Jon conceded. "But that's not the point."

Tyler looked to Jon. "She doesn't understand."

"No, you guys are the one's who don't understand," Ally said. She sounded pissed. "If we women let men do everything for us, what happens when you're not around? Huh?"

Tyler opened his mouth to respond, then shut it without saying anything.

"Exactly," Ally said.

"We can't drive off and leave her," Tyler said.

Jon stood. "You guys go. I'll take care of it."

Ally gave him a warning look. "Jon…"

"Thanks for dinner," he said.

He exited the restaurant. Hunching his shoulders

against the rain, he crossed the road and strode to where he knew Gabby had parked.

He could hear her talking to herself as he approached. "Stupid...freaking...mechanic..."

She'd managed to undo three of the four nuts and was using all her body weight to bear down on the tire brace to try to budge the remaining one. He noted with approval that she hadn't jacked the car up yet.

"Hey," he said.

She sat back on her heels and wiped the rain out of her eyes.

"Jon, I swear, if you've come out here to try to change my tire for me—"

"You got an umbrella?"

She peered up at him suspiciously. "Yes. It's on the backseat. Why?"

He didn't bother responding. He pulled open the rear door and glanced around until he spotted the umbrella. It was one of those stupid little ones that women always favored, all folded in on itself. Still, it was better than nothing. He shut the door and hit the button to open the umbrella. Then he stepped closer to Gabby and angled the umbrella so that she would be sheltered while she worked.

She looked up at him in silence for a long moment. "Thank you."

She meant it, too, he could tell.

"You're welcome. I don't suppose you'd let me loosen that nut for you?"

She thought about it for a second. "Yes. Thank you. That would be very helpful."

He handed her the umbrella and she shuffled to one side as he gripped the tire brace. He pushed experimentally. The brace didn't budge.

"Next time you get your tires checked, tell them not to use the air gun to finish up the nuts. Makes them too tight to undo by hand," he said.

"Don't worry, I've already made a mental note."

He braced himself, flexed his shoulders and gave the brace a good turn. He was beginning to get worried when it finally gave.

He looked at her with new respect. "Man. How did you get the other three off?"

"Determination. And a lot of four-letter words."

She handed him the umbrella and he moved out of the way. Gabby squatted and felt along the bottom of the chassis for the jacking point, then placed her jack and started winding. After a few turns of the lever she swore and yanked at the scarf around her neck, stuffing it into her pocket.

"Driving me crazy," she explained as she went back to work.

Jon watched as she wound the jack until the rear wheel was off the ground, wishing like hell she'd let him take over. A couple walked past huddled under their own umbrella, both of them giving him a dirty look when they saw a woman was changing the tire.

"It's okay. I do all the work in bed," he said.

He heard a splutter of choked laughter at his feet. The couple quickened their pace without saying a word. When he looked down again Gabby was grinning.

"This is killing you, isn't it?"

"Someone's going to take a picture of me and I'm going to wind up on one of those email chain letters under the title Man of the Year or something."

She laughed outright. "If it's any consolation, I'm not having much fun, either. But you gotta do what you gotta do."

It took her another fifteen minutes to remove the old tire, replace it with the spare, tighten the nuts, let the jack down and tidy everything away. Since the spare was a doughnut tire, she would have to get the damaged one repaired or replaced as soon as possible.

"Done. Thank God," she said as she turned from dumping the ruined tire in the trunk.

Despite his best efforts with the umbrella, she was soaked to the skin, her T-shirt and arms streaked with dirt from lifting the tires.

"You've got something on your face." He used

his thumb to brush a smear of mud from her cheekbone.

She looked at him uncertainly. "Thanks."

He spotted something on her neck. "What's that?"

She clapped her hand to her neck. "Nothing."

He tugged her hand away. Sure enough, she had a hickey. "I did that?" he asked, even though he knew.

"It'll fade."

She started to move away from him, but he slid his hand around the back of her neck to keep her still.

"Does it hurt?" he asked, smoothing his thumb over the angry-looking mark.

"No. Haven't you ever had a love bite?"

"No."

"Really?" She gave him a speculative look.

"I've led a sheltered life."

"Sure you have." He was still rubbing her neck and she swallowed and shifted nervously.

"Shouldn't we be fighting right about now?" she said, her voice low.

"Maybe we've got better things to do than fight."

Her gaze went to his mouth as he lowered his head. He pressed his lips against hers gently, tasting her lower lip with his tongue. Her lips moved against his, butterfly light. He cupped the back of her head with his palm and moved closer. She shivered and reached up to wrap her arms around his neck.

Heat grew within him, but he kept things light, wanting to show her that he had it in him to be gentle after the craziness of last night. She curled her fingers into his shoulders and followed his lead.

He lost track of time as he explored her mouth with his own. A passing car sounded its horn, its occupants calling for them to get a room. They broke apart. Gabby took a step backward.

"I should probably get you home," she said, not looking at him.

He let her hustle him into the passenger seat, mostly because he'd never seen Gabby shy before.

"I'll head back up Brunswick Street to St. Georges Road," she said as she started the car.

"Sure."

"Did you like your meal? I loved that smoky tomato thing I had with my starter. But I love anything smoky. You could smoke a piece of cardboard and I'd eat it."

"Could I?"

She flashed a look at him before concentrating on the road. "Sorry. I'm a bit nervous."

"Why?"

"I don't know. Maybe because I only know how to handle you when we're disagreeing."

"You want me to pick a fight?"

She smiled. "It's not the same if you fake it."

"I know."

Her smile widened and he asked the question that had been on his mind all night.

"Are you really okay about Tyler and Ally having a baby?"

"I'm happy for them," she said firmly. He got the sense she'd given the issue some thought. "I think they'll make great parents. And that kid is going to score some awesome nursery furniture."

He couldn't doubt her sincerity. She really was pleased for them. Whatever sway Tyler still had over her heart wasn't that powerful, then. Something in his chest relaxed.

"What about you?" she asked.

"What about me?"

"Are you happy for them?"

"Of course. Why wouldn't I be? They both seem to want it. Like you said, they'll make good parents."

He wondered if she could hear the lack of conviction in his voice.

"I thought you seemed a little tense when they made the announcement." She took her eyes off the road to glance at him. She didn't miss much, then or now.

"Did I? I guess I was surprised."

That, at least, was true. The list of things he and his brother had never discussed was as long as his arm, but he'd always assumed that, like him, Tyler would never risk having his own kids. Just in case. As far as he was concerned, the cycle of misery stopped here, period.

"Something occurred to me," she said as she signaled to make a right turn. "At my birthday dinner, when you didn't drink a toast to me—that was because you weren't drinking. Right?"

"You saw that?"

"I thought you didn't drink because you didn't like me."

He frowned. "I never didn't like you."

She made a rude noise.

"I thought you were a pain in the ass, but I didn't dislike you." He realized with some surprise that it was true. Through all their ups and downs, a part of him had always sought her approval. Why else had he kept trying with her?

"So you don't think I'm a pain in the ass anymore?"

She stopped at the curb in front of his apartment building.

"I think you have a great ass," he said. "Want to come upstairs?"

She smiled at his joke but her eyes were uncertain. "Look, Jon—"

"You have a nice neck, too."

She blinked. As though no one had ever paid her a compliment in her life.

"I don't think—"

"And you have a very sexy mouth."

"Jon—"

He silenced her with a kiss, his hand on her jaw as he slid his tongue along hers. She was breathless when he broke the contact. He could feel his own pulse thudding in his ears.

"Please don't tell me I have great breasts because I will know you're lying then."

"You have perfect breasts. They're like firm, ripe little plums. Juicy and delicious."

He ducked his head and kissed her through her damp T-shirt, smiling as he felt her nipple bead against his lips. He pulled it into his mouth, fabric and all, sucking gently. When he lifted his head she looked a little dazed, her pupils hugely dilated.

"Come upstairs."

"Okay."

JON LED HER THROUGH THE LIVING room and straight to his bedroom. Gabby caught her reflection in the mirror and pulled a face.

"God. I'm filthy," she said, looking at her dirt-streaked arms. Either she really did have perfect breasts or Jon was more hard up than she thought.

"You want a shower?"

"That might be a good idea."

He showed her the ensuite bathroom and handed her a clean towel. He started to leave the room then hesitated.

"You want me to wash your back?"

She flicked a glance at him through her lashes. The thought of him in the shower with her was enough to make her mouth go dry.

"Um, okay. If you like."

He gave her a slow, lazy smile. "I like."

She reached for her T-shirt and tugged it over her head. He yanked his T-shirt off. She toed off her sandals. He bent and pulled his boots off. A little surge of nerves hit her as she undid the button on her trousers. Last night, she'd been so crazy with need she hadn't had time to think. This was a little different and she had plenty of time to think about how bright the fluorescent lights were and how exposed she was about to be. She glanced at him, her gaze sliding over the round mounds of his pecs and down his ripped belly.

Screw it. She wanted him. She was going to have to get naked to have him.

She stuck her thumbs into the waistband of her panties and shed them along with her trousers in one sweep of her hands. She flipped the catch of her bra open, then let it slide down her arms. And then she was standing naked in front of Jon, staring at his naked body and very nice erection.

He was looking at her breasts. He reached out to cup the one he'd marked last night.

"Tell me that didn't hurt," he said quietly.

"It didn't."

They both watched as he ran his thumb gently over the bruise. Her nipple puckered and he shifted his attention to it, brushing his thumb back and forth over it until her knees started to shake. He shot her a knowing glance before moving closer. He placed both hands around her waist and smoothed them upward until her breasts were plumped by his hands. He looked at one, then the other, then made an approving noise in the back of his throat before bending his head to take her left nipple into his mouth. She braced herself against the tiled wall behind her as her body went up in flames. He nuzzled and sucked and kissed and bit and played with her breasts until she was panting and ready to fall over.

"Jon…" Her voice was a ragged whisper.

He lifted his head, a far-off look in his eyes. "Sorry. Got a little carried away."

"I'm not objecting. I just might not be able to stand up much longer."

He laughed, a low sound that made her clench her thighs.

"Let's get you clean so I can make you all dirty again."

He turned on the water and followed her into the shower. For the next ten minutes he slicked soapy hands over her body, exploring every dip and hollow. She returned the favor, chasing her hands across his body with kisses, tasting his skin, savoring the feel of warm skin over firm, hard muscle.

"Okay, we're done," Jon said as she slid her tongue into his ear while simultaneously stroking her hand up and down his shaft.

"Having trouble standing?"

He turned off the water and kissed her. "Having trouble being patient."

They fell onto the bed in a tangle of limbs. He rolled her till she was on her back and looked over her body with a hungry, approving eye.

"You drive me crazy," he murmured, then he started kissing her breasts again.

She kneaded her fingers into his shoulder muscles and arched her back as he began to trail kisses down her belly. She made a small excited noise and he shot her a deeply amused look as he slid between her wide-spread thighs. She didn't look away even as he lowered his head to take the first taste of her. She watched as he closed his eyes, savoring her, then she was utterly lost for endless, torturous minutes as he licked and lapped at her until the tension inside her reached a crescendo and she cried out her climax, her hands clutching his shoulders.

She collapsed onto the mattress, panting, while Jon kissed her thighs and her belly and worked his way up her body.

"Ask me how I feel about your—"

She pressed her fingers to his clever lips. "Trust me. I know."

He grinned. She pushed him onto his back.

"Condom?" she asked.

He started to sit up. "Back pocket of my jeans."

She liked that he didn't have a bulk pack in his bedroom. Not that she thought he was a saint, but still.

She found the condom and straddled him as she tore the packet open with her teeth. He was hot in her hands as she smoothed the latex on.

Taking him in hand, she raised her hips and slowly eased onto him. He closed his eyes, the muscles of his neck and shoulders tensing, his fingers tightening on her hips.

"Nice?" she whispered.

"Oh, yeah."

She started to move, riding him with smooth,

sure strokes. He teased her nipples and watched her through slitted eyes. She tried to make it last but she could feel herself tightening again.

"Jon," she said, leaning forward to kiss him.

He gripped her tightly and rolled, never leaving her, and suddenly she was on her back, legs spread wide, as he stroked into her.

She forgot to breathe as he pushed her over the edge a second time. She was still shuddering around him when he plunged deep and stayed there.

"Gabby," he grated, his jaw tight. She held the back of his head as he pressed his face against her shoulder and came and came.

She closed her eyes afterward, basking in the warm sensation of complete satisfaction. His body was heavy on hers, his heart thumping against her breast bone, his breath in her ear. She ran her hands lightly over his back, enjoying the bold valleys and planes of his body.

He rolled to one side and got out of bed. Thirty seconds later he was back, tugging the sheet over both of them and pulling her tightly against his side.

"Give me twenty minutes and I'll make it hard for you to stand again," he said, closing his eyes.

She smiled sleepily. "You're on."

She woke two hours later to find Jon's arm

wrapped possessively around her waist, his body curled around hers. She lay in the dark enjoying the purely physical pleasure of lying skin to skin with another human being again.

She'd missed this so much.

Not that it had ever been like this before.

She'd always enjoyed sex, but it had never been so intense, so consuming, so demanding as it was with Jon. Not even with Tyler.

Staring at the faint outline of the moon through the blinds on his window, she reflected that he was probably going to cast a long shadow over her future lovers.

Now there's a cheery thought.

Moving slowly, she eased out from under Jon's arm. She used the bathroom, then went to the kitchen for a glass of water.

Her thoughts shifted to the conversation they'd had on the way here. When Jon had asked her if she was okay with Tyler and Ally's pregnancy news, she'd honestly had to take a moment to understand what he meant.

She sipped the water. For someone who was supposed to still be in love with her ex, she was spending a lot of time naked with another man. A lot of time thinking about him, too. Just last week she'd been drunk and maudlin and ready to cry as she watched Tyler and Ally dance together, gazing into each other's eyes, talking quietly, communing with one another. Even now, she could still feel an echo of that pain. She envied their happiness. She missed the closeness of having someone to share her life with. She was lonely, and scared that it would always be that way because she'd put all her eggs in Tyler's basket and he'd turned out to be the wrong man.

It occurred to her that what she'd described didn't sound like love. It sounded like yearning, and maybe a little like grief.

All of which would explain why she was currently standing naked in Jon's kitchen, and why he'd been the starring attraction in her thoughts for quite some time.

Maybe she'd been a lot more ready to move on than she'd understood. Maybe she'd already moved on, in fact, on some unconscious level, and the rest of her was only now catching up. Maybe the angst and emotion she'd been experiencing in the past weeks was the curtain coming down on one phase in her life and rising on another.

She walked to the bedroom doorway. Jon was sprawled across the bed on his back, the sheets barely preserving his modesty. He looked ridiculously beautiful, his naked body stretched out, his sleek, powerful muscles loose and relaxed. It was impossible to see all that potent, undeniable masculinity and not feel a thrill of desire—not so long ago, this man had been inside her. They'd loved each other with hands and mouths and trusted each other with their pleasure. But it wasn't only desire she felt when she looked at him. Mixed in with all the earthy stuff was a fond sort of admiration for his pigheadedness, along with an appreciation of the care and skill he brought to his work and a grudging, growing understanding that his need to look out for others was the expression of a caring, nurturing instinct and not an attempt to control her or anyone else.

She liked him. She liked him a lot. The realization made her smile.

She returned to the kitchen to rinse her glass. She was placing it on the drain board to dry when she heard a noise. Thinking Jon had woken and was wondering where she was, she went to the bedroom. She saw that he was still asleep, his eyes closed. As she watched, his face creased into a frown and he moved his feet restlessly.

"No! Stop!" He moved his head, his body tensing.

She took a step toward the bed. He was obviously having some kind of bad dream.

"Stop. Don't. *Please*." His voice was low and anguished. He thrashed his legs, one of his hands opening and closing on the pillow. "I'll be good. Promise I'll be good."

Her chest tightened. He sounded so frightened. So scared. She climbed onto the bed and crawled to his side. "Jon," she said quietly, placing her hand on his shoulder.

"Leave him. Leave him. Please." His jaw was tight, his face distorted with fear.

She gripped him more firmly and shook his shoulder. "Jon. It's just a dream. It's not real."

His eyes opened with a snap and he jerked away from her touch. They stared at each other, then the lost, hunted look left his eyes and he lifted a hand to drag it over his face, effectively masking his expression from her.

She didn't say anything, giving him a chance to find his feet. His breathing sounded very loud in the quiet room.

"Would you like a glass of water?"

"I'm fine. Thanks." He slid off the bed without looking at her, walking to the bathroom and closing the door.

She sat in the dark, listening to the tap running. Thinking.

Tyler used to have nightmares. Not very often, not as violent as this, but still. Something bad had happened to the Adamson boys. Something ugly and sad. But she had already guessed that, hadn't she?

She looked at the bathroom door. She guessed that Jon standing on the other side trying to work out how to handle her. Maybe even how to get rid of her.

The more she thought about it, the more certain she was that the moment he exited the bathroom he was going to either ask her or force her to leave in some way. He was too much of a man to enjoy having exposed himself so fully. And he was too much of a man to ask for comfort.

She moved quickly, fixing the bed and smoothing the pillows before finally crawling beneath the sheet. When the bathroom door opened a few minutes later she was lying on her side, facing away and feigning sleep.

She could feel Jon hesitate, could feel him trying to work out what to do. After a long beat the bed dipped as he climbed in beside her. She stirred.

"What time is it?" she murmured.

"Nearly one."

"Mmm."

She didn't try to embrace him directly. Instead, she shifted so that the curve of her back pressed along his side. Offering him the warmth of human contact with no strings. She kept her eyes closed, and after a few minutes she felt the tension leach out of his body. He rolled toward her, wrapping his arm around her. She felt his lips on the back of her neck as he kissed her. She murmured her approval, and when he began to play with her breasts she rubbed her backside against him.

She let him take the lead, let him take what he needed, and they made slow love in the dark, a long, intense ride.

Afterward, he fell asleep with his head on her chest. She waited until he was well and truly out of it before she slid from the bed.

She would have liked to stay, for him as well as herself, but her survival instinct had finally kicked in. It had been a big couple of days, and Jon was a complicated man. It wouldn't be a bad thing to put a little distance between them. At least until she could get a grip on things.

She gathered her clothes and shoes and took them to the living room so she could dress without disturbing him. She glanced around as she fastened her bra. The couch was gray and square and cheap-looking, the coffee table made from frosted glass. A TV sat on a nondescript unit. Near the window there was a small dining table with two modern plastic chairs with thin metal legs, the kind that cafés favored.

There was no color, no flowers, no cushions. She glanced toward the kitchen, but even the counters were bare. A pair of sneakers sat outside the bedroom door, but apart from that there was not a single sign that anyone lived in the space. It made her feel sad to think of Jon living inside this sterile little box.

No wonder he doesn't mind playing bodyguard if this is what he's got to come home to each night.

For a moment she was tempted to return to bed with him. To hell with caution. To hell with what was bound to be an awkward morning after. This man needed a little warmth and comfort and softness in his life.

Go home, idiot. Before you do something really stupid. Before you get so far ahead of yourself you'll never be able to pull back.

She slipped on her shoes, then tiptoed to the bedroom and made her way to the side of the bed. He was still sleeping deeply and she stooped to press a kiss to his cheekbone. Then she ran a hand over his hair in a gentle caress.

"I have to be up early. I'll see you tomorrow," she said quietly.

He stirred. "Gabby. Where are you going?" He made a groggy grab for her hand.

"I've got an early start. Go back to sleep, I'll see you tomorrow."

She kissed his cheek again and eased from his grasp. She picked up her handbag and slipped out the door, telling herself she was doing the right thing, the smart thing, to put some distance between them.

Even if it felt wrong.

CHAPTER TEN

GABBY WAS BUSY AT HER COMPUTER when Jon arrived for work the next day. She looked up to find him standing in her doorway. His eyes were wary, as though he wasn't quite sure of his reception. She didn't need to be a mind reader to know he was embarrassed about his nightmare, now that he'd had time to review their night together in the cold light of day. No doubt he'd been squirming ever since he'd woken and remembered what had happened.

"Hey." She smiled.

"Hey. Sorry I was a bit out of it when you left."

He looked so uncomfortable, so uneasy.

"I understand. I wore you out. You're not as young as you used to be…"

As she'd hoped, his shoulders lost some of their tension and his mouth kicked up at the corner. "Just how old do you think I am?"

She knew exactly how old he was; she'd filled out his insurance forms.

"I don't know. Forty-five? Fifty?"

He came fully into her office, a playful glint in his eyes. "You're pretty funny."

"There's no need to be embarrassed. You put in a good showing for a man who's no longer in his prime."

"Is that so?" He started rounding her desk.

"Morning, Jon, Gabby," Dino called as he walked past her door.

Jon stopped in his tracks. "*Today* he comes in early."

"Dino's always had great timing."

He gave her a long look. "I'll see you later, okay?"

He exited and she let her breath out.

So much for keeping her distance and taking it easy. But it was hard to be sensible when she was busy remembering the way he'd washed her in the shower, and the way he'd made love to her with his mouth, and the way he'd curled his body around hers afterward....

"For God's sake," she muttered under her breath.

Anyone would think she'd never had sex before. *Not like that, you haven't.*

"Morning, Gabby. You got the details on the Montgomery quote? I need to check their specs again."

It was Tyler, a take-out coffee in hand. She tidied the already tidy pile of paperwork in front of her, trying to look as though she hadn't been sitting here, staring off into space daydreaming about having sex with his brother.

"Sure. Sure. Give me a second and I'll print it off for you."

"Did you get that tire sorted okay?" Tyler asked as she called up the file and hit the print icon.

"I did. Thanks."

"Did you let Jon do it?"

"I did not."

"You never cease to amaze me."

She knew he was laughing at her but she didn't care. "I let him hold the umbrella."

"Jon would have loved that."

"Oh, he did."

She collected the page from the printer and passed it over. Tyler scanned it briefly.

"Thanks." He folded it and tucked it into his back pocket. "I wanted to talk to you about something else, too."

To her surprise, he pushed the door closed before facing her. Gabby felt a little plunge of nerves in her belly. She couldn't remember Tyler *ever* wanting a closed-door meeting with her.

"Should I be bracing myself for bad news?"

"No bad news. I had a chat to Jon yesterday, and I haven't heard from him yet but I thought you should probably know what's going on. I've asked him to be become a partner in the business. Fifty-fifty."

Gabby blinked. "Wow. That's…not what I was expecting."

"We need someone to take charge of production. I figure with you on sales and admin, Jon on production and me on design, we're in good shape to meet our growth forecasts."

She nodded. Shock was starting to give way to the sting of hurt.

Why hadn't Jon mentioned this to her? Granted, there hadn't exactly been a huge amount of chat going on last night, but they were talking about a pretty significant offer here. A life-changing offer.

Maybe he didn't think it was any of your business.

It was a sobering thought.

"So, did he say when he might get back to you?" She hated herself for fishing.

"We left it open. To be honest, I think I kind of blindsided him. I've had the feeling the past couple of days that maybe he was thinking of taking off."

"Have you? Huh." She reached blindly for a paperclip and started playing with it.

"Shit. Sorry, Gabby. I know you and Jon are—"

"No, we're not. We're just…friends. Work colleagues, really." She could practically feel her nose growing longer with every lie.

"Well, so long as you know that was just me talking. Not Jon. I have no idea what he's thinking, to be honest. He plays things pretty close to his chest."

No kidding.

"It's cool. No worries," she said. She even threw in a smile to prove she was fine with everything she'd learned. "For what it's worth, I think it's a good idea. You guys complement each other."

"Glad you think so." He turned toward the door, patting his back pocket. "Thanks for the quote."

"Sure."

Gabby pretended to be absorbed in her work until she was sure Tyler was well and truly gone.

Maybe she was overreacting, but she felt as though she'd been slapped. A few hours ago, she'd been naked in Jon's kitchen, fretting about his depressing accommodation. She'd done her damnedest to offer him the comfort he didn't even know how to ask for after his nightmare, and she'd lain in his arms afterward, trying to be sensible about the growing sense of connection she felt to him.

And he hadn't bothered to mention the fact that his brother had offered him half of his very profitable business.

Her survival instincts had kicked in none too soon. Obviously, she and Jon had very different ideas of where this…thing between them was going. Which was fine. Neither of them had made any promises or representations to the other. Hell, a couple of days ago they could barely stand to be in the same room with each other without squabbling. Realistically, Jon was probably right to treat what had happened between them as a casual, inconsequential liaison.

It had felt like a lot more than that to her. All that anger and frustration they'd generated between them…the way he'd looked at her last night when they were standing in the rain…the way he'd curled his body around hers and held her so fiercely to his chest… None of that had felt inconsequential to her. It had felt real and meaningful and important.

But as she'd said to him only recently, it took two to tango, and it seemed as though the only tangoing Jon was interested in was the horizontal and not the emotional kind.

At least the way forward was clear now: keep her distance, keep her head, keep things light.

Be sensible.

JON TRIED TO CONCENTRATE ON adjusting the guide on the router but his mind kept circling to the events of last night like a dog chasing its tail. He was more than happy to review the good bits, but that wasn't the part his brain obsessed over. All he could picture was the moment he'd woken and found Gabby leaning over him, concern and pity in her face.

Pity. Because he'd had a big bad scary dream, like a little kid. And like a little kid he'd cried out and thrashed around and obviously woken her up.

He put down the router with more force than strictly necessary.

He'd thought he was getting a grip on the nightmares. He hadn't had one for nearly a week. He'd hoped that maybe the dreams had been a reaction to the fact that he'd stopped drinking, that he was finally breaking free from the quicksand that had enveloped him since his father's death.

Apparently not. Apparently he'd been waiting till he had an audience before he put on his next grand performance.

The only saving grace had been that she hadn't made a big deal out of it. He'd expected hand-wringing and amateur counseling when he'd exited the bathroom—instead, she'd been asleep. She hadn't said anything in her office, either. Which probably meant she wasn't going to. This was Gabby, after all. She wasn't exactly the queen of subtlety. If she wanted to know something, she asked.

The realization allowed him to move past his nightmare to think instead about the good parts of last night. Gabby's laughter. The look in her eyes when he'd started kissing his way down her belly.

Man...

Some women acted coy when it came to accepting pleasure in bed. They closed their legs and protested halfheartedly, even though they were quivering with need. Gabby had simply watched him with knowing, wicked eyes and sighed her appreciation. It had been that way every time with her—she knew what she wanted, and she wasn't ashamed of it, and she was hands down the sexiest, most responsive lover he'd ever had. Tyler must have been nuts to let her slip away.

Jon ground his teeth. He wasn't sure from which dark, reptilian part of his brain that thought had popped up, but he didn't want to hear from it again. The fact that Tyler knew Gabby intimately had always lurked in there somewhere, niggling at him, but he had refused to acknowledge it. He didn't want to think about his brother with her. Didn't want to imagine her undressing for him, moaning for him—

He shoved the piece of wood he'd been measuring along the workbench, sending a chisel flying into the wall.

He'd never been jealous of his brother, not even when they were kids. They'd had bigger fish to fry growing up, and as adults they hadn't seen each other enough to drum up any rivalry. Truth be told, he wasn't a jealous man. A perfectionist in his work, yes. A tough but fair boss, hopefully. But he'd never coveted another man's woman before, and this seemed like a particularly shitty time to start.

Gabby's not Tyler's woman. Not anymore.

He let the truth of the thought sink in for a beat. Then he returned the chisel to its place on the rack and took his marked-up timber to the bench saw along the far wall.

It struck him that it had been a long time since any woman had gotten him so worked up on so many levels. In the time he'd known her, Gabby had irritated him, infuriated him, engaged him and aroused him to the point where he'd lost control. Now, apparently, he was getting all dog-in-manger about her, too.

It was more than a little unsettling. His romantic history was littered with short-term relationships with women who had demanded little and received even less. He'd worked damned hard to keep them at arm's length, to make sure that no one expected anything from him apart from pleasure in bed and casual companionship. Yet here he was, knee deep in angst over Gabby without even trying.

At any other time, with any other woman, the realization would send him packing. The thing was, he really liked her. It seemed an obvious observation given all that had taken place between them. But it wasn't something he could say about all of the women he'd slept with over the years. He couldn't stop thinking about Gabby's sexy little body, and he enjoyed her mouthiness and straight-from-the-hip frankness. When he was with her he couldn't imagine being anywhere else—or wanting to be anywhere else, for that matter.

He thought about Tyler's offer. If Jon hung around, bought into the business…

He shied away from completing the thought. He was still on the fence about the offer. About a lot of things. Once he committed, there would be a lot of expectations, from all quarters.

He wasn't sure he was ready for them. The thing was, Gabby wasn't the kind of woman who screwed around. Every encounter they had bound them more tightly together. If he wasn't prepared to welcome those ties, he had no business sleeping with her again.

DESPITE HIS WARNING TO HIMSELF, Jon felt a definite thud of satisfaction when he entered the kitchen shortly after 5:00 and overheard Gabby talking on the phone with her mechanic. He was aware that she'd dropped her car off to have her tire repaired, but judging from her side of the conversation, it wouldn't be ready until tomorrow.

She ended the call and slid her phone into her pocket, clearly annoyed. "They promised me they'd have it done this afternoon. I should bill them for the taxi home," she said. "Why don't people ever do what they say they'll do?"

"I'll give you a lift," he offered before his brain had a chance to engage.

There was a long pause before she spoke. "That would be great, thanks."

"Let me know when you want to leave."

"Actually, I was going to have an early night tonight. So I'm ready when you are."

"I'll grab my gear." He walked to his workbench to collect his jacket, wallet and keys.

Given the kind of thoughts he'd been brooding over all day, he had no right to feel pissed that she'd had to think twice about accepting his offer. He should be glad she hadn't been jumping up and down, leaping at the opportunity to spend more time with him.

Except he wasn't.

He turned from pocketing his keys to find her standing outside her office, her purse in hand.

"Let's go," he said.

The afternoon sun was beating down on the

parking lot and the truck was warm when he opened it.

"Give it a second to air out," he said when Gabby started to climb in.

She dutifully waited. He watched her through the cab. He studied the elegant slimness of her neck before letting his gaze drop to her breasts.

In deference to the hot weather, she was wearing a green tank top with spaghetti straps, with a pink and green silk scarf around her neck. Unless he was wildly mistaken, she wasn't wearing a bra. If anyone had ever told him that he could get hard in an instant over breasts that barely filled his palm, he would have laughed. He'd always been a breast man, and he'd always been attracted to women with generous cleavages. Yet Gabby's handfuls were fast becoming an obsession for him. The delicate color of her nipples—the palest of peachy-pinks. The way they sat so high and firm on her chest, almost as though they were offering themselves up to him. The silkiness of her skin, so pale he was sure it had never felt the kiss of the sun.

He lifted his gaze and realized that he'd been well and truly busted. Last night when he'd admired her breasts, she'd been aroused. Today, she glanced at her feet, fiddling with the strap on her handbag. He remembered that pause before she'd accepted his offer of a lift.

"We're probably fine now." He climbed in and waited until she was settled, her seat belt on, before reversing. For the first few minutes the only sound was the hum of the engine and the sound of the air-conditioning blowing. Out of the corner of his eye he could see her hand moving restlessly on her thigh.

She was nervous. Maybe even worried about something. He hated the thought that the something might be him—and not only because he wanted to sleep with her again. He reached out and caught her hand in his. Her hand tensed, her fingers flexing. He glanced at her but didn't let go. Her wary golden eyes met his, and when she realized he wasn't going anywhere, her hand slowly relaxed in his.

By the time they stopped in front of her place, he'd only released her hand twice—once to make a turn, the other to change lanes—and both times her hand had tightened around his when he took it up again.

"Would you like to come up?"

He did. A lot. But he needed to know something first. "You hesitated before, when I offered you a lift home. But now you want me to come up?"

"I wasn't sure if it was a good idea."

"Right."

She twisted to face him more fully, her eyes scanning his face. "What do you think?"

He almost smiled. Almost. Typical of Gabby to lob the hand grenade back his way.

"I don't know if it's a good idea, either."

Her lips twisted into a wry smile. "Anyone ever told you you're the master of the nonanswer?"

"Anyone ever told you you're great at answering a question with a question?"

Her eyes crinkled attractively. He wondered how he'd ever managed to overlook her innate beauty.

"We could go on all night like this," he said.

"We could." She eyed him seriously for a second, her gaze searching. Then she leaned over the hand brake and kissed him. Her tongue traced the seam of his lips before he let her inside, then she slipped in deeper to tease him some more. He cradled her jaw in his palm and let his thumb sweep across her cheek. When she pulled back, she was flushed and her nipples were tight beneath the fabric of her top.

"Come upstairs," she said.

He switched off the engine. She took his hand when he joined her on the sidewalk. The foyer to her building had a security keypad, he was happy to see, and he waited as she punched in her code.

They took the elevator to the third floor. She

searched for her keys in her bag. He stepped close and bent to kiss the vulnerable hollow at the nape of her neck. She shivered and offered him a small smile before unlocking the door. She led him into her apartment and waved an arm to her right.

"Living room."

There were two couches placed either side of a fireplace, a two-seater in cream and a three-seater in charcoal. Bright cushions were scattered over both, a mixture of florals and stripes and polka dots. A deep green throw was folded over the arm of the charcoal couch, and a floor lamp that looked as though it had been made from a surveyor's tripod filled one corner. Sunlight streamed through wide-slatted white blinds, crisscrossing a bookshelf full of paperbacks and knickknacks with golden light.

Gabby pushed open a door on the right wall.

"Dining room in here. It's pretty pokey."

He glanced in to see a table with four mismatched antique chairs and a wall covered with an eclectic mix of photo frames. She retraced her steps before he had a chance to inspect her photos and waved toward another door.

"Kitchen. Bedroom is at the end of the hall, and the bathroom."

She was nervous again, her hands fidgeting at her waist. "Do you want a drink? Juice? Water?"

"Juice would be good."

"Do you want to stay for dinner? There's a decent Chinese place around the corner. We'll have to go pick it up, but it's walking distance..."

"Sounds good."

She disappeared into the kitchen to take care of the drinks. He used the opportunity to inspect her bookcase. Crime novels, a whole collection of vintage Nancy Drew hardcovers and a number of glossy coffee table books on interior design. As well as those, each shelf boasted a handful of trinkets—a glass paperweight with swirls of color trapped within it, two small but perfect teacups carved from what he assumed was jade, an old pipe made from burnished wood. It was the contents of the second top shelf that intrigued him the most, however—a collection of tin windup toys. A robot, a monkey, an elephant, a whale...

He picked up the monkey and wound the spring and watched as it marched across the shelf.

"Here you go." Gabby's gaze went to the marching monkey as she handed his drink over. "I used to collect them when I was a kid. I keep telling myself to throw them out but I guess I'm too sentimental..."

He didn't have a single memento from his childhood—unless he counted the small bump on his nose from when his father had broken it. Robert had been careful to rarely punish his sons to the point where they needed medical attention, but that one time he'd lost it completely and back-handed Jon across the face with all his strength.

The monkey had hit the end of the shelf and Jon turned it around to let it walk the other way.

"I like them. Especially this monkey," he said.

She passed him a folded menu but he handed it straight back to her.

"You choose. I'll eat anything."

"That's pretty much a challenge for me to order something really weird, like chicken feet with congee, you know that, right?"

"I dare you."

He wandered to the dining room while Gabby pondered the menu. He'd never paid much attention to the way people lived before but for some reason her apartment fascinated him. It was warm and eclectic and interesting and welcoming, full of little clues to her personality, like those whimsical windup toys.

"When I bought this place I had big plans to knock that wall down, open this up," she said, noting his interest in the smaller space.

"What happened?" He surveyed the offending wall with a professional eye.

"Oh, you know. Big plans, not enough money,

not enough time." She punched in a number and began to relay their order.

He inspected the dividing wall from both sides, considered the ceiling and the layout, tapped on the plaster. "This isn't load-bearing, so it wouldn't cost you a lot to knock it down," he said when she'd finished her call. "If you ran a lintel across here, you wouldn't even have to get the ceiling replastered, which is good because period cornicing is hard to match."

She came to stand beside him, tilting her head to look at the ceiling then at him.

"What are the odds, do you think, of it ever really happening?"

There was so much wry self-knowledge in her comment and her expression. When he'd first met her, he'd thought she was uptight, that she didn't have a sense of humor or know how to have fun. The truth was that she was funny and smart and she was more than up for a good time. As he knew only too well.

He stepped closer, sliding his arms around her. Her eyes widened as he smoothed his hands onto her backside, cupping her cheeks and squeezing them lightly. He encouraged her closer, until his hips were pressing against hers. He watched her gaze grow smoky as she registered his erection.

He kissed her, massaging her bottom, taking his time.

"What about dinner?" she said as he started peeling her top over her head. "They said it would be ready in ten minutes…"

He surveyed her breasts hungrily. "There's this thing called a microwave." He filled his hands with her breasts. His thumbs brushed over her nipples and he watched as they hardened. "You put the food in and push some buttons, and like magic the food gets—"

She cut him off with a kiss. "You had me at microwave." Then she took him by the hand and led him into her bedroom.

THE SMELL OF LEMON DETERGENT was sharp. He was at the kitchen sink, washing the dishes with Tyler. He could hear the television in the other room but nothing else. A good sign—his parents weren't fighting, which meant he and Tyler had a chance tonight.

He was too small to reach the sink and had to stand on an old soft-drink crate to wash properly. Tyler was on drying duty, carefully returning each piece of crockery or cutlery to its rightful place. Jon wasn't sure how the game started, whether he splashed Tyler first or the other way round. They stifled their laughter, not wanting to draw attention to themselves, splashing soap suds and water back and forth. Then Tyler upped the ante by twisting his wet tea towel and flicking it at Jon's legs. Jon waited until Tyler was busy drying a cup before grabbing the other tea towel and returning fire.

Tyler tried to dodge. His foot skidded on the soap-slicked floor. He flung out an arm to save himself and the cup in his hand hit the floor with a crack.

It shattered instantly and he and Tyler skidded to a halt, staring at what Jon now recognized as one of his mother's treasured Royal Doulton cups.

Footsteps sounded in the living room. His tummy dipped with fear. He knew what was coming now.

"*Oh!* What have you done?"

It was his mother, hands pressed to her chest as she stared, aghast, at her precious teacup. Behind her, their father filled the doorway, his face already darkening with rage.

"What's going on? What have you been up to?"

His gaze went from the china to their mother's face to Tyler, still standing frozen above the mess.

Jon opened his mouth to explain that it had been an accident, that it was his fault as well and that they hadn't meant it, but their father was already reaching for his belt, pulling the thick leather clear of his trouser loops. Jon kept trying to get the words out—if only he could explain, make them see that he and Tyler hadn't meant to be naughty, they'd only been playing—yet no sound came out.

Time slowed as his father wrapped the thick leather around his fist. Once, twice, three times, leaving the buckle end free. Then he stepped toward Tyler, grabbing him by the hair. Tyler's face twisted with terror, his mouth opening wide, tears sliding down his cheeks. His eyes begged Jon to do something, anything, to stop the pain.

Again Jon tried to speak, to make his heavy, leaden feet move but he was stuck to the floor, his tongue thick in his mouth, his throat tight.

"Please. I didn't mean it. I didn't mean it," Tyler pleaded as their father bent him over and raised his arm for the first blow.

Again those pleading eyes burned into Jon's, begging for help. For a way out. For safety.

Suddenly it was Gabby's face he was staring into and she was the one pleading with him with her big golden eyes and it was her terror he was standing by and witnessing and not doing a goddamned thing about as the leather whistled through the air—

"Jon. It's a dream. You need to wake up."

Jon clawed his way to consciousness. It was dark and he was in an unfamiliar bed, Gabby leaning over him. His heart was racing, pounding against his breastbone, and his body was damp with sweat.

"You're okay," Gabby soothed, her hand gentling his shoulder. "It was just a dream."

Shit.

Shame prickled through his body. Two nights in a row. Gabby must think he was a complete freaking head case.

"Are you okay? Do you need anything?"

She flicked the bedside lamp on and he blinked in the light. Her eyes were twin pools of concern as she watched him, her face tight with worry.

"I'm fine." He rolled out of the bed and looked around, disoriented.

"That door," she said quietly.

He shut himself in her black-and-white-tiled bathroom. His face in the mirror was haggard, the echo of old terror still sitting in the back of his eyes. He ran the tap and scooped water to his mouth, drinking deeply. He washed his face, then sat on the edge of the tub and braced his elbows on his legs and stared at the floor.

He couldn't take much more of this. Something had to give.

An image from his dream flashed across his mind's eye—Gabby, pleading with him to save her.

"Bloody hell." He shut his eyes but it didn't stop the tears from leaking from beneath his eyelids.

He wanted it to stop. He wasn't a saint, but he wasn't an evil man, either. He'd never gone out of his way to hurt anyone, physically or emotionally. He gave to charities, wasn't afraid to work hard, always did his part to chip in. He'd survived his childhood, made his own life, buried his father. And *still* it was with him. The guilt. The shame. The fear. And he just wanted it to stop.

His breathing was choppy with suppressed emotion and he forced himself to breathe past the constriction in his throat until he felt his heart rate normalizing. Big belly breaths, sitting naked in Gabby's bathroom while she worried about him on the other side of the door.

After a few minutes he stood and opened the door. The last thing he wanted to do was face Gabby, but he knew he had to. He walked out. She was sitting in the middle of the bed, knees pulled to her chest, arms wrapped around her legs.

"You okay?" She unfolded her legs and moved toward him. She was going to hug him, he knew. To offer him comfort.

He turned away and made a grab for his jeans. Out of the corner of his eye he saw Gabby pause, undecided. He dragged his jeans on, then pulled his T-shirt over his head and grabbed his boots.

"I'm going to go," he said, not quite looking at her.

"All right."

She pulled on a blue silk dressing gown and they walked to the door in silence.

He paused on the threshold, trying to find something to say that would make any of this okay. He couldn't think of a single freaking thing.

"Thanks for dinner," he said.

He leaned close and kissed her cheek, then ducked out the door. He stuffed his socks into his pocket and pulled his boots on in the elevator.

Once he was in the safety of his truck he leaned against the seat and let his head fall back.

Over the years, he'd called his father every name under the sun. He'd lain awake at night thinking of the things he wished he'd said and done to force his father to recognize his crimes against his own children. Jon had cursed the man, demonized him, tried to forget him—and even though he was dead and rotting in the ground, he'd never hated his father more than he did at this moment.

He had something good here. He could *feel* it. The business with Tyler. Gabby. But he couldn't get beyond this bullshit to let it happen because the past still owned him.

And for the life of him he didn't know how to break free.

Bone weary, he started his truck and drove to

his empty box. He would make it up to Gabby tomorrow. If she'd let him.

GABBY STOOD AT THE WINDOW, watching Jon drive away. Everything in her had wanted to go down there and throw her arms around him and tell him it was going to be all right. But Jon didn't want her comfort. He'd made that more than clear. He held himself as tightly as a fist and while he might let her in for sex, he wasn't about to share the other parts of himself with her.

Remind you of anyone?

She'd already played this game with one Adamson. She didn't think she had it in her to try again.

And yet she remained at the window until Jon's taillights disappeared into the night. Eyes gritty, she let the curtain fall. She made herself a cup of tea, working on autopilot.

She understood now why Tyler had been so keen to have his brother on board that he'd agreed to Jon's no salary stipulation. Jon was in crisis. The drinking, the not drinking, the weight loss, the nightmares… He put up a good front, standing around joking with the guys, arguing with her, sleeping with her, but he was in so much pain it was a wonder he could function.

She listened to the kettle boil and wondered if she should call Tyler. Jon had been so distressed.

Surely someone should be with him? Then she remembered what Tyler had said that morning. *I have no idea what he's thinking. He plays things pretty close to his chest.* Clearly, Jon wasn't talking to his brother, either.

She took her tea to the bedroom and sat against the pillows. Her chin started to wobble and she realized she was close to tears. She took a sip of her tea, then another. Slowly, the urge to cry passed.

She grasped the cup in both hands and stared at the amber fluid, trying to decide what to do. Keep trying to get through? Take what he was offering and ask no questions? Try to find some middle ground?

There was really only one thing she could do, and in her heart she knew it. She'd tried for years to get Tyler to open up to her, to no avail. His many small rejections had meant the death of a thousand cuts for their relationship. She couldn't do it again. She already felt too deeply for Jon. She already wanted to swoop in and save him and take away his hurts.

She needed to take a step back. She needed to protect herself. No more fabulous sex. No more letting her heart get ahead of reality. If Jon wanted to talk, if he needed a friend, she would be there for him. But she was not going to sacrifice herself to his cause. Maybe that meant she was selfish, but she couldn't keep taking body blows only to get up and let it happen all over again. She only had so many recoveries in her, and the way she felt when she was with Jon… She couldn't do it.

She fell asleep with the light on and woke with a start when the alarm went off at six. For the first time in months, she pressed the snooze button and rolled over. She didn't fall back into true sleep and when she resurfaced she felt worse instead of better. And she was late for work.

It was only when she was ready to head out the door that she remembered her car was in the shop. She called a taxi and went to the window to wait. It took her a moment to register the black truck parked out front.

She stared at Jon's familiar silhouette in the driver's seat, then dialed the cab company again and canceled her taxi. She locked up the apartment, then took the elevator to the foyer. Jon got out of the truck when he saw her approaching.

"I thought you'd need a lift. With your car in the shop…"

"I do. Thanks."

He looked terrible, drawn and tired. For a moment her resolve wavered. She stopped in her tracks, willing him to say something, anything, about last night. Willing him to give her some sign that she should hang in there despite her best instincts.

"Did they say when your car would be ready? I can take you to pick it up this afternoon if you like."

She pressed her lips together. Not quite what she'd been hoping for.

"Thanks, but they said they'd drop it off." She got into his truck. He started the engine and pulled into traffic.

"I was thinking we could go out somewhere nice on the weekend if you'd like. One of the guys was talking about the new seafood place at the Docklands. Or maybe you've got some place you want to try out?"

Her heart sank as she listened to the careful casualness in his voice. A nice dinner out was his way of making it up to her, of course, without actually acknowledging there was anything to make up for.

"I can't go out with you on the weekend, Jon."

"Okay. Maybe next week sometime, then?"

"Maybe I should rephrase. I can't go out with you, Jon. Full stop."

His hands tightened on the steering wheel. "Look, if this is about last night, I'm sorry. This not drinking thing has really messed with my sleeping patterns. I'm thinking about seeing the doctor for some sleeping tablets."

She wondered how long he'd worked on his explanation. All night, by the look of him.

"You never asked me why Tyler and I broke up."

He glanced at her, clearly surprised by the change of topic. "I figured it was none of my business."

Normally, she would agree, but this was a pretty unique situation and Jon deserved to know why she was drawing a line under what had happened between them.

"We saw each other for three years. At one point we were practically living together. But I never felt as though he'd really bought into the relationship." She glanced at Jon, but his gaze was fixed on the road ahead.

"You know those old fifties movies where if they showed a married couple in bed one of them always had to have their foot on the floor to get past the censors? That was how I felt Tyler was through our whole relationship—one foot on the floor all the time, never quite in the bed. There were all these no-go areas. His childhood, his parents, the nightmares he had sometimes."

Jon shot her a quick, searching look. She wondered if he knew these things about his own brother, if they'd ever talked at all. Knowing them both, she suspected not.

"I tried so many times to get him to talk to me about it. I waited. I begged. I got angry. And eventually I realized it just wasn't going to happen. That maybe he couldn't open up about it, and either I had to be prepared to accept a relationship that was based on sex and a few laughs and a bunch of other superficial stuff, or I had to walk away. So I walked away. Then a few years later, Tyler met Ally and the rest is history."

She fell silent for a moment, gathering her thoughts. "Some people might think I'm stupid for giving up someone I loved. But you've seen what he's like with Ally. There are no secrets between them. He let her in."

They arrived at the workshop and he pulled into a parking spot. She twisted to face him more fully.

"I want that, too, Jon. I want the man I love to let me in. I want to really be a part of his life. I want the highs and the lows. And I know I probably sound like some kind of crazy stalker, having this conversation with you after only a few days, but whatever is going on between us has felt like a lot more than sex to me right from the start."

He was studying the dash and she willed him to look at her. Finally, he did, and she could see how wary he was, how threatened he felt.

"I don't know what to tell you," he said.

She felt incredibly sad. "I know you don't. I guess that's what I was saying in a really round-about way. We obviously want different things. That's why I'm making it easier on both of us, Jon. Thank you for the past few days. And thanks for the lift."

She leaned across and kissed his cheek.

"For what it's worth, you're a great guy and I hope that one day you meet your Ally. When you're ready for her."

She slipped from the truck and strode quickly toward the building, blinking away tears. She told herself she'd done the right thing every step of the way. By the time she got to the showroom door, she still didn't believe it.

CHAPTER ELEVEN

JON WATCHED GABBY WALK AWAY from him. Everything in him wanted to call her back, to tell her that he didn't want to meet anyone else, that he hadn't even thought about another woman since she'd walked into her office and started giving him a hard time for using her computer.

He didn't move, didn't so much as lift a finger.

He hadn't been lying when he said he didn't know what to tell her. She'd been very clear about what she wanted in a relationship, but he had no idea if he had it in him to give.

A lovely ironic twist—after years of sidestepping commitment and keeping women at arm's length, he'd finally found someone he wanted to get close to, and he didn't know how.

So, that's it? You're going to let her go? The best thing that's ever happened to you?

Because that was one thing he knew without a doubt—he would never meet another Gabby Wade in his lifetime. She was unique, a small, fiery, feisty gem. She'd predicted he'd meet his own Ally one day. He didn't want an Ally. He wanted Gabby. Only Gabby.

The realization crystallized things for him. He had to act or he was going to lose her. He had to do something to show her that he wasn't interested in only sex and laughs. He was interested in her. In the life they could have together.

Galvanized, he got out of the truck and headed for the building. He strode straight through the showroom and into the workshop and started up the stairs to Tyler's office.

His brother was seated at the drafting board positioned to the left of his desk, poring over a blueprint.

"I'll do it. I'll buy in," Jon said without any preamble.

For a long moment Tyler simply stared at him. Then his lips curved into a big smile and he put down his pen. "Hey. That's great."

Jon walked to the visitor's chair and sat. "What happens next?"

Tyler used his legs to push his office chair to his desk and reached for a folder. "It's not rocket science, so it shouldn't take too long to work out a deal. But you'll need to get your own lawyer to go over it, and I think we should get an outside valuation."

"Sure. Whatever you think."

Tyler grinned at him. "I gotta tell you, you've surprised me. I was pretty sure you were going to turn me down."

"You and me both."

His brother eyed him shrewdly. "Is this about Gabby?"

Jon hesitated a moment. But there was no reason to hide his intentions. He wanted Gabby to be a part of his life. "Yeah. It is."

"Good."

Jon waited for him to say more, but Tyler simply turned to his computer.

"Did you get a chance to go over all the figures in the five-year plan?"

They talked business for a few minutes. Jon felt his shoulders loosening more with each second that passed. Now that he'd jumped, he felt free. Crazy, when he'd effectively tied himself to his brother for life.

"One of the things I want you to know up front is that I'll want some time off when the baby's born," Tyler said. "I figure I might as well take advantage of being my own boss, and I want to be with Ally in those early weeks as much as possible."

"But you'd still be available for design work?"

"Of course. But I'll leave it to you and Gabby to handle client meetings and that end of things.

I've been mucking around with some designs for nursery furniture. I was thinking it might be worth adding some pieces to the catalogue." Tyler talked about his and Ally's plans for the nursery for a few minutes.

Jon marveled at his brother's unwavering enthusiasm. Tyler was practically skipping and singing and clicking his heels he was so happy about Ally's pregnancy. He didn't seem to have a single doubt. Jon couldn't comprehend it.

"Aren't you worried?" The question slipped out before he could stop it.

"About all the stuff that could go wrong?" Tyler asked. "Sure. But Ally's got a great doctor and we're doing lots of research. It's a leap of faith. But I'd rather take the risk than not."

"I meant you. Aren't you worried about you?" Jon had started this, he figured he might as well finish it. "Aren't you worried you might be like him?"

Jon shifted in his chair, frustrated with his ability to articulate his feelings. It wasn't that he thought Tyler was in any way like his father. His brother was even-tempered and good-natured and there was no doubting his love for Ally. The odds were high that he'd be a great father. But there was no denying that their father's blood ran in their veins. For many years their only model of manhood—of fatherhood—had been a bullying, violent monster. That had to come from somewhere, and who was to say that it wasn't waiting inside either of them, waiting to be expressed?

Tyler put his pen down on the desk. "I know what you mean. Sometimes I hear myself say something, or catch sight of myself in the mirror and I see shades of him. That ever happen to you?"

"Every time I shave."

They both had their father's strong jawline.

"Yeah. When I was younger, every time I lost my temper, every time I wanted to rip someone's head off it would freak me out."

"I caught myself calling someone a bloody mongrel once. Made my blood run cold," Jon said. "Never said it again."

It had been their father's favorite epithet, usually spat in fury.

Tyler nodded grimly. "The thing is, we're not like him. He was like a little kid, needing to get his own way the whole time. He had no concept of self-control. You remember how he used to get when he was angry, smashing stuff, laying into us. I never once heard him take responsibility for his mistakes or failings. Not once. It was always about other people. I'm not perfect. Far from it. But I'm not like that. And neither are you, mate."

Tyler was so certain. So sure. For the second

time in as many days Jon felt a twist of envy. His brother had his shit all worked out, while Jon was still flailing around. Tyler had Ally, a baby on the way, a house that was a home, not just a roof over his head...

You've got Gabby.

Except he didn't. Not yet, because he'd let her walk away this morning without offering her any of the things she needed to hear.

But that was why he was sitting here right now, talking to his brother, right? Buying into the business, letting her know that he wasn't going anywhere.

That he was serious about her, about them.

It had taken guts for Gabby to put herself on the line this morning. The least he could do was try to match her courage.

But he didn't want to offer Gabby the least. He wanted to offer her the most. The best. Which meant he had some serious work to do.

THE DAY DRAGGED FOR GABBY. For the first time in her life she failed to find solace and distraction in her work. Her mind kept drifting to Jon, or she'd catch sight of him in the workshop or hear him talking and laughing with the guys.

In her gut, she knew she'd made the only decision she could. Everything had happened so quickly between them. She felt as though she'd been running downhill, arms flailing, out of control—and it wasn't until the last minute that she'd recognized that there was nothing but disaster waiting for her at the bottom of the slope.

She assured herself she'd stopped in time so often during the day that it almost became a mantra.

At five o'clock on the dot she packed up for the day. She wanted to be alone. Or at least somewhere Jon wasn't. Dino pretended to faint when she offered a general goodbye to the team and headed for the door, carefully avoiding looking directly at Jon.

Last night they'd left together and she'd shown him her apartment and they'd eaten beef in black bean sauce and fried rice and made love once on the couch and once in her bed.

Tonight she microwaved a frozen meal and watched six episodes of *Friends* back to back in an effort to short-circuit her circling thoughts.

The next two days ground by. On Thursday Jon made a point of coming into her office and chatting for twenty minutes as though they were old friends and she had to go into the bathroom afterward so no one could see her chin wobbling.

She didn't want to be his friend. She was sick of being the friend.

By the time she crawled into bed on Friday night she was feeling flat and teary. She missed Jon. In a single visit he'd marked her apartment indelibly with his presence. She looked at her bookcase and remembered him playing with her windup toys, and she went into the kitchen and saw him spooning Chinese takeout into bowls and laughing at her insistence that they eat with chopsticks, and in her bedroom she remembered how he'd pinned her against her pillows while he tortured her with his roving mouth.

Lying in bed, staring at the ceiling, she told herself it would get better. It wasn't as though she'd fallen in love with him, after all. She'd caught herself, just in time.

She woke to the sound of loud knocking. She prized an eye open and looked at her alarm clock. Barely eight. On a Saturday morning.

"This had better be good," she muttered as she rolled out of bed and grabbed her robe.

If it was her downstairs neighbor asking whether Gabby had seen her cat again, she was going to be seriously hard-pressed not to reach for the nearest blunt object. It had taken her hours to fall asleep, and even if it hadn't been exactly restful it had at least been better than being awake, mooching around pretending she wasn't the next best thing to heartbroken.

She shuffled toward the foyer, tying the sash on her robe as she went. Yawning hugely, she opened the door.

Jon stood on the other side looking better than anyone had a right to when she was feeling so low and he was the culprit.

"Did I wake you? Sorry. I assumed you'd be up."

"It's Saturday. I sleep in on Saturdays."

"Ah. Well, I'm here now."

He bent to collect a large black box, angled his shoulder and stepped forward, forcing her to fall back. Before she knew it he'd pushed past her and into her apartment and was placing what she now recognized as a toolbox down in her living room.

"I've got some wood I need to bring up from the truck, and some tools. Might be a few trips."

"Jon. Wait!" she said, but he was already disappearing out the door.

She scurried into her bedroom to pull on some clothes and tried to ignore the slow bubble of happiness rising inside her. She reminded herself that Jon was a closed book, that she was already dangerously close to being beyond help where he was concerned, that she had to remain strong no matter what he said to her when he came back. With his tools and his wood.

She'd pulled on a pair of jeans and a tank top

and was standing at the door arms crossed over her chest by the time he returned.

"One more trip," he said as he entered with a large piece of timber over his shoulder and a circular saw in one hand.

"Jon. Stop."

"I figure if I go at it hard, I can get everything but the painting done today."

He was about to step out the door again but she stood in his path.

"Jon. What are you doing here?"

"I'm knocking down your wall."

"Why?"

"Because you said you wanted it knocked down."

He was laughing at her with his eyes.

"I don't think that's a good idea."

He hadn't said a word when she told him where she stood the other day in his car. He'd let her walk away. She needed to hang on to that, even though he was standing in front of her looking beautiful, his hair still damp from the shower.

"Don't you?" He hooked a finger into the waistband of her jeans and pulled her toward him.

She tried to resist, but he was strong and she wound up pressed thigh to thigh with him, her neck crooked to maintain eye contact. Jon looked at her and the smile slowly faded from his mouth.

"A couple of days ago, Tyler asked me if I wanted to be his business partner."

Suddenly she was afraid to breathe. "I know. He told me."

"I signed the papers yesterday afternoon." He brushed his fingertip across her cheek. "I want this to work between us, Gabby. All those things you said the other day… I want that, too."

She'd indulged in a few pathetic fantasies over the past few days, but this was better than all of them. Jon was staying. He was going to be part of the business. And he wanted to make things work with her.

In case all of that wasn't enough, he was going to renovate her living room.

But still she didn't say anything. It was too perfect. She wanted it too much.

The smile faded from Jon's lips. "If things have changed for you, Gabby, I understand. But I'd still really like to fix your wall for you."

"Things haven't changed for me." She was more than a little afraid she was going to disgrace herself with tears. "I missed you."

"I missed you, too, Gabby. You wouldn't believe how much."

They kissed. She closed her eyes and rubbed her cheek against his. Jon's hands found her backside and she slid her hands beneath his T-shirt to run her hands over his belly and back.

She'd thought she'd never get to do this again. She'd thought they were over. She moved closer, seeking physical reassurance that he was real, that this was real.

"Hold that thought," he said.

She opened her eyes in surprise as he slipped away from her and moved toward the door.

"Where are you going?"

It had been three days—three very long days—since they'd had sex.

"I'm double parked, and I've got more tools I need to off-load," he said apologetically. "If we keep going, I'm going to need a cold shower before I can be seen in public."

"You're serious, aren't you?"

He closed the distance and dropped a quick kiss on her mouth. "Five minutes, tops."

He kissed her again and disappeared out the door. She stood staring blankly at the spot he'd been for a full ten seconds. Then her brain caught up and she closed her eyes and took a moment to simply savor the realization that Jon was here, and he was staying, and this was happening.

Against the odds. Against her expectations. He wanted her the way she wanted him.

Her eyes snapped open and she spun on her heel

and raced to the bathroom to turn on the shower. By the time she heard the door close she'd showered and was brushing her teeth.

She spat and rinsed, then walked naked into the hallway. Jon was crouching beside his toolbox, sorting through the top tray.

"What are you doing?"

He looked up and his gaze instantly became very focused. "I thought you were still in the shower."

"What are you doing?" she repeated.

A slow smile curled his mouth. "I'm taking my clothes off," he said, standing and whipping his T-shirt over his head.

"That's more like it."

She turned and sashayed into the bedroom.

"Have I mentioned you have a great ass?" Jon called after her.

"Come tell me again."

"I'll do better than that," he said as he appeared in her bedroom doorway.

He was naked, hard and pretty damned amazing.

And he was here. With her.

"What do you have in mind?"

AN HOUR LATER—A VERY STEAMY, toe-curling hour later—Jon pushed her out of bed.

"The clock's ticking," he said.

"Couldn't the clock tick while we're in bed?"

"Do you have any idea how hard it is to get a tradesman to turn up on a weekend?" he asked her as he pulled on his jeans.

"I'm trying to think of an appropriate comment that involves the lewd use of the word *tool,* but I'm drawing a blank."

She pulled on a tank top. Jon glanced at her. "Maybe you should wear a bra."

"Why?" She glanced down. Really, a bra was more of a matter of decoration for her than a necessity.

"Because I find it distracting when you don't."

She arched an eyebrow. "Do you now?"

He laughed. "I've handed you a secret weapon, haven't I?"

She eyed his big, broad chest. "You're doing all right over there with your nuclear warheads and whatnot, don't you worry."

The back and forth continued as they finished dressing and went to tackle her dining room wall. Jon had brought half a dozen disposable drop cloths and they covered her couches and dining set to minimize the clean-up. Every few minutes she stopped what she was doing to kiss him. Her heart felt full to overflowing.

He was here. This was happening.

Once they'd protected her furniture Jon picked up a big sledgehammer and adopted a wide stance.

"It's about to get noisy," he warned. He flexed his arms and the sledgehammer swung in a powerful arc, smashing a very satisfying hole in the wall.

"Cool," she said, inspecting the hole. "Can I have a go?"

Jon grinned. "Why did I know you were going to ask that?"

She held out a hand and he passed the sledgehammer over. She hefted it, assessing the weight. Heavy, but not too heavy. Copying his stance, she swung the hammer over her shoulder before slamming it into the wall with everything she had. A big chunk of plaster fell away, revealing the frame behind it.

"You have a talent for destruction."

She smashed another hole. "This is very therapeutic. People would pay to do this."

"I'd pay to watch you do this."

She looked over her shoulder to find him eyeing her backside.

It took an hour to break up the plaster and cut away everything but the top two feet of the stud frame. Jon got busy marking up the wood and by midday she had the bare bones of a lintel installed and a sense of how the larger space would feel.

"This looks so good!" she said, walking around and viewing the room from all angles. "I should have done this years ago."

"We're not finished yet, sweet cheeks," Jon said. "Gotta get the new plasterboard up, tape the joins, finish them with skim coat. Then we'll have to do something about the floorboards."

She wrinkled her nose at him. "*Sweet cheeks?* Really? You think that's me?"

"I thought we'd already covered my obsession with your butt."

"You're right, I almost forgot about that, sugar dick."

He burst out laughing. Gabby joined in and for a while they did nothing but laugh like idiots and lean against each other.

Finally, she wiped her eyes and looked at him.

"So that's a no on the nicknames, yeah?"

"Oh, yeah."

He crouched to mark up the plasterboard, and she lay a hand on his shoulder, just because she could. He looked at her, the laughter still in his eyes. Something big and warm and full expanded in her chest. He looked so happy, and she'd helped make him that way. He'd made her happy, too. In fact, she felt a little drunk with it.

It was three o'clock by the time they'd installed the plaster over the lintel frame, finished the joins and tidied up. After they'd packed everything back into Jon's truck, Gabby insisted on him taking her undercover spot beneath the building so that they could be assured his tools would be safe overnight, then they showered and made love again.

Gabby woke from a light doze several hours later to realize it was dark outside. Her stomach rumbled and she checked the clock.

"What time is it?" Jon asked, his voice gravelly with sleep. His arm slipped around her waist, pulling her back against his chest.

"Nearly seven. I'm starving. Pizza or Chinese again?"

"Pizza."

They walked around the corner to collect it, picking up a DVD from the rental place on the way.

"I hope you like it," Gabby said as they rode the elevator back up to the apartment. "*So I Married an Axe Murderer* is one of my favorite movies ever. It's funny and cute and smart—"

"I am prepared to love it, even if there is dancing and singing in it," Jon said solemnly.

She got an action replay of the expanding-warm-chest moment as he pulled her close and kissed her. She was going to reserve judgment until they hit midnight, to be safe, but she suspected this was pretty much the happiest day of her life. She'd gotten to smash stuff, she'd scored a new open living-dining space and she'd fallen the rest of the way into sloppy, profound, death-do-us-part love with a beautiful, kind, sweet man. Hard to beat that.

Her step faltered as they exited the lift.

"You okay?" Jon asked.

"Yeah. I'm good."

She smiled a reassurance at him and handed over the key so he could let them into her apartment.

Love. She was in love with Jon. It felt a little scary admitting it to herself, even though she'd been catching glimpses of it out of the corners of her eyes for the last few days. She'd fallen so hard and fast. Like a rock.

Admit it. You were gone the moment he showed up on the doorstep this morning.

Although Gabby was beginning to suspect she'd been gone the moment she looked into his eyes that very first day and that she'd been fighting a desperate rearguard action ever since. To absolutely no avail.

"Plates or out of the box?" he asked as they walked into the living room.

"People don't eat pizza off plates. That's an urban myth."

Jon grinned at her. "*I* never would. But people get strange ideas sometimes."

She felt a terrible urge to sit in his lap and wrap her arms around him and tell him all the different reasons she loved him. Because he was honorable and because he was kind and because he was funny and because he cared and because he was tender and generous…

She took one step toward him, then caught herself.

It was too early. They were on Day One. She could hold her horses for another day or two. She might even hold out for three days before she lay herself utterly at his feet.

They ate their pizza in front of the TV, Gabby pointing out all her favorite parts of the movie to him and reciting key pieces of dialogue along with the characters. The third time she did it, he pulled her close and kissed her thoroughly.

"What was that for?" she asked dazedly.

"You're adorable."

They stretched out along the sofa, Gabby's back pressed to his chest, one of his arms snugged around her body. She pretended to watch the screen while inside she was swooning.

She was adorable. Which implied that he adored her. Definitely this was the happiest day of her life.

Jon's hand slid from her hip to her belly, his

palm warm through her tank top. She wriggled against him a little more and realized he was hard. She glanced over her shoulder at him.

"Do you want to—"

"Let's finish the movie first."

The hand on her belly began to move in small, teasing circles, slipping beneath the waistband of her shorts and getting closer and closer to the top of her panties but never quite close enough. Desire mounted inside her and she found it difficult to concentrate.

"Jon…" she said, moving restlessly.

"Watch your movie," he whispered in her ear.

He slid his hand into her underwear. He started to stroke her, and she gave up any pretense of watching the screen and spread her legs for him. He made an approving noise as he slicked his fingers along her sex.

She moaned as he slid a finger inside her. He stroked her gently, steadily, lovingly, and it wasn't long before she was quivering on the edge of climax. He nuzzled her ear and whispered dirty beautiful things to her as he pushed her over the edge. She fell back against him afterward, limp and exhausted. After a few minutes she opened her eyes and realized the film had finished.

"I missed the end. Did you like it?" She twisted around so she could look at him.

"It was the best movie I've ever seen."

She laughed.

"Come to bed, Gabby."

He made love with her again, then turned her on her side and curled his body around her and held her close. They talked quietly about what they might do tomorrow—drive to the beach, maybe eat fish and chips on the sand—and she slowly drifted off to sleep feeling warm and sated and precious.

Best. Day. Ever.

THE FOLLOWING WEEK PASSED IN A blur of great sex and laughter. Gabby couldn't remember when she'd been so happy. Jon stayed at her place every night. They worked their way through her favorite take-out places and decided that Thai was the best so they had it two nights in a row. She made him watch more of her favorite movies and he retaliated by taking her to the motor show at the exhibition buildings in the city.

When Saturday rolled around again, she felt as though she was living in a bubble of happiness. Having Jon in her life was like upgrading from a cathode tube TV to a plasma screen—everything was brighter, sharper, crisper. Every day brought new discoveries. The fact that he was incredibly ticklish behind his knees and would literally howl for mercy if she attacked him there. The knowledge that he wouldn't eat brussels sprouts no matter what the inducement. The growing realization that despite his size and controlled demeanor, inside he was incredibly sensitive and gentle and kind.

They spent Saturday putting the finishing touches on the living room, sanding and painting the walls and patching the floor. Jon came up with the clever idea of stealing floorboards from her closet to fill the holes created by the removal of the wall, claiming that a patch in the closet would be less noticeable than new floorboards in the main room. The result was a near perfect match and they celebrated with dinner at a small but expensive Italian restaurant.

"One of us should really learn to cook," she said as they scooped up the last of their shared dessert, a mouthwatering tiramisu.

"I'd hate to force you into such a traditionally feminine role," Jon said, deadpan.

"Funny. I was thinking exactly the opposite thing about you."

They went home and shared her bathtub before making love and falling asleep in each other's arms.

Gabby woke with a start in the early hours. For

a moment she didn't know what had disturbed her, then Jon moved restlessly beside her.

"No. Please. *Please.*"

Dread thumped in her belly. Another nightmare.

"Jon. Wake up," she said, shaking his shoulder firmly. His skin was damp with sweat, the muscles beneath his skin tense.

Jon's eyes snapped open. She could see the exact moment reality descended on him. *It was a dream. I'm in bed. Gabby's here.*

He closed his eyes for a beat. Then, without looking at her, he stood and left the bedroom.

Dread thumped in her belly again, but she shook it off. This was hard for him. She had to be patient. Whatever issues Jon was battling, they weren't going to go away overnight, and his attitude was not going to do a one-eighty shift so quickly, either. But he wasn't in this alone now.

She was no expert, but he was clearly dealing with the aftereffects of trauma. It was likely he needed help, to talk to someone who understood these things. Knowing him, it would be an uphill battle to convince him to seek professional help, but she was determined. For both of their sakes.

And the first skirmish in that battle was to get Jon to stop closing doors between them so she could, at the very least, offer him the comfort he so desperately needed.

She pulled on her robe then tapped on the bathroom door.

"Jon?"

There was a long silence. "I'll be out in a minute."

She stood, undecided. He had a right to privacy, but her gut told her that nothing good or productive was happening in there.

"I'm coming in." She opened the door.

Jon sat on the edge of the tub, his muscles tight, his legs braced wide, his back bowed. Atlas, shouldering an impossible burden.

Her heart swelled with compassion. He glanced at her briefly before looking away. She knelt beside him on the cold tile and put her hand on his knee.

"Tell me what's going on," she said softly.

"It's nothing you can do anything about." He kept his gaze fixed on a spot on the floor. His leg felt like granite and he was vibrating with suppressed emotion. She had the sense that if he could, he'd fling her hand off and push her away.

Well. As she'd already acknowledged, this wasn't going to be easy. "You can't keep going on like this. And please don't tell me it's because you've stopped drinking. I know there's more to it than that." She kept her voice gentle but firm.

She had to get through to him somehow.

"It'll go away. It did last time."

"Last time? You've had nightmares before?"

He nodded, the barest dip of his head.

"When?"

"When I first went to Canada."

"Tell me about them. What are they about?"

His shoulder jerked impatiently. "They're not worth talking about."

"They obviously upset you. That must mean something."

He remained silent.

"Jon. Please talk to me. I'm worried about you. I care for you. I hate the thought of you dealing with all this on your own."

"Talking won't change anything."

"It might make it less powerful. Like opening the closet and shining a light on the bogeyman."

He shook his head. She knew what he was thinking: that she didn't understand.

"Okay. What about Tyler, then? I'm guessing this is about your childhood. Tyler must know what you're going through—"

"No."

"You need to talk to someone. You can't just let this eat away at you. And I mean that literally. How much weight have you lost lately?"

"I'm fine."

"No, you're not. You've had three nightmares in the past two weeks. Please tell me you don't think that's normal or acceptable. I can only imagine how hard it must be to put your head on the pillow every night, knowing what might be waiting for you."

"It'll get better."

"Will it?"

He still refused to look at her. She shuffled forward on her knees so she was in his direct line of sight, forcing him to engage. She knew he wanted her to leave him the hell alone, but even if she didn't love him, she didn't have it in her to walk away from someone who was in so much pain.

"What about a counselor? Someone who specializes in abused children?"

"Gabby... Just leave it, will you?" His face was set in stone.

"Or maybe there's a survivors' group. Somewhere you can go and talk to other people like you—"

He surged to his feet in an explosive burst. *"Will you freaking drop it?"* His voice echoed loudly in the small space.

She looked up at him, towering over her, naked and angry and scared. She stood.

"Jon—"

"No. You don't know what you're talking about. I appreciate the thought, I really do, but you've got no idea and talking or whatever isn't going to change anything. So leave it. Okay?"

"Do you think this makes you weak? Is that it? Because—"

"For God's sake, Gabby, get out of my head. I don't want you in there, I didn't invite you and it's *none of your freaking business!*"

He said it so forcefully she actually took a step backward. She blinked a few times. She felt as though she'd been standing in a wind tunnel, as though she'd been battered and bruised by his vehement, angry rejection.

Without saying another word, she left the room. She collected Jon's clothes, then she took them to the bathroom and left them on the floor. She retreated to her bedroom doorway and stood there, arms wrapped tightly around herself, holding herself together. Just.

She could hear him dressing. The hiss of his zipper. The metallic clink of his belt buckle. The thud of his boots. Then there was a small silence and he stepped out.

They looked at each other in silence for a stretched moment.

"Gabby—"

"It's okay. I get it. I've been here before. I know the drill."

She walked to the front door and held it open

for him. She stared at the wall, waiting for him to leave. After a moment he moved past her. She didn't give him a chance to say anything, swinging the door shut between them and turning the bolt. She waited to hear the sounds of his departure. It seemed to take a long time for them to come.

Why does happiness speed by so fast while pain seems to last forever?

Numb and shaken, she sat on the couch. Mere hours ago, she and Jon had shared dessert and talked about what they'd do after Dino's anniversary party the following day. He'd held her close and made her body ache with his clever hands. He'd made her feel so damned precious and loved.

She pressed her fingers to her lips, but her chin started wobbling without her permission. She could feel the pain cracking open inside her.

So much hope. She'd really thought they had a chance. How stupid was she? He might have knocked down her dining-room wall, but he'd kept his own walls firmly intact. He was prepared to sleep with her, to laugh with her, to whisper sweet, dirty nothings in her ear. He was prepared to put down roots, to buy into Tyler's business. But he wasn't prepared to share his pain or weakness or fear. He wasn't prepared to tell her about his past.

He didn't trust her. For whatever reason. Maybe he didn't think she was up to it. Maybe he thought

she wouldn't understand or that she'd judge him.
She didn't know.

All she knew was that she had been in exactly
this spot before and she knew it was impossible
to share a life with someone who didn't trust you.
Impossible to put your trust in their hands when
they kept themselves guarded. There was no true
intimacy, no connection.

I can't do, I can't do it, I can't do it.

The first tear slid down her cheek. She closed
her eyes.

Jon needed her so badly. He needed her more
than he needed air. She knew it in her bones. But
she couldn't do this again. She couldn't give him
all of her and get carefully rationed parts of him
in return. It would kill her. It would curdle her
love into resentment and anger and it would de-
stroy anything good between them. Worst of all,
it would leave her with nothing but pain or loss.

Not that she wasn't dealing with that now. But
it could have been worse.

*How could it have been worse? Tell me how this
moment, right now, could hurt more? Tell me how
I could love him more and feel his loss more?*

A distressed sound escaped her throat. She
bowed her head as her grief overflowed. Her hands
gripped her thighs and she held on for dear life as
the tears came in earnest.

Her chest ached with hollowness. She felt so empty. So lost. So alone. The night, the weekend, the coming week, the rest of her life stretched ahead, bleak and unimaginable.

She reached for the phone. There was only one person who might come even close to understanding.

"Hello?" Tyler answered on the third ring, his voice thick from sleep.

"I need you," she said brokenly.

"Gabby? What's wrong? Are you okay?"

"No. Jon just left. Can you come over?"

"I'll be there as soon as I can. Hold tight."

She loved that he didn't hesitate. He'd always been a good friend to her. The best of friends.

She huddled on the couch, waiting for the buzz of the intercom to announce Tyler's arrival. Instead, there was a knock on her door. She opened it to find him standing there, hair mussed, T-shirt inside out.

"How did you get in?" she asked, even though she wanted to throw herself into his arms.

"I know the code. Remember?"

He opened his arms and she walked into his embrace. His arms closed around her, warm and strong. She tried to give herself over to the comfort of familiarity but after a couple of seconds she pushed herself from him and took a few steps backward, shaking her head. Tyler looked at her quizzically.

"Sorry," she said, feeling sad and helpless. "You're close, but you're not the one I want."

She knew he understood what she meant.

"Come on."

He led her into the living room and they sat on the couch. She pulled her knees tight to her chest and he watched her, compassion on his face.

"Jon and I have been seeing each other. In case you hadn't noticed."

"I noticed."

"He's been practically living here. We've spent every night together. He fixed my living room—" She hiccupped as more emotion welled up.

He waited patiently.

"We had a great day today," she said, trying again. "Really, really lovely. Then Jon had one of his nightmares."

"Jon has nightmares?"

"Three in the past two weeks that I know of. He's under siege, Tyler. God knows how many hours of sleep he gets a night. Each time he's had one, he's bailed in some way. This time, I thought he'd stay, that we would talk."

She took a deep, shuddering breath.

"But he didn't want to talk. He didn't want me to touch him. And when I tried he told me it was none of my business. That he didn't want me in his head."

She started to cry again, remembering the utter, harsh rejection of the moment. Tyler moved closer and put his hand on her back.

"It's okay, Gab. It's okay."

"No, it's not, because I love him. I love him so much and now I have to try to get over him and I don't think it's going to happen. He's a part of the business and I'll see him every day. *Every day.*"

The full horror of it hit her as she contemplated the future. Jon in her life, in her workplace. Sexy and funny and kind—and completely, profoundly off-limits to her.

"I'm going to make you a cup of tea. You got a box of tissues somewhere?"

She swiped at her wet face with the back of her hand. "In the bathroom."

Tyler brought her tissues then disappeared into the kitchen. She blew her nose and mopped at her face. When he returned with a mug she was feeling moderately calmer.

He sat opposite her. "I know I'm supposed to say something profound here, but this isn't really my area of expertise. I do know he cares for you. Ally and I have both seen the way he is with you."

She sniffed and fiddled with the scrunched-up tissues in her hand.

"Maybe it's a matter of time. Of waiting him out. You've got to understand, the way we were brought up… We got really good at surviving on our own, you know? From a young age. We never had anyone we could trust, anyone who was there for us."

Gabby knew all this.

"But you trusted Ally."

"Yeah. I did."

"And you never trusted me." She said it without accusation. It was simply a fact.

He shook his head. "It's not as black-and-white as that. Ally and I… There was this connection, right from the start."

She nodded, smiling sadly. He was making her point for her. "I get it. I do."

"Give it time, Gab."

"How long? A year? Two years? I waited three years for you to trust me, Tyler, and you never did. It's taken me nearly four years to get over you. I've known Jon for two weeks and I'm so in love with him I feel like my chest is going to cave in. So how long should I sit around and hope?"

Tyler shrugged helplessly. "You know I can't answer that."

"I know. No one can."

She fiddled with the tissues some more.

"Why don't you drink some tea?"

She looked at him. "I need to resign."

The decision had been sitting in the back of her mind since Jon walked out the door and she'd understood exactly how deeply she'd invested in the dream of him.

"Come on. You're upset. This is not the time to make big decisions."

"It's exactly the time, because otherwise I'll let myself get sucked into sitting around in perpetual hope. I can't do it again, Tyler. I...can't. I love him too much to see him every day, knowing he's in pain, knowing he won't let anyone close to do anything about it."

"We can't run that place without you, Gabby. And, frankly, I don't want to. You're as much a part of T.A. Furniture as I am."

"You'll find someone else."

"I don't want to."

"I need to do this, Tyler. For me. You don't know what it's like loving someone who doesn't love you in the same way. It kills a part of you. Makes you feel like maybe there's something wrong with you, something that's stopping them from fully committing."

Tyler looked anguished. "Look, I know I hurt you. If I could take it back, I would. That was about me. Or maybe it was about us, about us together not being right. But there is nothing wrong with you."

She nodded her understanding of what he was saying, but it didn't change anything.

"I'm not accepting your resignation. Not tonight. Not until you've had time to think about this. Really think about it."

"Fine. But I'll feel the same way tomorrow."

A half-amused, half-worried look crossed his face. "Jesus, you're stubborn."

Tears welled as she thought about all the times Jon had accused her of the same thing. How pathetic to think she would even miss their fights.

She did a mental calculation of how long it would take to find someone and train them to replace her. Probably six weeks, possibly eight. It seemed like a long time, but she couldn't simply walk out. And it was better than the alternative: staying. Waiting. Dying a little every day. Or, worse, giving in and embarking on the kind of relationship Jon was open to. Giving him all of herself while she accepted the crumbs from his table.

I deserve better. And so does he. He just doesn't realize it.

Sitting up straighter, she wiped her tears away. She was strong, her mother's daughter. She could do this.

JON HAD TO DRIVE INTO THE CITY to find a bar that was open. He ordered a beer with a whiskey shot and knocked them both back in a matter of seconds. He ordered another round and waited for the alcohol to make the world a better place.

Five beers and five shots later, he still couldn't get the scene in Gabby's bathroom out of his mind. He'd never spoken to a woman that way, just as he'd never manhandled anyone the way he'd manhandled Gabby that night in her office. She'd seen the worst of him, that was for sure.

Don't worry. She won't be coming back for a third helping.

He'd blown it. He'd seen the look in her eyes—he'd hurt her viscerally tonight. Really got at her. He'd meant to, too. Anything to stop her poking and prodding at him.

God forbid she learned how freakin' weak he really was. Far better for her to think he was a bully who only wanted her for sex and good times.

He signaled for another round. Maybe if he drank enough, he could fill the gaping hole in his chest.

The rest of the night melted into a blur. He had no real recollection of leaving the bar or getting home. He'd been with it enough to get a cab instead of attempting to drive. When he woke it was full daylight and his mouth tasted and felt as though something had died in it. He peered at the clock and groaned.

It was nearly twelve. His stomach lurched and he took a few deep breaths to get his nausea under control.

He moved to the edge of the bed and sat up in stages, giving his woozy head a chance to equalize. Finally he was ready to contemplate standing. He didn't move, however. There didn't seem much point in diving into the day. He'd planned to spend it with Gabby. Go to Dino's anniversary party together, head to a movie afterward. Obviously, that wasn't going to happen. He'd be lucky if she so much as smiled at him again.

If only he hadn't had another nightmare.

If only she hadn't pushed.

If only he wasn't complete screwed in the head.

She'd been trying to help him, and he'd sent her away. He'd seen the sympathy and concern in her eyes and rejected it unequivocally.

A pathetic voice in the back of his head piped up with an offer of hope. Maybe if he went to her place and tried to explain…

What would he explain? About his childhood? About the fact that, for the life of him, he didn't know how to move beyond the rage and hurt that was his father's legacy? About the fact that he

couldn't look at his brother without feeling profound, bone-deep guilt at his failure to protect
him?

Yeah, that was really going to win her over. That
was really going to bring the light of love back to
her eyes. What woman could resist the lure of a
man who had abandoned his younger brother to
brutality? No doubt Gabby would jump him on
the spot, she'd be so turned on and touched by his
confession.

You didn't deserve her anyway.

A knock at the door brought his head up. His
first ridiculously hopeful thought was that it was
Gabby, but he quickly dismissed it. There was
no reason for her to seek him out after what he'd
done.

He walked to the door and opened it to find
Tyler. His brother gave him a once over.

"Big night?" He didn't sound surprised.

"What's up?"

"I wanted to talk to you. Can I come in?"

Jon stepped aside and waved him in. Tyler
strode in and surveyed the small space.

"Cosy," he said.

"You want a coffee?"

"You look like you could do with one."

"I'll take that as a yes." Jon grabbed a fresh
filter and spooned coffee into it.

"I wanted to talk to you about Gabby."

"What about her?"

"I want to know if this thing between you is serious. Are you in love with her?"

He gave Tyler a cool look. "Are you here in your capacity as Gabby's ex or as her employer?"

"I'm here as her friend. And yours, if you'll ever let your guard down enough to let me in."

Jon busied himself organizing mugs and milk.

"And there it is—the patented Jon Adamson silent treatment. Great. A cure for every evil, a solution to every discussion."

Jon banged the mugs onto the counter, temper rising. "What do you want me to say? If you've spoken to Gabby, you already know I screwed up. You want me to bleed on the rug for you? Fine. I think she's amazing. I think you were nuts to ever let her slip through your fingers. I feel privileged to have known her, even for a little while. She's smart and tough and funny and unbelievably hot and for a while I deluded myself into thinking we could have a future together. But the delusion is over."

He glared at his brother. "That enough for you, or do you want more?"

Tyler stared at him, a long, searching look that bored down into Jon's soul. "What's going on with you? You think you don't know how to be happy because we had a shit childhood? You think you're like the old man, that you'll turn into some kind of sadistic asshole if you let yourself get close to someone?"

"I know how to be happy. Gabby made me happy."

That shut Tyler up for a moment. Coffee was dripping into the carafe. Jon ran a hand over his bristly chin.

"She said you've been having nightmares."

Jon sighed. "Yeah."

"What are they about?"

He shook his head.

"Mate, you think you've got something special going on in your head that I don't know about? You think I haven't been there?"

Jon met his brother's eye. "It's different."

And it was. He'd been the older brother, the big one, the tough one. The one who was supposed to protect. Tyler didn't remember, or maybe he did but was prepared to forgive. But Jon wasn't.

"You're like a frickin' bank vault, you know that?" Tyler said. "Like a brick wall. No wonder she'd rather quit and walk away than try and get through."

Jon's head whipped around. "What?"

"Yeah, exactly. Gabby's resigned."

"You didn't accept it? She loves that place. It will fall apart without her."

"She doesn't want to have to see you every day."

The pain in his chest was so real he almost lifted his hands to check for a wound.

"Then I'll bow out of the partnership," he said after a long moment.

"As if she's going to let you do that."

"You can't let her go."

"She's not my indentured servant, she's my friend. I don't want her to go, but if this is what she needs to do, then I won't try to stop her."

"You're nuts. She's upset, she's not thinking straight."

Tyler shrugged. Jon looked around for his car keys. Tyler might not be prepared to talk sense to Gabby, but he was. She might not want him in her life but she'd damned well listen if it killed him.

Too late he remembered he'd left his car in the city. With a bit of luck it would have been towed by now.

"Can you drive me over to Gabby's place?"

"She's not there. Dino's anniversary party, remember?"

"Fine. Take me there."

Tyler gave him a critical head to toe. "No offense, but you might have a better shot if you didn't stink like a brewery."

Jon looked down at his sleep-crumpled clothes. "Give me five minutes."

He strode into the bathroom and ripped his clothes off. Two minutes under the shower, deodorant, toothpaste, mouthwash.

He reappeared in the living room, glancing at his brother as he strode to the door.

"I'm driving," he said.

THE VERY LAST THING GABBY wanted to do was attend a party celebrating the tenth anniversary of someone else's happy marriage. But Dino and Lucia were her friends, and she had contributed to the weekend for two in Sydney that the company had bought as their gift. She had to go.

Her eyes were still red-rimmed from crying, but she did her best with mascara and eyeliner. She dressed in the skinny black jeans and flowery sleeveless shirt her sister had bought her for her birthday. She added a beaded necklace. There. She looked exactly like a heartbroken thirty-three-year-old woman who had been weeping all night and who was now trying to put on a brave face. Bully for her.

She gathered her phone, purse and keys. Ever since Tyler had left she'd felt numb. Simply… empty. She'd cried and wailed, she'd whined and complained. There was nothing left to do but take action.

In the cold light of the morning after, her decision to leave seemed even more smart and necessary than it had during the heightened angst of the small hours. She could not see Jon every day and not keep loving him. And she refused to flush more of her life away loving a man who was incapable of letting her in.

A pretty simple equation. With only one solution.

She drove to the suburban bistro hosting the party with the intention of staying the absolute bare minimum of time. An hour or two, tops. A noisy restaurant with a highly patronized children's playground attached was not her idea of joy right now.

She parked near the entrance so she could make a quick getaway and got out of her car. She was collecting her bag from the passenger seat when Tyler's truck drove past. She lifted her hand in greeting then froze when she saw Jon was behind the wheel, his face like thunder.

A little clutch of panic gripped her. She guessed Tyler had told him about her resignation. She squared her shoulders. So what if Jon didn't like it? It was nothing to do with him.

She started walking toward the entrance.

"Gabby."

She considered ignoring him, but figured it was better to get whatever it was he wanted to say out of the way before they went inside. This was a happy occasion after all.

She swiveled to face him as he approached. He stopped a few feet away from her. She was vaguely aware of Tyler hovering, but all her attention was on the angry man looming over her.

"Tyler said you've quit. Are you nuts?"

She pretended to think about it. "Don't think so, no."

"You love that place."

"It doesn't matter."

"Yeah, it does. If you're leaving because of me, don't. I've already spoken to Tyler. I'm backing out of the partnership deal."

"No."

"No?"

"I won't let you do that. You're good for the business and Tyler needs you." She eyed him steadily. "And you need it. You need it more than anyone."

She could see she'd thrown him. All the anger left his face and his shoulders softened.

"Don't do this."

"I have to. There's nothing there for me anymore."

He looked pained. He took a step toward her. "That's not true. You know how I feel about you."

Her treacherous, weak heart ached for the pain in his voice and face. "I thought I did yesterday. But I realized I was wrong."

"You weren't wrong. I've never felt like this before, Gabby. Believe me. And I'm trying my best to give you what you want but this stuff doesn't come easily to me."

"I know. But I don't want to be some sort of penance you have to endure, Jon. I want you to love me as freely and openly as I love you."

She smiled as she saw the ripple of reaction across his face. "See? You're not even comfortable with me saying it, are you? You let me in only so far but no more. You're so busy protecting yourself there's no place for me in your life. You don't trust me with your secrets or your pain or whatever it is, and you don't trust me with your heart."

She blinked away tears. Surely she'd cried enough last night. Surely her bloody tear ducts could give her a break for five freaking minutes.

"None of that is true."

"Isn't it? Then what happened last night, Jon?" He looked away.

She gripped the strap on her handbag. "I need to go. Dino and Lucia are expecting me."

Jon caught her arm. "Don't go."

She put her hand on his and squeezed it, looking into his eyes, willing him to understand. "Give me one good reason to stay. Tell me what your dream was about last night."

His expression immediately became shuttered. "None of that stuff matters."

Everything in her went cold as she watched him retreat. This man was so precious to her, but what kind of a life would they have without trust?

"It matters to me. And I think it means everything to you."

She pushed his hand from her arm and turned toward the entrance.

"Gabby."

But he didn't try to stop her this time. Her legs were shaking and she felt as though she was going to be sick as she entered the foyer. Ally popped up from a chair near the coat check, her face showing concern. Gabby guessed she'd been waiting for Tyler, since Tyler had come with Jon.

"Gabby. Are you all right?"

"N-no." She was doing her damnedest not to cry, but tears were still leaking out of her eyes.

Ally looked around. "Come on, in here."

The coatroom was unattended and Ally pulled Gabby inside and shut the door.

"This is about Jon."

"Yes."

"And your resignation."

"Yes."

"You know that Tyler and I love you too much to let you go, don't you?"

Gabby gave up the fight to stop the tears. "I have to go, Ally, I have to. I can't love another man who can't love me back."

Ally's face was creased with sympathetic understanding. "Jon isn't Tyler."

"Oh, I know. It never hurt this much with Tyler. Not even close. I guess that should have told me something, huh?"

"Jon cares for you a lot."

"I know. But how am I supposed to build a life with someone who quarantines parts of himself away from me, Ally? What if we had children? How would we ever discuss anything real?" Gabby threw her hands in the air. "Listen to me, talking as though any of that was ever really a possibility. As if Jon would ever have let me get close enough for any of that to happen."

Ally reached out and captured both of Gabby's hands in hers, squeezing them earnestly. "I think you're wrong. I love you and Jon too much to give up on this. Give him a chance, Gabby. I know you want to protect yourself—I know how powerful that instinct is. But you don't get the good stuff without risking the bad. And he is worth it.

When you first meet him he seems so closed off and unapproachable, but inside he's sweet and so incredibly fiercely protective of people he cares about—"

"You don't have to sell him to me. I love him."

"Did you know he hassled Tyler about hiring an assistant for you? And that he came over to our place the other night beside himself because he thought he'd hurt you?"

Gabby shook her head.

"Stay. Take back that stupid resignation, and fight for him."

Ally made it sound so easy.

"You're worth it. He's worth it, too," Ally said.

She pulled Gabby into a hug. Gabby let her head rest on her friend's shoulder for long moments.

"You know, when Tyler first told me about you I thought I'd hate you," she said, sniffing.

Ally laughed. "I know. I should probably have hated you, too—the gorgeous, sexy ex still working with my man. But I didn't."

"Me, either."

Ally kissed her cheek. "I'm going to back off now, put away my Dear Gertrude hat and leave you to it. But think about what I said, okay?"

Gabby nodded. "I will."

"You might want to hit the bathroom before

you join the rest of the gang," Ally advised with a small smile.

"Mascara?"

"Oh, yeah."

They exchanged one last hug before Ally slipped out of the room. Gabby took a couple of deep breaths and tried to work out what to do. She wanted so much to believe what Ally was saying. But the memory of Jon's rejection was lodged like a splinter in her mind. And minutes ago she'd given him a second chance to offer her something—anything—she could latch on to, and he still hadn't been able to get past his own defenses.

And yet…

She loved him. She wanted this so badly.

Her head spinning, she decided that maybe a cloakroom wasn't the best place to make the most important decision of her life. Certainly she couldn't make it alone. She owed Jon and herself at least that much: a conversation that wasn't muddled by fear in the middle of the night or conducted publicly in a parking lot.

First, she needed to fix her face. She went in search of the bathroom.

JON STARED AT THE BEER SOMEONE had put in front of him. Last night he couldn't get enough of the stuff and now he couldn't even muster enough interest to lift the glass to his mouth. Carl and Kelly were swapping jokes next to him, cracking each other up as usual. Jon didn't have it in him to pretend to be anything other than what he was right now, which was shattered.

He was more messed-up than he knew. Gabby had offered him a second chance—a third chance, really—and he still couldn't come to the party.

I want you to love me as freely and openly as I love you.

That was what she'd said. She'd boldly told him that she loved him—and he hadn't been able to come even close to articulating his own feelings for her.

She should run a mile. She should run and keep on running from a screw-up like you.

But she wasn't. He'd thought he'd blown it last night but he'd realized he still had a chance with Gabby. If he was man enough to take it.

She wanted the truth? He'd give it to her. Tell her about all the times he'd cowered to one side and let his father beat the living crap out of Tyler. How he'd said nothing while his little brother got kicked or whipped or punched. How he'd abandoned his brother the second it was legal for him to bail on school and leave home and make his own way in the world, never once looking back.

How he hated himself for being such a coward, for never standing up to the old man. And how even at the very end he hadn't been able to stand up to him. Because that was why he'd left it so late—too late—to come home. Because he didn't know how to face Robert. Because he'd been afraid his father would take one look at him and know how much of a hold he still had over Jon's life.

Sweat prickled beneath his arms as he thought about sharing any of his shame with Gabby. She was so straight and strong and brave. He could only imagine what she would think of him, a woman who thought she could take on the world. She thought he was her match, but he wasn't even close.

Kelly gave him a nudge and gestured toward the outside part of the restaurant with his chin.

"Going outside for a smoke," he said.

Suddenly a cigarette seemed like a great idea. Jon had taken up smoking again when he'd first learned about his father's illness and while he'd managed to kick the habit before Christmas, right now he figured he could do with something to calm his nerves while he thought about how to tell Gabby what she wanted to know.

"Mind if I have one?" he asked.

"Yeah. Sure. Didn't realize you smoked." Kelly shot him a curious look.

Jon went outside with the guys and made small talk while he sucked nicotine into his lungs. They'd chosen a spot near the playground and he watched the kids run around while he pretended to listen to Carl talk about the weekend's cricket score.

He would find Gabby, and he would take her out to Tyler's car and he'd tell her. Lay it all in front of her. If she wanted to walk after she heard what he had to say…well, so be it. He wasn't going to beg. She had to know what kind of a bargain she was getting.

A little kid dodged around the table near them and tripped over a dip in the concrete. He sprawled at Jon's feet, his hands stretched out to break the fall. Jon instinctively crouched to check on him.

"Ow, that had to hurt. You okay, little guy?"

The kid scrambled away from him, shooting him a fearful look. Small and scrawny, Jon guessed he was seven, maybe eight.

"You all right there?" Kelly asked. He had two kids of his own, Jon remembered. "Your hands okay?"

The kid nodded, not making eye contact, smoothing his palms down the sides of his jeans. Jon guessed they hurt like hell, but he wasn't going to admit it. Ducking his head, the kid sidled away from them before breaking into a run again.

Jon stood, staring after him. "You think he's all right?" he asked the other guys.

Carl shrugged. "You know what kids are like. Made of rubber. You saw the way he bounced back. They don't know what fear is at that age."

Jon nodded, even though it had seemed to him that the boy knew plenty about fear. The way he'd looked at Jon…

"Another brewski?" Kelly asked, and Jon saw they were ready to go inside.

"Might stay out here a bit longer." He wanted to get his head sorted before he saw Gabby again. Wanted to make sure that he had all the things he wanted to say ready to roll. Because she was too important for him to screw this up.

"You want another one?" Kelly offered Jon his cigarette pack.

"I'm good, thanks."

The guys left. Jon propped his back against the fence around the playground. He closed his eyes and lifted his face to the sun, thinking. Maybe he should simply start at the beginning.

My father was an unhappy man who should never have had children.

The sound of a low, angry voice broke his concentration. He looked toward the noise. At the other end of the area, a burly guy with receding hair was talking to the little boy who had performed the face-plant in front of Jon. The kid stood, head lowered, as his father laid into him.

"I told you not to run off. You think it's not enough that I have to work all week to put food on the table and clothes on your back without having to run around after you all weekend, too? When I tell you to stay put, you stay put. You hear me?"

The kid said something that Jon couldn't hear.

"Don't you lie to me, you little mongrel. You think your old man's stupid? Huh? You think I don't know when a runt is trying to pull the wool over my eyes?"

Jon looked around, waiting for someone—security, staff, *someone*—to step in and tell the guy he couldn't talk to his kid that way. A couple of other parents were supervising their children. Jon watched as, one by one, they all looked away while the man continued to abuse his child. *Nothing to see here, la, la, la.* Nobody wanting to make a fuss, make things uncomfortable or awkward.

"Look at me when I'm talking to you. Always sneaking around, hiding in corners. You think I don't know what you're up to? Huh?" The man grabbed his son by the arm, gave him a shake. The kid's head rocked on his neck.

A woman lifted her little girl from a nearby swing and headed for the exit. Jon's gut was hard with tension, his shoulders cracking with it. Someone needed to intervene. Couldn't they all see that the kid was in danger? He couldn't understand why no one was saying anything.

"You know what? That's it. You've ruined it. We're going home." The man hustled his son toward the gate. When he tripped his father gave him another hard shake, nearly pulling him off his feet.

"You're more trouble than you're worth, you know that?" He started across the parking lot, heading for a late-model sedan, almost dragging the boy.

Everything in Jon went hot, then cold.

He knew what would happen when they got home. He knew exactly what kind of pain was waiting at the end of that drive.

He was moving before he could think twice about it. His stride long, he closed the distance between them.

"Hey!" he bellowed.

The guy looked across at him, scowling. "What's your problem?"

"You think it's okay to talk to your kid like that? Drag him around like that?"

The father's eyes grew hard. "He's my kid, so why don't you mind your own business?"

"So you can take him home and beat the shit out of him? I don't think so."

"You are way out of line, asshole."

Jon moved closer, his hand curling into a fist. "I know exactly who and what you are, you pathetic weak-assed coward. I bet you've never picked on someone your own size in your life. I bet you specialize in women and children. I bet you get your rocks off proving what a big guy you are, smacking your kid around the house."

The other man's face was mottled with fury. He dropped his son's arm and pushed him away, squaring up to Jon, his fists raised.

Jon made eye contact with the boy. "Go back to the playground where it's safe."

The other man took his shot while Jon was distracted. The blow sent his head back on his neck. Pain blossomed along his jaw. He tasted blood in his mouth.

He grinned at the other man. "Thanks. I was really hoping you were going to do that."

Then he moved in for the kill.

AFTER FIXING HER MAKEUP, GABBY joined the group and did her best to look happy for Dino and Lucia. She watched Jon go outside with a couple of the guys and decided she wasn't ready to talk to him yet. She needed to be clear about what she wanted, what she was prepared to accept. She was sitting with Lucia's aunt and uncle when people started surging toward the exit. Gabby looked around, bemused, and spotted Lucia standing near the bar, her hand pressed to her mouth.

Gabby crossed to her side. "Are you okay?"

Lucia grabbed her arm. "Do you know where Tyler is? There's a fight out there. Someone said something about it being one of our guys..."

Gabby whirled on her heel and tried to see what was happening outside, but there were too many people gathered on the edge of the parking lot. A chill of prescience ran down her spine as she looked for Jon's dark head and broad shoulders among them.

She couldn't see him.

She thought about how angry and bleak he'd looked when she left him. Surely he wouldn't have picked a fight with someone?

She headed for the exit, her steps urgent as she made her way through the voyeurs hovering near the windows. Her high heels skidded on the stones outside and she took a second to catch her balance before pushing her way through the crowd.

"Excuse me. Excuse me. *Move!*"

She spotted a familiar back in the crowd and sidled up to Dino. "What's happening?"

He turned to her, his olive skin unusually pale. "Where's Tyler? We need Tyler. Carl and Paul tried to get him off but he's lost it—"

Time seemed to slow as Gabby looked past his shoulder and saw that Jon had another man pressed against the side of a car, one big hand gripping the neck of his T-shirt while he pulled back his other arm for a punch. Kelly and Paul stood nearby looking helpless, while a small, brown-haired boy watched the fight with tears running down his face.

"Jon!" she screamed.

Jon punched the man, sending blood spraying across the car. The other man's body flopped loosely and she had the sense that the only thing keeping him upright was Jon's grip on his T-shirt.

"Careful, Gabby!" Paul warned as she darted past.

Gabby ignored him, her focus on Jon, on the arm he was positioning for another punishing blow. She lunged forward, grabbing his arm with both hands, her body slamming into his. She could feel the anger and adrenaline vibrating through him, could feel how hot his skin was, how tense his muscles.

"Stop, Jon. Stop!"

He stilled the moment he felt her touch, his head jerking around toward her. It took a moment for him to return from whatever dark, angry place he'd been lost in to focus on her face.

"Let him go."

Sirens wailed in the distance. Jon hesitated, then dropped his arm, released the guy and stepped back.

His opponent's face was shiny with blood, his bottom lip split open, his nose possibly broken. He slid along the side of the car a few feet before he caught himself and lowered himself more slowly to the ground. A couple of people stepped forward to help him, but Gabby was too busy inspecting Jon to pay much attention.

"Are you okay?" Her heart was pounding out of control as she scanned his face and body for injuries.

"I'm fine." Jon searched the crowd.

Her hands trembled as she caught his chin so she could inspect the cut at the corner of his mouth and what she suspected was going to be a bruise on his right cheekbone. If anything had happened to him...

He tried to pull away from her.

"I can't see him. Where is he?" At first she didn't understand who he was talking about, then she remembered the little boy. She searched the crowd and spotted him talking with Lucia. The other woman crouched beside him, her arm around his thin shoulders.

"Lucia's got him. Dino's wife. See? Over there. He's okay, Jon."

He followed her pointing finger. "Someone needs to look after him. Make sure he's okay."

He seemed disoriented. As though he was only just coming back down to earth.

"Lucia's got him. She'll take care of him," she repeated.

A police cruiser flashed into the parking lot, stopping a few feet away. "He can't go back there, Gabby." Jon caught her hand and she saw that his knuckles were swollen and bleeding. "They can't send him back there. Someone has to protect him."

She wrapped both her hands around his injured one. She didn't understand why he was so concerned about the boy, but his distress was very real—she could feel him trembling with it.

"He's okay now."

Jon shook his head. "No, he's not, you don't understand. His father hits him. They can't send him home with the man."

Understanding dawned on her.

This wasn't a random fight, some belligerent guy Jon had somehow tangled with.

This was a rescue.

She searched his face urgently. "How do you know that, Jon? How could you possibly know that?"

"I know."

There was so much bleak knowledge in his

eyes that she believed him, without a question of a doubt.

"I'll make sure the police know. I'll call Child Protection myself. Whatever it takes." She held his eye so he knew it was a promise.

"Thank you." His smile was relieved, grateful, infinitely sweet. "Thank you, Gabby. You're so good and strong. I love you."

Tears filled her eyes. On what planet, in which lifetime had she thought she could walk away from this man? This amazing, amazing man who had put his body, his freedom, his future on the line in order to protect a little boy he didn't even know?

"I love you, too, Jon. So much."

He lifted a hand to touch her cheek, then he kissed her. She could see the police approaching out of the corner of her eye. She blinked away tears and lifted his hand and kissed his knuckles gently.

"The police are here."

Jon took a deep breath, nodded. She squeezed his hand reassuringly.

"You want to tell us what happened here, sir?" one of the policemen asked.

Gabby kept a grip on Jon's hand as he turned to face the music. They were in this together now.

No matter what.

THE NEXT FOUR HOURS PASSED IN a blur of a
nxiety and frustration. Both Jon and the other
man, Ian Patterson, were taken into custody and
driven away in separate police cars. Gabby followed Tyler and Ally to the local station, but by
the time they'd arrived Jon had disappeared into
the depths of the building and no one was willing
or able to tell them what was going on.

Tyler busied himself organizing a lawyer for his
brother while Gabby called Child Protection to
talk to them about Campbell Patterson, Ian's son.
She'd made a promise to Jon that Campbell would
be taken care of, but even if she hadn't there was
no way she could turn her back on a child who
was so obviously at risk.

She learned that the best way forward was for
her to make a notification of abuse, which would
be anonymous in order to protect her from repercussions. She was assured that a team from the
organization would visit Campbell at home, either
today or tomorrow, to investigate the situation.
Dependent upon what the team found, charges
could be laid, or Campbell might be removed from
the house and taken to a close relative—kinship
care—or into temporary foster accommodation.
There would be a court hearing to sanction any
decisions the team made, and if alcohol or drug
abuse were suspected, Ian might be ordered to

attend detox services or take anger management sessions.

Gabby's throat was hoarse by the time she'd finished talking with the social worker. She ended the call and rubbed her temples, hoping against hope that she'd done enough to ensure that Jon's act of bravery had not been in vain.

Ally passed her a bottle of water. "He's in the system. He's not an isolated little kid anymore."

"Plenty of kids still slip through the cracks, even if social services are looking out for them," Gabby said.

"So we follow up. We do whatever it takes."

Gabby nodded. Ally was right. This was the beginning of the fight, not the end.

It was another hour before Jon was brought to the front desk. He looked tired, and the bruise on his cheekbone had turned an ugly purple-gray. Gabby shot to her feet the moment she saw him. She gripped her hands tightly together and waited impatiently while Jon signed his bail papers, the lawyer by his side. The moment he was finished, she crossed the waiting room and threw her arms around him. He hugged her tightly, his big hands splayed across her back, his head lowered so he could press his cheek to hers.

"Are you okay?" he asked, his voice low.

He was the one who had spent the past five

hours in police custody and he was concerned about *her* feelings?

"I love you," she fiercely. "I love you, Jon Adamson."

His hold tightened and he turned his head to press a kiss to her cheek, then her lips. Finally, they broke apart. She could see the question in his eyes and she touched his arm reassuringly.

"I've spoken to Child Protection. They'll be investigating either today or tomorrow."

Some of the tightness left his face. "Okay."

Tyler and Ally were hovering toward the rear of the waiting area. Tyler came forward when Jon caught his eye.

"Next time you want to be a hero, give me a call. I'd be happy to ride shotgun," Tyler said.

"You mean be charged as an accessory," Jon said drily.

"That, too."

Tyler clapped Jon on the back, but Gabby sensed that what he really wanted was to hug his brother. Their restraint and uncertainty with each other made her chest ache. She saw Ally blinking away tears, as well.

She wasn't the only one who wished things could be different between these two men.

They discussed Jon's police interview briefly and the lawyer informed them that based on his clean record and the mitigating circumstances, Jon would probably receive a good behavior bond. The lawyer promised to be in touch the moment he had further details.

Together they walked out into the parking lot. Jon shook his head.

"I can't believe it's still light out. I feel like a week has passed."

"I know," Gabby said, reaching for his hand. She wove her fingers with his.

"We should get something to eat," Tyler said. "Why don't you guys come to our place and we'll grab some take-out?"

Ally put her hand on her husband's arm. "I think Jon and Gabby might want a bit of time alone."

Tyler looked nonplussed, as though the notion had never even occurred to him. "Right. Sure."

Gabby smiled. "We'll see you tomorrow," she said as she pulled her keys from her bag.

During the drive home she filled Jon in on everything the Child Protection people had told her. Jon asked a few questions and she knew that he would be on to Child Protection first thing tomorrow, following up the situation.

She and Jon were both silent as they rode the elevator to her floor. She glanced at him as they approached her door.

"Are you hungry? I can manage an egg on toast. Or there's breakfast cereal."

"They gave me a sandwich in lock-up."

"Very civilized of them."

"They were just doing their job."

She waited for him to precede her into the apartment. "They ought to give you a medal."

Jon rolled his shoulders as though he was trying to shrug off her words. "I didn't do much. I did the bare minimum."

"That's not true, Jon. You stepped up. Stopped that kid from getting another beating. You could have even saved his life."

They faced each other in her small entry hall.

"Don't make me out to be something that I'm not, Gabby." He said it quietly, firmly. With utter conviction.

Gabby watched him carefully. She didn't want to push—not tonight when he'd already been through so much—but she wasn't about to let this slip by.

"You did a good thing today, Jon."

"It was one thing, and it doesn't come even close to making up for all the times I did nothing."

Everything inside her went still at his words.

"I'm not sure I understand what that means," she said, but an idea was forming in her mind.

It was so simple and so sad that it made her want to howl for this man.

He walked into the living room, crossing to the bookcase. He picked up the windup monkey, fiddled with him for a few seconds. She followed him into the room but resisted the urge to go to him. This was hard enough for him and she understood that he wasn't able to accept her comfort.

Yet.

"He used to hit us. When we were kids. Used to lay into us with his belt or whatever was on hand."

He was talking about his father, she knew.

He glanced at her quickly before concentrating again on the toy in his hand.

"One time he perforated Tyler's eardrum. Nearly knocked the teeth out of his head he hit him so hard. Another time he locked him out of the house even though it was the middle of winter." His hand closed tightly around the toy. "And I let him. I should have stepped in. But I didn't."

While a part of her reeled, a clear-sighted part noted that Jon had said his father hit both him and Tyler. Yet he hadn't mentioned any of his own injuries or punishments. It was all about Tyler. In Jon's mind, his own suffering was so unimportant, so negligible, it didn't even rate a mention.

Jon looked at her, his face tight with strain.

"That's what my dream was about last night.

Me standing by while Dad beat Tyler." His lips curved into a parody of a smile. "Probably not what you wanted to hear. Not exactly noble hero stuff. But it's the truth. And if it changes things between us…I get it."

His words hit her like a blow to the solar plexus.

"Jon…"

She crossed the room and threw her arms around him, holding him to her so tightly that her joints ached with the intensity of the embrace.

"You were a kid," she said, her voice choked with emotion. "A little kid."

He stood stiffly within her embrace. Unable to accept her love. Her understanding.

"I was the eldest."

"You were a kid. Fourteen months older than Tyler. What chance did either of you have against a grown man?"

"I should have at least tried," he said doggedly.

She loosened her hold so she could look him in the face. "He was your father. He was the one who was supposed to protect you from the world. You were a victim. Just like Tyler. You were kids. *Both of you.*"

He stared at her. So much doubt in his eyes. So much guilt.

"You've been carrying this around for years, haven't you? My God."

She couldn't stop the tears from welling. Angry tears, sad tears. She ached to think of how much he had punished himself because of what he perceived to be his crimes.

His self-imposed distance from his brother. His exile to Canada. His refusal to let her—or, she suspected, anyone—close.

"Don't cry." He cradled her face, his thumb sweeping across her cheek to catch her tears.

"How can I not cry? You were a little boy, Jon. An innocent, defenseless little boy. You deserved love and protection. Instead you got violence and fear and you've been blaming yourself all these years, taking all that ugliness on yourself—" She gulped in a breath, everything in her wanting to make this right for him, to make him see. "That boy today. Campbell. If he has a brother at home, or a sister, would you blame him for not getting between them and his father? Would you think he was wrong or evil or weak?"

"It's different."

"Tell me how. Tell me how your situation was different."

Jon stared at her. She could see his mind working, could see him fighting to step back from beliefs he'd carried with him for a lifetime.

"Have you ever talked to Tyler about any of this?"

"No."

"Why not?"

Jon shrugged, but the answer was in his eyes.

"You're afraid he'll confirm it for you, aren't you? That he'll tell you it was your fault. That he blames you."

A muscle flickered in his jaw. She knew she was right.

"Talk to him. Ask him. Because I guarantee that he is going to say the exact same thing I did."

Jon started to say something, but his voice cracked. He cleared his throat and tried again. "You don't know that."

Gabby searched for the one, perfect thing to say that would take away his pain. Nothing came to her. She suddenly understood that this wasn't her battle to fight.

She couldn't do this for him. Nothing she could say would convince Jon that he deserved the same compassion and understanding that he'd offered Campbell Patterson today. He needed to unpack his own beliefs, sort through his own history. Reconfigure the past.

And there was only one person who could help him do that.

She spun away from him and grabbed her car keys. "Come on. We're going to talk to your brother."

For a long moment he didn't move. Then he put the toy on the bookshelf and walked past her to the door. It occurred to her as they pulled out of the underground garage that Tyler and Ally might not be home. She glanced at Jon. He was so tense and wound up she prayed that they were. He'd carried this burden for long enough. She wanted it gone tonight.

Even though she knew it would take years for him to truly let it go.

Her anxiety dropped a notch when she stopped in front of Ally and Tyler's house and saw Tyler's truck in the driveway. She glanced at Jon, noting how taut the tendons in his neck were. Again she wished she had the power to fix this for him.

But when had life ever been that simple or easy?

Jon had the car door open the moment she stopped the engine. Now that they had stepped onto this road, he wanted it done. To stare down the barrel and face whatever was coming.

Gabby caught up with him on the path. She reached for his hand and held it as they walked to the door. Everything that crossed her mind to say seemed trite or useless. She settled for squeezing his hand.

"I love you," she said simply.

His hand tightened around hers, but he didn't say anything. She had the feeling that maybe he couldn't, that maybe right now it was all he could do to prepare himself to face what he believed would be his brother's condemnation.

He raised his left hand and knocked.

JON'S HEART WAS RACING AS though he'd finished a sprint. He swallowed, trying to ease the tightness in his throat. Gabby slid her arm around him.

"Trust me," she said.

Her gaze was steady. Reassuring. He remembered what she'd said to him back at her apartment.

You were a little boy, Jon. An innocent, defenseless little boy.

Rationally he recognized her words made sense. He had been a child, just as Tyler had been. Just as Campbell was. Yet something in him couldn't release the guilt, the sense of responsibility. Tyler was his younger brother. It had been Jon's job to protect him. To save him. And he'd failed.

The door swung open. Tyler looked surprised to see them.

"Hey," he said, his questioning gaze going from Jon to Gabby and back again. "I thought you guys wanted time alone."

Jon swallowed again. "You got five minutes?"

Tyler frowned slightly before stepping back and swinging the door wide. "Sure, come on in."

Jon was aware of his brother's unspoken curiosity as Tyler led them to the living room. Ally was stretched out on the couch, a *Home Beautiful* magazine open in her lap.

"Hey," she said brightly. "Didn't think we'd see you two for a couple of days at least."

Jon tried to smile and failed. "I, ah, wanted to talk to Tyler."

Ally's expression immediately sobered. "Okay. Sure." The magazine slid from her lap as she sprang to her feet. "Gabby and I can go inspect the seedlings I planted in the yard. Can't we, Gabby?"

Gabby looked at Jon. He saw the question in her eyes. She'd stay with him if he wanted her to. She'd do whatever he needed. The unwavering, steadfast warmth in her gaze humbled him and gave him the faith he needed to raise their joined hands to his mouth and kiss her hand before letting it go.

She rested her fingertips on his arm—the smallest of acknowledgments and reassurances—before turning to Ally. "You know I know next to zip about gardening, right?"

"It's easy. You buy the pretty pots from the nursery, you stick them in the ground. If they die, you buy more. If not, you brag like there's no tomorrow."

The two women chatted as they left the room,

their voices echoing up the hallway as they headed for the door.

Jon stuck a hand in his back pocket and stared at the floor, trying to muster the courage to say what needed to be said. He could feel his brother waiting. Wondering. The sound of the door clicking shut echoed through the house and for a moment the world was silent.

"Grab a seat," Tyler said after a beat.

Jon shook his head. No way could he do this sitting down. "I'm all right. You sit if you want."

Tyler eyed him warily. "Mate, you're starting to freak me out a little here. What's going on?"

Jon took a deep breath. He felt sick. As though he was going to lose his lunch. "I need to talk to you about Dad."

"Okay."

"I need to tell you— I want to say—"

Jon swallowed bile. His heart was pounding, his stomach churning. Hands down, he'd never been so terrified in his life.

It was one thing to throw himself on Gabby's mercy, but she hadn't been there. She hadn't suffered through his inaction. She loved him, for whatever misguided reason, and she wanted to believe the best of him.

But Tyler knew. He'd been there. He understood exactly how Jon had failed.

"I wanted you to know I'm sorry." Jon finally choked the words out. He forced himself to hold his brother's gaze. "I let you down. I should have done more, and I want you to know that there isn't a day that goes by that I don't think about it."

Tyler frowned. "Let me down? When have you ever let me down?"

A trickle of sweat ran down Jon's spine. "You don't have to keep up the happy families routine. I get that you want to forgive and forget, but that doesn't change anything. I should have stopped him. Should have protected you. But I didn't. And I'm sorry. More than you'll ever know."

For a moment Tyler seemed frozen. Then he swore, short and sharp, his face distorted by the strength of his emotion. "Unbelievable. This shit gets better and better. I think I've got a grip on it, that it's finally over, and something else comes up."

Tyler took a step to his right, then stopped. He lifted a hand to his face, dashed his knuckles across his eyes. When he looked at Jon his eyes were shiny with tears. "You know what I think about every day? Standing watching Dad beat the living crap out of you and feeling guilty because I was glad it wasn't me. Which is freaking great, isn't it, when you've been walking around feeling guilty about not protecting me all these years? Just freaking great."

Jon stared at his brother. "You have nothing to feel guilty about."

"But you do? What do you think he would have done to you if you'd fought back, Jon? He would have pounded you into the ground. He would have annihilated you." Tyler stepped closer, his expression belligerent. "Is this why you went to Canada? Is this why you've been knocking back Ally's invitations, shutting me out? Because of some stupid misguided sense of responsibility?"

Jon was still stuck on the issue of his brother's guilt. Couldn't let go of it. Couldn't Tyler see that he'd only been surviving? That he'd been making the best of a lousy, terrifying situation, taking comfort wherever he could find it?

"You were just a kid."

Tyler surprised Jon by grabbing both his arms and shaking him, his fingers biting into his biceps.

"*So were you, Jon!* Don't you get it?"

Suddenly his brother's arms were around him and he was being crushed to Tyler's chest.

"All these years. What a freaking waste," Tyler said. "Both of us punishing ourselves. Bloody hell."

His brother's shoulders shuddered and Jon knew he was fighting tears.

"Shit," he said, but by then it was too late, the first tear was sliding down his cheek. He returned his brother's embrace tenfold, hanging on for dear life as years of grief welled up inside him.

"I came home because I wanted to make it up to you," he said brokenly, finally acknowledging the truth that had been sitting inside him for months. "I wanted to ask for your forgiveness."

Tyler hugged him tighter. "Well you can't have it, because you didn't do anything wrong. Neither of us did. We were both victims. Both of us."

Jon sniffed mightily, on the verge of totally losing it. Tyler squeezed him for a brief second before loosening his grip and stepping back from their embrace. Neither of them looked at each other as they struggled to regain their composure. Jon used the hem of his T-shirt to wipe his face. When he looked up, Tyler was doing the same.

He smiled sheepishly. "Don't tell Ally I did that. She's been campaigning for me to start carrying a handkerchief."

Jon raised his eyebrows. "What does she think you are, a Sunday school teacher?"

"That's what I said."

Jon smiled but it didn't hold long. He felt as though his world had been tipped on its axis, all his beliefs overturned. He'd held on to his sense of responsibility for so long. Blamed himself. Punished himself. And all the while Tyler had been on the other side of the world, flagellating himself over the same issue.

"Why did they even have kids?" It was a question he'd asked himself over and over. There had been so little love and patience and so much anger and resentment.

"Ally and I have talked about that. I don't think they knew any better. Back in those days, you got married, you had kids. End of story. Tough luck if you'd made bad choices or weren't suited to it. Tough luck if you had no idea how to manage yourself and your own moods, let alone take charge of two little kids."

He sat and Jon followed suit.

"It wasn't just that. He hated us. When his blood was up, he really hated us," Jon said.

The memory of his father in full fury still made him flinch.

"Well, according to Mom, we brought all that on ourselves."

He made a rude noise. "Right. Leaving the back door open equals a backhander across the face."

"Sure. Just like leaving a wet towel in the bathroom equals a thrashing."

"She should have done something. She should have stopped him."

"Yeah. She should have," Tyler said.

Jon looked at his brother. Warmth flooded his eyes again but this time he didn't fight the tears. Talking about this stuff, airing it, somehow made it smaller. More manageable and less dirty and shameful. He felt…released. Lighter. And the tears were part of that, whether he liked it or not.

Tyler studied his hands, lost in his own thoughts. "Do you remember the time when he took us to the beach on holidays?"

Jon winced. "Yeah. I remember."

They talked for over an hour, exhuming old memories, sharing insights and observations, making connections. Hearing his brother's version of events that had lived large in his memory helped scale Jon's own demons down to size. And there were good memories among the bad. Moments of laughter that he hadn't consciously thought of for years. The time he and Tyler built a tree house in the backyard. The time they'd been given a bike each by a friendly neighbor who'd been clearing out his garage. Long afternoons by the river, flying out over the water on the tire swing while their Tarzan cries echoed in the trees.

At some point Jon registered that it was pitch-black outside.

"Gabby," he said, shooting to his feet.

She'd be worried. Wondering how this had all gone.

They found Gabby and Ally in the bedroom, leafing through copies of Ally's extensive magazine collection. Gabby's head came up when he appeared in the doorway, her gaze scanning his face intently. He smiled faintly and held out his hand. Sliding off the bed, she crossed the room and wrapped her arms around him and lay her head on his chest.

Jon rested his cheek on the crown of her head.

One day he would find the words to thank her for pushing him to talk to his brother. Right now, he wanted to savor the feel of her in his arms.

Ally insisted on cooking pasta for them all, claiming that such a stressful day demanded some serious carb loading. And no one argued with her.

IT WAS AFTER TEN O'CLOCK BY THE TIME Gabby and Jon returned to her apartment.

She led him straight to the bedroom. Toeing off her shoes, she crawled to the head of the bed and patted the mattress beside her.

"Come here."

He sat on the edge of the bed to pull off his boots, then he joined her. He tried to take her in his arms, but she shook her head.

"No," she said, and she guided his head onto her breast and wrapped her arms around him. There was a lot of him and not quite so much of her, but it was the best she could do and it was what she needed to do to show him that she was there for him and that he was loved. She pressed a kiss to his temple and stroked his hair and breathed in the warm, manly smell of him.

She loved him. So very much.

"I think you should move in," she said eventually.

He turned his head slightly to kiss her chest.

"Is that a yes?" she asked, even though she knew.

"You know it is."

She bit her lip, then finally allowed herself to voice the question that had been top of her mind since Jon had appeared in the doorway of Ally and Tyler's bedroom.

"I don't need to know all the details of what you and Tyler talked about. I don't need to know any of the details, really. I just need to know that you don't blame yourself anymore."

"I don't want to have any secrets from you."

Precious, powerful words.

He sat up, crossing his legs so that he was sitting beside her. He picked up her hand, tracing the delicate bumps of her knuckles with his thumb.

"Tyler told me that he'd felt guilty for being relieved when Dad laid into me and not him."

Deep inside, Gabby flinched. That two of her

favorite people in all the world had carried around such terrible burdens made her feel infinitely sad.

"And what did you say?"

"I told him that he was a kid. That none of it was his fault."

"And he told you that you were a kid, too, right? That you were both kids and that you didn't stand a chance against an adult?"

He smiled at her vehemence. "Yeah. That's what he told me."

She eyed him. "You believe him, don't you?"

"I'm thinking about it."

But there was a small smile at the corner of his mouth. Tyler had gotten through, as she'd hoped. Their shared experience had given Jon a new way of looking at the past.

"Thinking about it. I see." She pushed away from the headboard and closed the distance between them, climbing into his lap and wrapping her arms and legs around him. "Think about this, Jon Adamson. You are the most honorable man I know. Even when you didn't like me much you were worried about my personal safety. You tried to stop me from making a fool of myself, you drove me home and offered me good advice."

"The argument could be made that I was probably desperate to get you naked. Even if I wasn't ready to admit it at the time."

She ignored him.

"You don't do anything that you aren't one hundred percent committed to. You're extremely tough on yourself. You hassled Tyler into hiring an assistant for me, and today when I tried to quit, you offered to give up the partnership with Tyler because you wanted me to be happy." She laced her fingers behind his neck and looked deep into his gray eyes.

"Does that sound like the kind of man who would let people down? Ever?"

He smiled slightly. Almost shyly. But he didn't deny it or try to turn aside her words.

"I think the man I described might even be a bit of an overachiever in the taking responsibility area. He might even be a bit overbearing and overprotective sometimes," she said.

His smile broadened. She was glad to see light in his eyes. She knew there would be days ahead when they would talk about what had happened to him again—when and as he needed to—and she was going to do her damnedest to persuade him to talk to a professional. But right now he deserved a little lightness and a lot of love.

"This man we're talking about might even sometimes verge on being patronizing when he thinks he knows better than others."

He kissed her, his tongue sweeping into her

mouth. Then he flopped back on the bed so that she was sprawled on top of him. She'd barely caught her breath when he rolled to cover her, his weight pressing her into the mattress.

"Hey. I wasn't finished," she said. "I hadn't gotten to your really good qualities yet."

He ducked his head to bite her nipple through her top. She gasped, then made an approving noise when he soothed the bite with his tongue.

"I think you're finished," he said.

She reached to cup the side of his face, suddenly very serious. "I am, you know. You did me in. The moment I met you, my goose was cooked."

"You cooked mine first. Asking if I wanted a coffee while I was using your computer without permission. What kind of a hard-ass does that?"

"The kind who loves you with everything she's got," she said, tracing his cheekbone with her fingers, her eyes locked with his.

He turned his head to kiss the center of her palm. "Thank you for not giving up on me, Gabby."

"You're worth it. A million times over."

He trailed kisses down her belly. She smiled to herself, knowing where that trail ended.

She made a correction in her mental diary as he popped open the snap on her jeans. Last Saturday wasn't the best day ever. Today was. A tougher day, by many measures—especially if they counted the hard stuff that had happened in the early hours of the morning. But still a very, very good day because they were here in her bed and Jon loved her and at long last there were no secrets between them.

Jon pulled down her zipper and licked the skin he'd exposed. He glanced at her, a wicked glint in his eyes.

She settled against the pillows.

Of course, she was willing to revise the best day decision on a regular basis. Say, every day.

Because she had a feeling that they were all going to be pretty damned spectacular with this man by her side.

EPILOGUE

Seven months later

"IT'S REALLY QUIET IN THERE. Too quiet," Jon said, springing to his feet. He paced, striding from one end of the small waiting area to the other.

"Relax. Royal Margaret has the best maternity wing in Melbourne. Ally's got a gazillion specialists at her beck and call."

"She was calling out before. Why has she gone quiet all of a sudden?"

Jon ran an agitated hand through his hair. Gabby stood and stepped into his path.

"She was swearing like a trooper because she was in pain. But if she's not in pain anymore, that's probably a good sign, right?"

"I guess."

He looked so worried. She placed her hand over his heart.

"Everything's going to be all right," she said.

Her hand looked ridiculously small against the breadth of his chest but Jon lost the tight look around his eyes.

"I just want everything to be okay."

As always she was touched by the depth of his feeling. He had a big heart and she knew Tyler's happiness meant a great deal to him.

"Hey."

They both spun around to face the bedraggled, worse-for-wear figure standing in the doorway.

"Tyler. Is everything okay?" Jon asked, taking a step toward his brother.

"Yeah. We're all good." Tyler's face lit with a slightly dazed, beatific smile. "We had a little girl. She's so tiny. Ally wants you guys to meet her."

Jon didn't say a word, simply stepped forward and threw his arms around his brother. For a moment they held one another, fists thumping on each other's backs.

Gabby sniffed away the threatening tears. Maybe one day she would get over the fierce sense of satisfaction and rightness she felt whenever she saw these two men together, enjoying one another, loving and appreciating one another. But not yet.

The brothers parted and Gabby stepped forward to offer her congratulations. She could feel the damp fabric of Tyler's T-shirt as she hugged him.

"Hard work, huh?" she said.

"If you want to know what the definition of *use-*

less is, stand around while your wife gives birth. Come on."

He gestured for them to precede him to the birthing suite. Inside, Ally lay propped against a pile of pillows, one hand resting on the tiny pink and red body lying on her chest.

She looked exhausted, her hair matted to her forehead, dark circles beneath her eyes. She gave them both a weary smile.

"Hey. Come and meet our little girl—Alana Rose Adamson," she said.

"Oh, that's so beautiful," Gabby said.

"We think so," Ally said.

Tyler went to his wife's side, sliding his arm around her shoulders. Gabby and Jon approached tentatively.

"She doesn't bite," Ally said.

"We don't want to overwhelm her," Gabby said.

Her gaze was glued to the small figure curled on Ally's chest. The baby's face was creased, her eyes shut. Her hands were clenched into tiny fists, her legs pulled up tightly. A shock of dark hair covered her head.

"Hello, Alana Rose," Gabby said.

"She's so tiny," Jon said.

"No, she isn't, trust me," Ally said drily. "She has a head the size of a bowling ball."

"Can we touch her?" Gabby asked.

"Of course," Tyler said.

Gabby reached out and ran her finger ever so gently across the baby's shoulders. The baby moved in her sleep.

"She's beautiful," Jon said, so softly that Gabby almost didn't hear him.

He reached out and touched one of the baby's hands. The hand unfurled, tiny fingers wrapping themselves around Jon's much bigger index finger.

A bemused smile broke across his face. Gabby met his eyes and couldn't help but smile in return.

The past seven months hadn't been perfect. There had been highs and lows. Jon's court case where he'd been sentenced to a good behavior bond, as his lawyer had predicted. Teething pains when he'd moved into her apartment and she'd had to adjust to sharing her space with someone. And, much to her frustration, Jon was still resisting talking to a professional—although she hadn't given up hope on that one yet.

But through it all they'd kept talking and sharing, and her respect and love for the man standing beside her had only grown deeper and more encompassing.

Her heart expanded yet again as she watched him gently caress his new niece.

Jon Adamson was a keeper. A gentle giant. A loving brother. A good friend.

And he was all hers.

Some girls really did have all the luck.

* * * * *